"I didn't know that was Oscar's Kit
sitting with you. She sure is a
cute little thing, ain't she?"

A tic tugged at Clay's brow as he shook his head, causing
him to press a finger to his temple. The eerie sensation had
him saying, "Kit Becker?"

Clay's mind was spinning, as was his stomach. He took the
stairs leading up to his office above the Land and Claims
Office two at a time and threw open the door, his heart
skipping several beats.

Kit.

Katie.

Katherine.

Kit.

Damn.

Katherine Ackerman was Kit Becker.

"Aw, hell," Clay muttered as he fell onto his desk chair.

What was she up to, pretending to be someone else? A
growl rumbled out of his throat. What was he up to? He'd
kissed her. Kissed his ward. And furthermore, while holding
her on the train, he'd thought about doing a whole lot more
than kissing.

* * *

Inheriting a Bride
Harlequin® Historical #1127—March 2013

Author Note

Behind every book is a story, and here's the one behind *Inheriting a Bride*.

What first came to me was the scene of Clay tossing Henry into the pond. Over the next few days I realized Henry wasn't Henry, but Kit, and that intrigued me, had me wondering why Kit was pretending to be a boy. As the story started to unfold I came to the conclusion that I needed to know a lot more about gold-mining in the 1800s before I could put pen to paper, so I started researching.

The internet is marvelous, but unless you know where you're going it can be like throwing a dart. Lucky for me, one of my searches landed on the amazing website of a "hobby" miner. It provided me with a vast amount of information, but I was still floundering. I needed specific questions answered in order to grasp an understanding of the process so I could import the needed bits and pieces into my story. Not because the book explains gold-mining in the 1800s, but because if I understood the process, and all that went along with it, I could then gain a deeper understanding of Clay and the issues he faced in becoming the guardian of his partner's wayward grandchildren.

I emailed Mr. Ralph, the owner of the website, and asked if I could interview him. Bless his heart, he not only agreed, and spent a considerable amount of time on the phone answering my questions, he sent me several emails with links to amazing sites, including videos.

I wrote Clay and Kit's story, but Chris Ralph gave me the backbone—the information I needed to get to know my characters and really tell their story. Without him—a man I will probably never meet in person—I would have never been able to write *Inheriting a Bride*.

Life is like that—it puts people into our lives just when we need them. Strangers or not. Remember that, believe it, and you'll see it in your life, too.

I sincerely hope you enjoy Kit and Clay's story.

INHERITING A Bride

LAURI ROBINSON

H HARLEQUIN® HISTORICAL

Recycling programs
for this product may
not exist in your area.

ISBN-13: 978-0-373-29727-6

INHERITING A BRIDE

Copyright © 2013 by Lauri Robinson

Printed in U.S.A.

To Chris Ralph, for so generously sharing all of his
knowledge and insight on gold-mining.

LAURI ROBINSON's

chosen genre to write is Western historical. When asked
why, she says, "Because I know I wasn't the only girl who
wanted to grow up and marry Little Joe Cartwright."

With a degree in early childhood education, Lauri
has spent decades working in the nonprofit field and
claims once-upon-a-time and happily-ever-after romance
novels have always been a form of stress relief. When her
husband suggested she write one, she took the challenge,
and has loved every minute of the journey.

Lauri lives in rural Minnesota, where she and her
husband spend every spare moment with their three
grown sons and four grandchildren. She works part-time,
volunteers for several organizations and is a diehard Elvis
and NASCAR fan. Her favorite getaway location is the
woods of northern Minnesota, on the land homesteaded by
her great-grandfather.

Chapter One

Northern Colorado, 1885

A variety of passengers scurried across the wooden platform of the Black Hawk depot, but only one held Clay Hoffman's attention, or better yet, his irritation. Women had a way of annoying him, and this one was in a tizzy, waving her hands, gesturing toward the train as she spouted off to Stan Thomas, the porter. Though he had no doubt the man could handle the situation, Clay moved to the depot door. Perhaps her luggage had been damaged or something. Loads had been known to shift during the ride up the mountain from Denver. That was why he was giving this woman, dressed in her canary-colored finery, the benefit of the doubt. His sister insisted he needed to do that once in a while. Therefore he was trying, but in reality, not getting too far. Old habits and all that.

"Clay?" Stan motioned for him to approach. "This is Miss Katherine Ackerman from Boston, Massachusetts."

Clay nodded, stepping closer and briefly assessing the woman, whose fancy bird-yellow outfit included a feathered hat with a lacy veil falling almost to her nose. Some might claim she deserved a second look, but he had no time for women, pretty or not, and turned his gaze to Stan, waiting to hear what the issue was.

"I'm inquiring as to the whereabouts of one Samuel Edwards," she said before Stan could speak.

Clay's insides froze as he narrowed his gaze on the little veil hiding most of Katherine Ackerman's face. "Why?"

She lifted her chin a bit higher. "That is between Mr. Edwards and me. Now if you'll be so kind as to—"

"No," Clay said. The fact she'd called Sam "mister" told him all he needed to know. The kid was barely seventeen. Anyone who knew him knew that.

"No?" she repeated. "No what?"

Clay had a dozen questions about what a woman such as this—clearly from out East, by the sound of her nasally little voice—would want with Sam, but none of them mattered. She would never meet his ward. That, of course, should be Sam's decision, but Sam liked his privacy and Clay knew women. This one even smelled like trouble—all sweet and flowery. He turned to the porter. "Was there something else she needed?"

Stan, one of the finest railroad men in the territory, hesitated and then cleared his throat. "Miss Ackerman was a bit upset by the, uh…accommodations on the ride from Denver."

What a surprise. Train rides up a mountain were very different from train rides across the plains, and those out East, no doubt. Going down wasn't any better. Judging by her appearance and attitude, this woman wouldn't be happy about anything unless it was the very best, which made Clay's spine tighten. He rerouted his thoughts.

Sam had never been out of the mountains, but the kid's father had, and a part of Clay always wondered if someone would show up, claiming to be a relative. With a single nod, Clay turned to the woman. "I apologize if your train ride was uncomfortable." It wasn't his usual policy, but she'd already wasted enough of his time. "Stan," he said to the porter, "refund the passenger's fare and give her a ticket back to Denver."

"Denver?" she all but sputtered. "I don't want a refund," she added snootily. "I want to know the whereabouts of Sam—"

"I," Clay informed her, nerves ticking, "am Sam's representative. I'll deliver a message to him for you."

"No," she said. "I prefer to talk to him in person."

"That's not possible," Clay retorted, his voice just as clipped as hers. His hackles were rising by the second. Outside of a few miners, Sam didn't interact with people much, and Clay respected that.

"Why not?"

"Are you a relative of his?" He might as well get to the bottom of it.

She swallowed but didn't answer, and the little veil made it impossible for him to see more than her chin and pert lips, which were drawn into a pucker.

Just as he suspected. A woman after the kid's money. "Sam's not a social person," he said. "If you want to give me a message—"

"No," she interrupted. "I—"

"Fine," he snapped. "Refund her money, Stan." Clay spun around and started making his way toward the other end of town. That was the second person asking about Sam in less than twenty-four hours. A message from Big Ed over at the general store had arrived this morning, saying a trapper was asking questions about Clay's ward, and now this woman turned up. The first incident wasn't too much of a surprise; Sam's father had been a trapper, and others probably wondered what had become of the boy. But a snooty woman from out East made no sense at all. The ride to Sam's place next to the Wanda Lou was a long one, and Clay had a thousand other things to do. But Sam was his responsibility, and warning him about this woman couldn't wait. Plus he had some business to follow up on, anyway—a miner causing a bit of trouble. Best to nip it in the bud. The kid didn't like taking the train, preferred to borrow a mule from the mine to haul his furs to Black Hawk, and had left town only a few hours ago.

Clay swallowed a sigh as he started up the street. Good thing he'd brought his horse with him on the train from Nevadaville this morning. The ones at the livery here were as barn sour as they came. If luck was with him, he could finish his business and still catch up to Sam before nightfall.

Kit Becker stared at the man walking away, half in utter disbelief, half in relief. Encountering Clayton Hoffman this early in her adventure was not in her plan. She wanted to meet Sam first. Had to meet Sam first. The desire to lift her veil so she could see the man more clearly, even if it was just his back, was hard to curtail, but she kept her hands at her sides. The veil was part of the disguise she needed to maintain.

"Right this way, Miss Ackerman."

It was a moment before Kit realized the porter was addressing her. She hadn't gotten used to the name. She had used the alias so her grandfather's solicitor, Mr. Watson, wouldn't learn she had left Chicago. Purchasing her ticket under a different name guaranteed a bit of time in her search for Samuel Edwards. That was another name that made her want to shake her head. Why hadn't Gramps told her about him? It just didn't make sense. Both he and Grandma Katie knew how badly she'd always wished their family was larger, and this past year, since their deaths, her loneliness had grown overwhelming and she'd wished it even more.

"Ma'am?"

Turning to the man dressed in his bright blue suit with gold buttons, she sighed. "I don't want a refund. I just wanted...oh, never mind." The train ride that had left her wanting to kiss the ground was no longer a concern. Finding her only living relative was. She dug in the drawstring bag on her wrist, pulled out a coin to hand to the man. "I apologize, sir, for the fuss, but I'm fine now. Would you be so kind as to see my luggage is taken to the hotel?"

"Yes, ma'am, but Mr. Hoffman said—"

"I am not concerned about Mr. Hoffman, or his refund." She spun around and stepped off the platform, wondering where to start her search. All she knew was that Gramps had traveled to Black Hawk. Her eyes, practically of their own accord, turned in the direction Clay Hoffman had taken. He most definitely knew where Samuel Edwards was.

"Did I hear you say you want to see Sam Edwards?"

Somewhat startled, and cautious, since the gruff voice had the hair on her arms standing up, Kit turned slowly. The man who'd stepped up beside her was huge and covered from head to toe in animal skins. She swallowed.

"I'm a friend of his," the burly man said. "Saw him just a few hours ago."

Kit willed herself not to shiver. People just looked different here from how they did in Chicago, she told herself. At least this one did. "Could you tell me where I might find him?" she asked, flinching at how her voice cracked.

"He headed back to Nevadaville."

She couldn't help but glance at the train. Embarking on another ride up the side of that mountain was the last thing she wanted to do. She'd seen how easy it would have been for the entire locomotive to fall over the edge, tumble end over end down into the ravine. Gramps had never mentioned how treacherous the train rides were out here. The journey from Chicago had been fun, but not long after the locomotive had rolled past the fancy homes bordered by tall shade trees, and the rows of manufacturing buildings of Denver—the moment they'd started to chug uphill—the trip had become quite night-marish, downright nerve-racking. Not right at first. To the west she'd seen Pike's Peak, boldly crowning the mountain range with regal glory. The sight had left her breathless, but then the train had crossed a bridge. Not a bridge like they'd crossed before, but a *bridge*. With nothing but emptiness below it. She could still hear the echoing rumble that had bounced off the mountainsides and sent her scrambling away from the window.

The way the train rocked and rolled on the narrow tracks, she'd half wondered if the metal wheels would bounce right off the rails and the whole thing, herself included, barrel down the mountain slopes that fell away on both sides. She'd tried to keep her gaze averted from the scenes outside, but something kept making her sneak peeks at the landscape, which varied from deep gulches to steep inclinations covered in pines and spruces and reaching thousands of feet into the air. Reading the bills advertising a list of shows available at Nevadaville's newly built opera house—everything from single magicians to full performances of *Hamlet*—had been a pleasant diversion. A necessary diversion. For each quick glance out the window had left her insides rolling.

"He didn't take the train."

The man's voice pulled her from the memory, and turning, she waited for him to elaborate. Anything would be better than climbing back in that rolling box on wheels.

"He took the trail," the man said. "He's headed to the Wanda Lou."

Excitement zipped up her spine. That was Grandpa's mine. Now hers and, according to the will, Sam's.

"The trail?"

He nodded, but it was the gleam that appeared in his narrow eyes under those dark, bushy brows that made her stomach flip. "I could show you," he said.

Barely able to contain the shivers this time, she shook her head. "No, thank you, that won't be necessary." She'd find someone else to assist her, which had her mind going to Clayton Hoffman. Grandpa's partner or not, there was no way she'd ask for his help. If he discovered who she was, he'd send her back to Chicago immediately.

Kit gave the frightening-looking man a parting nod, and recognizing her luggage being toted across the street by two young boys, hurried to follow them to the hotel. The boys waited as she checked in, and then carried her bags to her room. By the time they left, with coins in hand, she'd come up with her next disguise. A boy traveling the trail to the mine wouldn't fetch a second glance.

That might have been the longest night of his life. It had left a kink in his back as hard as a boulder. Clay stretched, flinching slightly at the ache, and then blew into the swirl of steam rising from his battered cup. When the coffee entered his mouth, instead of familiar appreciation, sharp, clawlike tendrils of repulsion dug into his shoulders and his throat locked up. Shuddering, he issued a silent curse and spat. Twice.

As another shiver raced over him, hitting every muscle and making him vibrate from head to toe, he tossed the rank coffee out, splattering dew-covered blades of spring grass.

How was *that* even possible?

Nothing, not even the sulfur-infused air of the gold smelters, stank this bad. Breathing through his mouth, he turned toward the other side of the fire pit, where the source of the eye-watering, nose-burning stench sat.

Head down, with an ugly leather hat hanging almost to his shoulders, the kid sipped his own cup of coffee, quite unaffected by the way his odor had corrupted the brew.

How he did so was unfathomable to Clay. He'd slept with his hat over his face just so he could breathe, and he'd been ten feet or more from the kid, on the other side of a smoldering fire.

Regretting the waste, but unwilling to dare a second taste, Clay picked up the flame-darkened pot sitting beside the fire, dumped out the contents and carried both the cup and pot to the trickling creek forging its way across the rocky ground and around squat trees.

Far enough away to breathe, Clay filled his lungs, and rinsed the utensils in the slow-moving water. Mountaintop-cold, the creek was only a foot wide and barely ten inches deep, but farther along the trail, where the water collected before rolling downhill again, there was a pond.

One that would do quite efficiently.

The thought floundered for a moment, but ultimately, there was no other option. Time was awasting, as his old partner used to say. After stuffing the gear in his saddlebag, Clay grabbed the pommel of his saddle and carried everything toward his horse. "Time to move out."

The kid—Henry, he called himself, though Clay knew when someone was lying—didn't glance up. He did empty his cup into the dying embers, and then threw a couple handfuls of dirt over the coals before he pulled the hideous hat farther down on his head and stood.

Tightening the saddle cinch, Clay tossed another glance over his shoulder, to where the skinny kid, shoulders drooped beneath a filthy black-and-red-plaid shirt that should have been turned into a rag months ago, stood staring at the snuffed-out fire. The ride wouldn't be pleasant, but the pond wasn't too far, and if Clay held his breath, he might just make it.

Mornings, no matter what season, were chilly in the Rockies. Most months, apart from July and August, you could see your breath before the sun made her way over the snow-capped peaks to brighten and warm the hills and gulches. The pool would be cold, icy even, but there was no way he could tolerate that stench all the way to Black Hawk.

Sticking a foot in the stirrup, Clay hoisted himself into the saddle and then held out a hand. "Come on, Henry, climb up."

Arms folded across his chest and head down, the boy gave a negative shake. "I'm thinking I'll walk."

"Walk?"

Henry nodded, at least the hat did. Actually, Clay had yet to see the kid's face, other than a dirt-encrusted chin and neck. He'd found "Henry" last evening, crouched beneath a half-dead ponderosa pine.

It had been obvious someone was following him yesterday, but figuring it was the trapper who'd been asking after Sam, Clay had continued on. Eventually, he had caught up with Sam, who'd informed him the trapper was an old family friend. Clay had told Sam he'd be out to the mine in a day or so, and had doubled back, expecting to come across the trapper and ask him a few questions. Instead he'd found Henry.

Clay shook his head at his own luck lately. Now he had another task, taking the foul-smelling Henry to Clarice. He'd decided that last night, even before persuading the kid to share a pan of beans and the warmth of a fire.

Henry appeared to be at that tough age—thirteen, fourteen maybe, but no older. His voice still had that squeaky pitch that didn't go away until age fifteen or so. Younger kids, ten and below, were easy to convince how nice Clarice's society house would be to live in, but older ones often disputed it.

Orphans were a commodity mining towns produced, whether anyone wanted to admit it or not, and Clarice, with a heart bigger than Gregory Gulch, had set her mind to taking care of those ill-gotten children. Every last one of them.

Clay looked around at the trees growing out of the mountainside, at the gleaming snow still clinging to the peaks as if warding off the changing season, at the pastel-blue sky dotted with white balls of fluff—anywhere but at the kid. He could let Henry be, and head back to Nevadaville, where an assortment of other duties waited. But he'd never forgive himself if he left a kid out here. A conscience was a hell of a thing sometimes.

"Well," he said offhandedly. "I guess that's your choice."

The hat nodded.

"You got any grub?" Clay knew the boy didn't, but wanted him to admit it, let the knowledge solidify in his stubborn little head.

"I—"

The shrillness of the squeaky voice could have sent the birds out of the trees.

It must have bothered Henry, too, because he cleared his throat and, with imitation gruffness, said, "I'll get by."

Acting as if he was pondering the day, Clay glanced around again. "That horse I saw last evening, the one I figured was yours, probably didn't get too far. I could help you catch it this morning. Then you'd at least have your bedroll and such."

"You—" Henry cleared his throat again. "You will?"

"Sure. Come on, let's take a gander." Once more he held out his hand.

The kid hesitated.

Clay gave the boy a moment, letting him think about his options. For all his gruffness, he was scared. The way his shoulders twitched and his feet fidgeted belied his crustiness.

"Suit yourself," Clay said, when enough time had ticked by. "I don't have all day."

The kid shuffled forward, and moments later, after he had stuck a foot in the stirrup, grabbed Clay's hand and awkwardly swung himself behind the saddle, Clay wished he'd never made the offer. The brief reprieve of being upwind made the stench that much worse.

Breathing into the crook of his arm, and holding his neck muscles tight, lest he start gagging, Clay kneed his mount, heading straight for the pool of water. The horse he'd seen yesterday was back in Black Hawk by now, that was certain, which was where they were headed. Riding double on the mountain trail all the way to Nevadaville would be too dangerous.

Stinking to high heaven or not, by climbing on this horse, Henry had probably saved Clay's life. If Clarice ever got wind of him coming across a child and not lending aid, she'd kill him. Clay grinned, knowing his sister would do no such thing. But, he acknowledged, she'd sure as heck never let him forget it.

Women were like that, reminding men of blunders, making their lives miserable. He was dually glad he'd sworn off them. Kids, too. His old partner's will had saddled him with enough youngster worries to last a lifetime, and Clay's own past mistakes had taught him life's greatest lesson concerning women. There wasn't a one in the lot who wouldn't lie to get what she wanted. The opera house he'd built in Nevadaville was a constant reminder of that.

Even with such heavy thoughts, by the time the pool of sparkling blue came into view, Clay was damned near light-headed. The front of his coat was pulled up over his nose, had been for several miles, but it didn't help.

He could still smell the noxious odor, and his burning lungs desperately needed a breath of fresh air.

"Why we stopping?" Henry asked in that mock rough voice.

"Andrew needs a drink," Clay answered without breathing.

"Who?"

Leaping to the ground, Clay moved to the front of his mount while sucking air deep into his lungs. "My horse."

Henry climbed down, in an almost delicate and sissy way. His toes searched for the ground, and he didn't let go of the saddle until both feet were safely planted. Tugging on the hat brim, as if it wasn't already as low as it could go, he asked, "Your horse's name is Andrew?"

"Yep, after Andrew Jackson, the seventh president of the United States." A man didn't know how sweet air was until he missed it, and Clay couldn't seem to get enough. He led the horse closer to the pool, glorying in every deep breath.

"I kno—" Henry cleared his throat again. "I know who Andrew Jackson was."

"Do you?"

"Y-yes."

Justification took to wallowing in Clay's mind. The sun had crested the mountains and was heating the air, but not the water. Even months from now, at the height of summer, it would still be icy cold. It really couldn't be helped, though. He couldn't ride for hours without breathing. Walking wouldn't be any better and would double their travel time. Long ago he'd learned that when something needed to be done, it was best to jump in and get it over with. He'd known Henry for only a short time, but he'd learned a lot about him.

One, he stank, which said he didn't like baths.

Two, he prickled easily, which meant he'd argue.

Three, he stank.

Clay flinched, thinking about what was to come, but he couldn't stand here pondering all day. Taking a deep breath, he walked to the back of Andrew, patting the horse's rump affectionately and trying to look casual.

Henry sidestepped, as if suspicious.

Clay shot out an arm, catching the kid by the collar.

"Hey! Let go!"

"I will in about three steps," Clay assured him, grabbing the waistband of his britches with his other hand.

"Put me down!"

As promised, three steps later Clay let go, pitching the boy into the pond.

"You—" The resulting splash stifled Henry's high-pitched protest.

Folding his arms, Clay watched the water swell up to engulf the youngster, hat and all. Henry would be mad enough to spit bullets when he surfaced, but at least he'd smell better.

Clay grimaced, feeling more than a little sorry for the boy. That water had to be bone-chillingly cold. Maybe he should have offered a deal—a bath for a ride to Black Hawk. Concern tugged at his conscience as the ripples slowly faded, but when the pond turned smooth and glassy, his heart slammed into his throat.

"Aw, shit!"

He didn't bother to remove anything, just ran. When the water hit his thighs, he dived toward the exact spot where he'd pitched Henry.

Pin prickles of cold stung his eyes as he searched the murky depth. Catching a flutter, he reached out. His fingers snagged material and he tugged. Heading upward, he towed the kid, adrenaline pounding through Clay's veins with every stroke of his arm and kick of his feet. His head broke the surface and he tugged harder, thrusting the kid above the waterline. The first thing he heard was spitting and sputtering.

Clay's heart fluttered with thankfulness, and gasping for air himself, he shouted, "Why didn't you tell me you couldn't swim?" Holding Henry by the waist with one hand, he used the other arm to tread water, orientating himself by searching for the bank where Andrew stood.

"Why'd you try to drown me?" Henry shouted between sputters.

Clay kept one arm around the kid and used steady strokes with the other to pull them through the water. "I didn't try to drown you." They neared the shore and he lowered his legs. The slick soles of his boots slipped on the rocky bottom several times before he found solid footing. "I was giving you a bath."

"A bath!" The kid's squeaky voice sounded downright self-righteous.

Clay bent to pluck his hat out of the water, having lost it when he dived in. A thought occurred to him and he twisted, ready to get his first good look at Henry. Dumbfounded, he stared. The shabby hat, now black instead of dirt brown, with water dripping off the floppy brim, was still on the kid's head.

As if he knew what Clay was thinking, Henry grabbed the brim with both hands and held on tight. The kid spun, an action that made it appear he was about to shoot back beneath the water. Clay caught the tail of the well-worn shirt and started walking toward the grass-lined bank.

Squirming and digging his heels into the creek bed, Henry fought him every step. Clay, shivering from the icy water and damn near steaming at the same time, gave a hard wrench to pull the kid out of the water.

A rip sounded and the cloth went slack.

"Aw, shit," Clay mumbled. He hadn't meant to tear the shirt off the boy's back any more than he'd meant to drown him. His patience, though, was running thin. He spun and this time caught Henry around the waist. Hooking him next to his hip, Clay carried the kicking and squirming kid out of the water before they both ended up with pneumonia.

Andrew snorted and, with haughty horse eyes, looked at Clay as if he'd lost his mind. At that moment, he could have agreed with the animal. One-handed— not trusting the kid to stay put—he untied his bedroll.

"Here." He lowered Henry so his feet touched the ground, and offered him a blanket at the same time.

The kid took a step back, head down and arms folded across his chest.

Clay flipped open the blanket, intending to drape it over the scrawny shoulders, but the boy took another step back and spun around. His shirt had ripped from hem to collar, straight up the back. The wet, frayed ends were stuck to wide strips of cloth wrapped around his torso.

A chill that had nothing to do with the temperature or his dripping clothes shivered up Clay's spine. Along with it came a horrendous bout of ire. "Henry," he asked, barely able to keep a growl out of his voice, "who beat you?"

"No one," the kid answered gruffly.

Clay shook his head, disgusted with himself. The poor kid probably stank like he had due to a salve or poultice on his injuries. Why hadn't he asked, instead of tossing the boy into the pond? He took a step closer. "I see the bandages, Henry."

"Ban…" The kid's arm twisted backward and his fingers searched the opening. "Those aren't bandages," he scoffed, flipping around. Drops of water dripped from his hat brim and plopped steadily onto his soaked, torn shirt.

Though he wanted to wrap the blanket around the kid, who was now visibly shivering with the after-effects of his icy dip, Clay didn't move closer. Injured children were no different than injured animals. The thing to do was tread carefully, but firmly. "I know bandages when I see them."

"They're not bandages. Just give me the blanket."

An odd sensation tickled Clay's spine. Henry's tone no longer held that note of gruffness. Actually, the way he stood, with one hand stretched out, the other folded across his chest, was like a woman shielding herself.

The shiver inching its way up Clay's back turned into a fiery flash that all but snapped his spinal cord. "Tarnation," he muttered, leaping forward to snatch away the floppy hat.

Wet strands of long hair fell in every direction, and squinting eyes full of fire and ice glared at him.

"It's you!" he declared, as the fire reached his neck.

"Yes, Mr. Hoffman, it's me," Katherine Ackerman assured him. She stepped forward and grabbed the blanket from his hand, wrapping it around herself with a quick flip of her wrists. "I'll probably end up with pneumonia, thanks to you."

The woman before him looked nothing like the snooty canary he'd met at the station, and gazing at her now, sopping wet, in tattered boy's clothes, with her mass of wet hair plastered to her head, Clay experienced a humorous rumble erupting. He pinched his lips to hold it in, but it burst from his chest with enough pressure that he had to toss his head back to let the entire bout of laughter out or else choke on it.

"I don't find anything funny, Mr. Hoffman," she screeched above his hooting.

"That's because you're not seeing what I'm seeing."

Caught up in laughing, Clay didn't see her move until it was too late. Pain shot up his shin from where the toe of her boot struck him. He hopped on one foot and grabbed his other leg, applying pressure to stop the stinging.

Knowing that only time would ease the ache, he let go, and turned around to discover her using his other blanket to sop the water from her hair. As she finger-combed the tresses and squeezed the ends with the blanket, he wondered how all that hair had fit under one floppy hat. Furthermore, how had he not noticed he was a she?

"What are you doing out here, Miss Katherine Ackerman from Boston, Massachusetts?"

"You know." She bent, flipping her hair forward. The tresses almost touched the ground as she wrung them out with her hands and then shook them.

Moving away from the spray of droplets, he walked over to sit on a boulder and empty the water from his boots. "How would I know?"

Her hair made a graceful arch as she flipped her head up and turned to cast him a look—one of those glares that women produced and expected everyone to understand. And if truth were told, hers was quite adorable. Clay frowned at the thought, and went back to dumping water from one boot and then the other.

"You know I'm tracking Samuel Edwards."

Her smugness, mixed in with that nasally accent, was charming. Clay stiffened and tugged on a boot. There was nothing about her, including her accent, that was charming, pleasant or even likable. She was like every other female gracing this earth—a conniving little imposter. This one even went so far as to dress up as a boy just to get her way.

Clay pulled on the other boot and stood. "Sam. His name's Sam." Walking across the grass, he didn't stop until he stood right before her. "And you, Miss Katherine Ackerman from Boston, Massachusetts, are not tracking him."

The way she sighed, the way she rolled her eyes, even the way she squared her shoulders irritated the pants off him, but her answer, "Yes, Mr. Hoffman, I am," downright infuriated him.

"No, you're not. If there's anything you want to talk to Sam about, it goes through me."

After an icy glare, she spun around.

"What do you want with him, anyway?"

She lifted her chin snootily and glanced over one shoulder. "That, Mr. Hoffman, is none of your business."

He didn't know if he wanted to insult her by laughing or by paddling her bottom. She deserved both. Instead he went with logic. "Tell me, Miss Ackerman, how do you plan to track him? You've lost your horse, have no supplies and…" he pointed a finger from her toes to her nose, wondering how to describe her appearance "…look like a cat caught in a downpour."

"Thanks to you," she spat.

"I'll accept—" he looked her up and down pointedly "—your wet clothes are my fault, but I didn't have anything to do with your horse." He leaned closer to whisper, "It was probably the stench that got to him, too."

"Oh," she screeched, throwing the blanket off her shoulders.

The humor tickling his insides at her reaction faded. A moment later he wondered if she was being attacked by a swarm of insects, but then assumed, by the way she peered down the front of her shirt, searched the ground and patted her neckline, that she was looking for something.

"It's gone."

"What's gone?" he asked.

"My pouch. It must have fallen off in the water." She grabbed the blanket off the ground, furiously searching its folds.

Still unaffected, he made a halfhearted effort of glancing around. "What pouch?"

"It was a little bag, about this big." She held up a thumb and forefinger. "And brown, with little beads on the string pulling it closed."

"What was in it?" Now, almost wondering if it held the Ackerman family fortune, given the way she searched, he scanned the earth more seriously.

"It must be in the pond." She spun, shooting past Andrew.

The horse snorted and sidestepped, blocking Clay's

pursuit. He shoved his way around the animal and caught her arm. "You aren't going to find it in there."

"I have to. It must have slipped off when I dived for my hat."

"When you dived for your hat?"

"Yes, it was sinking almost faster than I could swim."

Clay clutched her arm a bit more firmly. "You dived after your hat?"

Her gaze scoured the water, as if she could see into the depths below. "The pouch must have slipped off my neck then."

"I thought you were drowning." Clay wanted to shake her. He twisted her instead, so he could glare straight into her face, upturned nose and all. "I jumped in an ice-cold pond to save you, and you were chasing a sinking hat?"

"You jumped in to save me?"

"Yes," he all but growled.

"Why?"

"Because I thought you were drowning." His voice rose with each word.

"That was unnecessary. I'm a perfectly good swimmer," she replied, as her gaze went back to the pond.

The ire eating inside him was wasted on this woman, as was any more time. He let go of her arm and strode toward Andrew.

"Where are you going?"

Ignoring the urge to reply, he picked up his blankets.

"Aren't you going to get my pouch?"

Acting calm wasn't too hard, not when it so obviously irritated her. He folded the blankets in half and then began to roll them up to fit behind the saddle.

"You can't leave."

A smile tugged at his lips. "Yes, Miss Katherine Ackerman from Boston, Massachusetts, I can." He tucked the roll behind his saddle, securing it with the leather straps.

"But—but I can't stay here, not without my pouch."

The tremble in her voice had him turning around. Again he questioned, "What was in that pouch?"

She shrugged.

"Why is it so important?"

"Because it's an amulet." She glanced around and then whispered, "Without it…well, I could be attacked by mountain lions or bears."

Laughing long and hard was in Clay's near future, yet he held it in, considering the seriousness of her gaze. "Where'd you get it?"

"An Indian chief in Black Hawk," she answered.

Running Bear, sitting on the front porch of Big Ed's store, no doubt. The Indian would sell anything, including his medicine pouch, it appeared, to gain enough money to buy a few sticks of Adam's Black Jack. The man, who was not a chief, was completely addicted to the licorice-flavored chewing gum. "Tell me, Katherine," Clay started, a bit surprised at how easily her name rolled off his tongue. "How did he come about giving you the amulet?"

"I was at the general store, buying supplies for my…" she paused to glance around nervously "…adventure pursuing Mr. Edwards, and the owner of the store refused to sell me a gun."

Clay held in the shudder rippling his shoulders. It appeared Big Ed wouldn't go so far as to do just *anything* to make a sale. He'd have to remember to thank the man. A gun and Miss Katherine Ackerman from Boston, Massachusetts, would be a precarious pair. Lethal even. "Oh," Clay said, while waiting for her to continue.

"Well, I was a touch miffed, you see."

"A touch?"

"Well, a mite miffed."

He nodded in agreement. As if a mite was more than a touch. What came next? A pinch? A bit? A tad?

"Yes, well," she continued, "as I was leaving the building the chief was sitting on the porch. He, um, told me all about the lions and bears in this area. I asked him how his people have survived so long without being eaten by them."

Bows and arrows, guns, knives, tomahawks, but mainly brains, Clay thought, but asked, "Oh? And what did he say?"

"He said they have secret ways. We talked a tad longer, and then he agreed to sell me an amulet that would repel bears and mountain lions."

"A tad." Clay nodded, knowing it would come up. It was hard to say if she was acting, or truly this gullible. Still dripping wet, she didn't look to be a whole lot older than Sam, and nothing like the snooty woman at the train depot yesterday morning. "Tell me, did you look inside that little pouch?"

She cringed. "It didn't smell very pleasant."

"You don't say?" Clay pressed a hand to the center of his forehead, right where it had started to hurt. Running Bear had probably put a dead fish in there. It was a wonder she hadn't attracted bears and cats instead of repelling them.

Andrew let out a snort, and Clay turned to pat the animal's neck. *I know, boy. I know she's loco.* "Well, Katherine, Andrew and I have to get going. We'll give you a ride back to Black Hawk, or you're welcome to forge out on your own, chasing down Mr. Edwards, as you called him. It's up to you."

Kit was so engrossed in the way he said "Katherine," not to mention quite enthralled that Clay Hoffman's eyes were the exact same shade of blue as the bearded irises she'd planted near Gramps and Grandma Katie's memorial stone, it was a moment or more before she realized he was waiting for her response, and then she had to pull up her acting voice. "Well, of course I'm returning with you. I couldn't possibly remain out here without the amulet."

The memory of the foul-smelling medicine bag was enough to make her shiver from head to toe. Yet she might need it again. The smell worked wonders in keeping others at bay, which was why she'd bought it.

She should be miffed at Clay for throwing her in the water as he had, but truth be told, it was amazing he'd stood the stench as long as he had. Of course, he didn't realize she'd taken the pouch off last night and laid it near his side of the fire pit. She'd thought it would keep him on his side of the fire—which it had. Her initial fears had been more centered on coming across the fur-covered man in the wild, but a pompous gold-miner that held her livelihood in the palm of his hand was just as bad. That's what Clay Hoffman was. And miners were a breed of their own—that's what Grandma always said. Therefore Kit disliked every last one of them.

The man may have had Gramps duped, but his cocky grin and twinkling blue eyes couldn't fool her. She'd have to deal with him, that was for sure, but first she had to learn exactly who Sam Edwards was, without Clay Hoffman learning she was Kit Becker and not Katherine

Ackerman. If he discovered her identity, she might never learn the truth. She sighed. All in all, this was turning out to be far more complicated than she'd imagined.

He'd hoisted himself into the saddle and held out a hand. Given her choices, she took it, shoved a foot in the stirrup he made ready and climbed on the big roan behind him, barely flinching at the sting the movement caused. Squirming, making a more comfortable seat out of his jumbled bedroll, she grabbed the back swells of the saddle. "Ready, Mr. Hoffman."

"Are you now?" he replied, sounding somewhat sarcastic.

Kit let it slide, just as she had most of his other comments. Now wasn't the time. Besides, his eyes had told her more than his words had, anyway. Laughter had twinkled in those blue eyes at some of her exaggerated comments, and that reinforced how good of an actress she was. Of course, she'd never acted previous to this trip into the wilds of Colorado. But she was well-read. Books were her life, had taught her many things, including the importance of gaining the upper hand.

She wiggled a bit more. Her backside had taken to stinging again, and the bindings around her chest grew more and more uncomfortable. The strips of cotton were shrinking as they dried, no doubt, this being their first washing.

He twisted, tossed a quick glance over his shoulder, and she flashed him a grin, a syrupy one. Clayton Hoffman was not what she had expected. He couldn't be much older than her, seven or eight years maybe, making him twenty-eight or twenty-nine. Much too young to be her grandfather's partner. She'd truly anticipated an old geezer with one foot in the grave. A cringe had her sending up a silent plea, *No offense, Gramps.*

The smile that formed on her lips was real. She could hear his answer.

None taken, Kitten.

If Clayton Hoffman wasn't sitting right in front of her, she might have talked to Grandpa Oscar a bit. Asked him how he and Grandma were getting along up there in heaven. But since now wasn't the time or place, she was content just to smile, glad she still had this connection with the people who had raised her and loved her with great devotion. Grandpa Oscar's trips to Colorado had been tough on Grandma Katie. She'd always fretted something terrible the entire time he was gone, and a piece of Kit was happy they were now together for eternity.

"So, Miss Katherine Ackerman from Boston, Massachusetts, how do you know Sam?"

She bit her lips, holding in mirth at just how ridiculous the name sounded when he said it like that. Katherine Ackerman had been her birth name, but she'd never been to Boston. "I don't know him," she answered, pulling up her best actress voice. It had taken practice to acquire a Bostonian accent. A woman she'd met on the train from Chicago to Denver had been her inspiration, and pride welled at how she was able to sound just like the woman had. She'd mastered it as well as the rough voice she'd used for her Henry disguise. "I want to meet him."

Clay Hoffman repositioned his hat before he asked, "Why?"

"Because I want to meet a miner." *This particular miner, to whom, for some unknown reason, Gramps willed one half of his estate.* It was all so frustrating. Sam's name had never been spoken in her presence, nor a second partner ever mentioned. Clay Hoffman was a different matter. Gramps had talked nonstop about him.

"Sam's not a miner," he said.

His back had stiffened, as if he was bracing himself for her argument, and though she did want to insist Sam was a miner, and she would meet him, Kit bit her tongue to keep from arguing. Once back in Black Hawk, she'd just rent another horse and search for him again. Of course, she'd have to come up with another disguise.

"I read a playbill on the train, about the opera house in Nevadaville," she said, aloud. "Does it really seat four hundred people?" Having read the advertisements on the train could prove beneficial. Gramps had never mentioned the opera house, but they must certainly have a wardrobe full of costumes, and Nevadaville was only five miles from Black Hawk, by train.

"Yes, why?" he answered, sounding skeptical, almost angry.

"Boston has several wonderful opera houses, and I'm curious what one in the wilds of Colorado would look like." That sounded plausible, didn't it? Surely Boston had an opera house. Chicago did, and she truly enjoyed watching the plays. If that silly horse she'd rented hadn't run off, she wouldn't be worrying whether Boston had opera houses or not. She'd be finding out exactly who Sam Edwards was.

The best laid plans of mice and men, she quoted silently, pressing a hand to her temple. Once she knew the truth, she could decide what to do. The only thing that made sense was that Grandpa had another family. One not even Grandma knew about. It was unfathomable, yet why else would Gramps have included Sam in the will, and at the same amount as her? Clay Hoffman seemed as protective over Sam's identity as Gramps's solicitor, Mr. Watson.

It appeared no one wanted Kit to know the truth.

"So, Miss—"

Interrupting Clay, not done contemplating her thoughts, she leaned forward and whispered, "You don't think there's a bear or mountain lion following us, do you?"

Chapter Two

His back stiffened again and Kit swore she saw his neck quiver slightly.

"No, I don't believe there are any bears or mountain lions following us. They are few and far between in this area."

Gramps had never mentioned the animals, so she figured they weren't an issue, yet he hadn't mentioned Sam, either. "I sure do wish we'd found my amulet," she whispered.

"I'm sure the *chief* will sell you another."

She puffed out her cheeks, really wishing for a moment of quiet. "Oh, do you think so?" She'd come up with bears and mountain lions off the top of her head. A woman from Boston would be afraid of such things and believe an amulet from a chief would save her—and it had proved useful. Once in Black Hawk she'd ask the old Indian if he had another one. It had cost only a package of chewing gum. He'd been the one to tell her if she put a dead fish in it no one would come close to her, and had even told her where to find the fish.

"Yes," Clay answered.

Thankfully, he let the conversation slip then. The

scenery was quite beautiful, all lush and green, just as Gramps had explained. Her fingernails dug into the thick leather at the back of the saddle and a shiver skirted up her spine. Kit held her breath, refusing to remember how frightful the train ride into Black Hawk had been.

Clay glanced over his shoulder, and she tried, but knew the smile on her face wobbled. He stared harder and she averted her gaze, glancing at the surroundings.

"You doing all right back there?"

"Um, yes," she mumbled.

"You sure?" Those blue eyes were frowning, and he shifted as if trying to get a better look at her. His movements had her repositioning and glancing around. The mountains weren't as intimidating while on horseback. Zigzagging around the Rockies in that train had instilled a fear inside her like she'd never known. Grandma Katie would have been appalled to hear her talk so, but Kit had to tell the train agent how offensive the ride had been. Then again, Grandma would be upset that she'd left the house empty and embarked on this journey at all. Maybe it was a family trait—fear of train rides— for it appeared Sam didn't like trains, either, considering he'd taken the trail to Nevadaville. That was a nice thought, knowing she and Sam already had something in common.

"You sure?" Clay Hoffman repeated.

"Yes," she answered. "I'm fine. Just fine."

"The mountains make you nervous?" he asked, looking straight ahead, but nonetheless drawing her full attention.

Kit squared her shoulders. "No."

"You aren't a very good liar, Miss Ackerman."

She drew in a determined breath. Agreeing with Clayton Hoffman was not something she'd do, no matter how accurate he might be.

Kit let silence speak for her. It was a damnable situation, as Gramps would say—this one she found herself in. Yet she'd have to put up with Clay in order to get back to Black Hawk.

Wiggling, she repositioned her bottom on the bedroll. Her clothes were drying quickly and not overly uncomfortable, but the dampness irritated the spot on her backside that had grown tender yesterday while she'd been riding the rented horse.

The animal, white with liver-colored spots, had been gentle enough, but slipping about in the saddle while the horse picked its way over the rough trail had been quite tedious, and the thick wool of the britches Kit had bought from the Chinese washwoman at the hotel had chafed her bottom from the constant motion. There was one spot in particular where she wondered if there was any skin left.

It was a while later when Clay glanced over his shoulder again. "You sure you're doing all right?"

"Yes, I'm fine, thank you," she lied, flinching at another sliver of pain commencing in her bottom. Tightening her leg muscles, she held her breath, hoping that would help.

His gaze roamed over her face in such a way Kit felt as if she were a newspaper being read.

"Are you hungry?" he finally asked. "We didn't have any breakfast. I have some jerky and bread."

Would she be able to get back on the horse if she got down? The tenderness had grown stronger, now throbbed as painfully as it had yesterday when she'd climbed off her rented horse. That's when the animal had run off, while she'd been nursing her injury, much too sore to chase after it. Kit eased her weight onto the opposite hip and held in a groan. "How much farther is it?"

"To Black Hawk?"

"Yes."

"It's only about five miles as the crow flies, but ten or more for us."

A heavy dread settled on her shoulders. "That far?"

"Yes. Have you forgotten how far you traveled yesterday?"

No, she almost blurted, though her backside was a constant reminder. "It didn't seem that far," she admitted from between clenched teeth. He might as well have said a hundred miles. The way her bottom throbbed she'd be lucky to make it one, let alone ten. The horse's gait, though smooth and even, made riding on one hip impossible. She placed a hand on the animal's glossy-haired rump, which rose and fell with each step, and braced herself against the movement. "Maybe we could get down and rest for a while. I'm sure Andrew would appreciate that."

"We'll stop at that next plateau." Clay pointed a short distance up the hill. "There's a set of trees that'll give some shade. The higher the sun gets, the stronger the rays become."

Kit nodded, knowing full well he couldn't see her actions. But short of groaning, it was the best she could do. Setting her gaze on the terrain, she tried to focus on something besides the pain, knowing the more she thought about the stinging, the worse it became. It was like that with most things—the harder you thought or fretted, the larger they became. Gramps said that all the time. It was true about his will, too.

And Clayton Hoffman. A year ago, when she'd first learned of the terms of Grandpa Oscar's will, she'd accepted everything readily enough, too filled with grief to really care. But now that she'd been on her own for a year, and the pain of her grandparents' passing was easier to deal with, she'd discovered she needed to know the truth. Others didn't understand the driving need inside her. How could they? They had families. She had no one. Not a single person on earth related to her. The gaping hole that left inside her was indescribable, and it seemed to be sucking the very life out of her. An old ticket stub to Black Hawk she'd found in one of Grandpa's books had seemed like a sign, and no matter what she discovered, it would be better than not knowing.

Mr. Watson, Grandpa's solicitor, certainly didn't understand. Not only did he refuse to give her any details, he said she couldn't go to Colorado, leastwise not without Clay Hoffman's permission—a man she'd never met, only heard about from Gramps.

It appeared that he—Clay Hoffman—was not only her financial guardian, he was in charge of everything: her finances until she was twenty-one, and several other aspects of her life until she turned twenty-five. If she waited until then she'd die of loneliness.

Impulsive, that's what Grandma Katie had always called her. Kit hadn't minded then, and she didn't mind now. If a few hastily laid plans would reveal the truth, it would be well worth it. The spontaneous trip across the country had become an adventure for her, one that instilled a sense of excitement and freedom she'd never known.

Other than the sting in her backside, which at this very moment was letting itself be known with renewed force, the trip had been painless—terrifying at times, but painless.

"Here we are." Clay drew the horse to a stop.

A sigh of relief built in her chest, but she couldn't let it out. Thinking of climbing off the horse instantly doubled her anxiety. The now constant ache said movement would hurt. Severely.

The way Clay swung his knee over the saddle horn and bounded to the ground as effortlessly as a cat jumped off a branch had every muscle tightening from her head to her toes. Kit chewed on a fingertip, both to redirect the pain and to contemplate how she could manage without—

"Oh!"

Hands had wrapped around her waist, lifted her and planted her feet on the ground all in one swift movement. Regaining fortitude while clouds literally swirled before her eyes seemed impossible, and her breath caught inside her lungs at the smarting sting shooting down her legs. Eventually, she managed to squeak, "Thank you."

"You're welcome," he said, already leading the horse to a patch of grass. "I noticed dismounting isn't a strong suit for you."

His back was to her, but the humor in his voice couldn't be ignored. "Dismounting?" she asked, as indignation sprouted out of that fiery sting. "I'll have you know I'm a quite accomplished rider."

"Oh?" He was looking at her over one broad shoulder. His grin, which was way too appealing for a man of any age or rank, brightened his entire face, and those blue eyes twinkled as if someone had dropped stardust in them. "You ride around Boston, do you?"

Firelight, the little pony she'd had while growing up, came to her mind. The Shetland had been as white as snow, and the two of them had worn out the grass in the back paddock.

"I assumed you'd travel about in gold carriages, complete with velvet seats and little tassels hanging off the hood," he continued, while digging in his saddlebags.

The fact he'd described the buggy—white, not gold— that was parked in her carriage house back in Chicago should irritate her. In reality, it made her smile. "Jealous, are you?"

"No."

His cheekbones were slightly tinged red. That, too, excited her in a unique and secretive way. "I think you are."

"You think wrong, Miss Katherine Ackerman from Boston, Massachusetts." He held up a canvas bag and nodded toward the grove of trees. "Hungry?"

She turned to follow, which was a mistake. The first step had her gulping. Walking was worse than riding. Picking a slow trail, pretending to scrutinize the lay of the land, she made her way after him.

"A little sore?" That irritating grin of his was back.

"No," she lied.

"That why you offered to walk earlier?"

She cast him her best "you're annoying me" gaze.

He grinned and sat down, digging into the bag.

By the time she arrived at his side, he'd laid out several pieces of jerky, a crusty loaf of bread, broken in half, and two apples on a blue-and-white-plaid napkin. But it was the ground, which looked as hard as the leather-covered train seats had been, that held her attention. If she sat, she might never get up, yet her stomach growled as her eyes darted toward the food.

He stood. "I have to get the canteen."

She nodded absently, still wondering how painful sitting would prove to be. Perhaps she could stand while eating. If he'd hand her the food, she wouldn't even need to bend over.

Still contemplating options, she glanced his way when he returned. Along with the canteen, he had the two blankets that made up his bedroll. Quite honorably, he folded one and then the other, and stacked them on the ground.

"Try that," he said, patting the blankets.

Kit pressed her tongue against the inside of her cheek and met his gaze.

"It's obvious, Miss Katherine Ackerman from Boston, Massachusetts, that you're sore from being in the saddle too long."

"Obvious?"

He was a large man, with broad shoulders and bulky arms covered in a tan flannel shirt and leather vest. But the kindness simmering in his blue eyes made him look like a proper gentleman who might come calling on a Saturday night.

That thought did something to her insides, had things stirring around in a very peculiar way.

"Happens to everyone now and again." He held out a hand, inviting her to take the seat he'd prepared.

The stirring inside her grew warmer, something Kit thought she should question, but instead, another unusual instinct had her accepting his offer by placing her hand in his. He flinched sympathetically as she lowered herself, and his compassion somehow eased the sting as she settled onto the blanket. "Thank you, Mr. Hoffman." Feeling a need to justify something—whether her abilities or the odd things going on inside her—she added, "I have ridden before."

His brows arched enigmatically. "I've no doubt you have, *Katherine*." Clay handed her a long strip of jerky and forcibly bit the end off another piece. He chewed slowly, sitting there beside her and gazing across the hillside.

She wondered why he'd emphasized her name so. The way he said it made her heart skip a beat. Kind of like when she'd thought of him calling on Saturday nights. No one had ever called upon her any night of the week, so where on earth had that thought come from? Pondering, she let her gaze wander along the same skyline as his.

It was a picturesque sight, the mountainside decorated with newly leafed trees and patches of bold green grass, along with pines and spruces, unfathomably dense, that grew in the most unexpected places. Even during the train ride, which had had her stomach flipping and her temples pounding, she'd been in awe at the beauty of the Rockies. Gramps had told her about it, but up close, the wild and raw grandeur was astounding. Romantic, even.

"So," Clay said, interrupting her ponderings, "why the getup?"

She swallowed and licked the salt from the jerky off her lips. "The getup?"

His eyes roamed from the hole in the tip of one boot to the plaid shirt hanging loosely about her shoulders.

"I figured a boy riding in the hills wouldn't gain much more than a second glance," she said.

They were silent for a while, other than the crunch of teeth sinking into the apples, which were surprisingly sweet and crisp considering they must have been bouncing around in his saddlebags. When he'd pitched his apple core toward Andrew, and the horse had snatched it up quickly, Clay asked, "And the bandages?"

Kit felt the heat rise on her cheeks, but didn't bow her head or look away. "I told you, they aren't bandages."

"Then what are they?"

The sting of embarrassment grew. "If you must know…"

He waited patiently as she finished her apple and tossed the leftovers to the expectant-looking Andrew. Feeling more than a touch flustered, but knowing he wouldn't let up until she answered, she said, "I couldn't wear my…" she lowered her voice "…normal garments beneath the disguise, so I wrapped myself." She'd read about that in a book, and it had worked remarkably well.

"Wrapped yourself?"

She nodded.

"Why?"

If it wouldn't be excruciating, she'd have bounded to her feet. Instead she tried to explain her reason vaguely. "The disguise would not have worked as well if I hadn't."

The humor glittering in his eyes made a new bout of something akin to anger sweep up her spine.

"I suspect it wouldn't have," he said, stopping his knowing gaze on her torso.

The way her breasts tingled had her shooting to her feet. Flinching and catching her breath at the sharp pains and dull throbs that resulted, she couldn't stop from grasping her backside with one hand. Gritting her teeth, she prayed for the burning sensation to ease.

"Here."

Not realizing she'd closed her eyes, Kit was surprised to see him standing beside her, holding out a small tin. "What's that?"

"Salve."

"For what?"

He glanced around as if assuring their privacy, and then leaned closer to whisper, "For the saddle sore on your rump."

"My r—" She swallowed the rest of the word, aghast.

"Yes, your rump." Though he looked as if he was about to burst out laughing, he didn't. "Saddle sores are a common ailment, and nothing to be embarrassed about." His expression turned serious. "They're also nothing to mess with. Especially once the boil forms."

The intense heat of mortification covered her face. "I do *not* have a boil," she insisted.

"Maybe not yet, but you will by the time we get to Black Hawk if you don't take care of it." He took her hand and laid the tin in her palm. "Go behind the trees and rub some on."

Right now, she was willing to try most anything. The pain had become unbearable. "Will it hurt?" she asked.

"Yes."

She snapped her head up. The laughter was gone from his eyes. Sincerity and honesty shone there instead. A large lump formed in her throat. "Yes?"

He nodded. "At first it's going to sting like h—really sting, but within a few minutes it'll ease up and soon the spot will be numb. You won't feel a thing the rest of the way to town. At which point you'll want to have Doc look at it. He may need to lance it."

Her insides shook. "Lance it?"

Again there was nothing but truthfulness in Clay's gaze. That and compassion. "Go on," he insisted, turning her about by grasping her shoulders. "Andrew and I will wait here."

Kit wished she had an alternative. Well, she did, but the thought of a boil wasn't much of a choice, and she honestly didn't think she could climb back on Andrew the way her backside stung—as if she'd backed up against a cookstove. "You won't peek?"

Clay fought the urge to laugh. It wasn't funny. Her backside had to be stinging as if she'd sat on a hornets' nest. He doubted there was a person alive who hadn't ended up with a saddle sore at one point in his or her life. Including him. But she looked so darn cute. "No," he assured her. "Neither Andrew nor I will peek." The flicker of annoyance dancing in her coffee-colored eyes had a grin tickling the edges of his lips. He winked. "Yell if you need help, though."

The chuckle that her glare ensued died as Clay watched her gingerly pick a path behind the trees. She was in serious pain. He walked to Andrew, keeping his eyes focused on the scrap of snow clinging to the farthest mountain peak. "The balm will help," he told the horse, fighting the urge to turn about and see if anything was visible between the aspens behind which Katherine Ackerman from Boston, Massachusetts, had taken refuge.

Clay tossed his head with a touch of frustration. He really had to stop calling her that. She gave him one of her little looks every time it rolled off his tongue. Maybe that's why he did it. He certainly didn't like her. She was as annoying as bedbugs.

A tiny screech had him spinning about. "Are you all right?" he called.

"Yes," she answered, sounding somewhat winded with pain.

"Give it a minute," he shouted. "It'll ease."

"It'd better!"

Smiling, he reached down to tighten the saddle cinch strap he'd loosened when they stopped to eat. She had grit, he had to give her that. All in all, she was quite remarkable. Katherine Ackerman from Boston, Massachusetts. Once again, he chided himself. "Katherine" just didn't fit her. It seemed too formal for someone so youthful and charming. Maybe she went by Kathy.

Leading Andrew to the blankets, he proceeded to fold them into a neat pad for Kathy to sit on. Nope. Kathy didn't fit her, either. He turned toward the woods, where she was tenderly stepping from between the trees. Now dry, her hair had turned straw colored and hung in spirals around her shoulders, while the ends bounced near her elbows.

It was all he could do to stop staring. Spinning around, he laid the bedroll behind the saddle. As soon as he got Miss Katherine Ackerman from Boston, Massachusetts, back to Black Hawk, he'd see she got on the next train heading east, and he'd never think about her again.

"Thank you." She handed him the tin. "You were right. It stung like the dickens at first, but now I can't feel a thing." Her eyes twinkled as brightly as specks of gold in a creek bed as she leaned a bit closer and whispered, "I can't thank you enough for that."

His throat thickened, and for a moment Clay thought about something he hadn't contemplated in years: kissing. Her lips seemed to have been made just for that purpose.

He managed to mumble, "You're welcome," as he took the tin and stuck it back in the saddlebag.

Once he'd climbed into the saddle, he held one stirrup on top of his boot for her to use as he took her hand. After she'd settled onto the blankets, he asked, "You set?"

She grasped the saddle with both hands near his hips before answering, "Yes, thank you."

He clicked his tongue, setting Andrew moving, and held his breath at the way his skin near her hands tingled. He'd have been better off riding all the way back to Black Hawk smelling the foul kid Henry. "What was in that pouch, anyway?"

The tinkle of her soft giggle tickled his neck. "A dead fish."

"Really?"

"Well, parts of one, anyway. I'd stuck it in there."

"Why?"

"In case someone caught me tailing Mr. Edwards. I figured the smell would keep them at bay."

Clay had almost forgotten that part—that she was looking for Sam. "All this just to meet a miner?"

"I've always wanted to meet a miner."

I'm a miner, Clay had an unusual urge to say, but of course didn't. He'd asked Sam yesterday if he knew a young woman from Boston, but the boy had had no idea what he was talking about. So Clay had decided there was no reason for the two of them to meet, and all the more reason for him to send her back to Boston as soon as possible.

He glanced heavenward, as if Oscar could see him. *Why me?* he asked. *Why didn't you leave someone else in charge of your will and your wayward grandson?*

Chapter Three

Clay was still asking the same question the next evening when he sat across the fire pit from Sam outside a small cave not far from the Wanda Lou, the gold mine owned by the two of them and Oscar's other grandchild, a young girl named Kit who lived in Chicago. It had started out simple enough. Nine years ago, he and Oscar had agreed to continue the partnership his father, Walt, and Oscar had formed years before. That joint venture had been for the Wanda Lou when she was little more than a hole in the side of Clear Creek Mountain—named for the creek that split to flow both eastward and westward off the mountaintop, and carried specks of gold all the way down on both sides.

Staring into the light of the fire, watching the flames spout sparks into the air, Clay was more than a touch reflective, given all that had happened lately. And there was a wall of frustration in his head due to the fact he couldn't get a set of big brown eyes out of his mind.

She was in more places than his mind. That woman had gotten right under his skin. "So," he asked, "you've never heard of Katherine Ackerman?"

Sam let out a sigh. "I already told you, no. And I

ain't got no relatives in Boston. My pa didn't have any family."

"And you were just in Black Hawk to sell your furs?"

"Yep, got a good price for them, too." Sam removed his hat to scratch his head, which was covered with an unruly mop of red hair. "Why would a woman from Boston want to talk to me?"

Clay wished he knew. His gut said it was because of Sam's inheritance. All in all, that came down to the only explanation. "You haven't sent any wires? Discussed the will with anyone?" He'd already asked, and for the most part believed Sam when he said that he hadn't.

"No, why would I do that?"

There was no reason, Clay knew. But he also knew Sam was relatively unknown, even in the mountains he'd lived in all seventeen years of his life. That was the way of most trappers, and Sam was especially shy around people.

"Maybe she's here to see your opera house," Sam said. "Folks come from all over for that."

The unexpected tightening in his jaw had Clay shifting. The opera house was a part of Nevadaville and brought in a good income, so he'd buried the memories associated with it—and Miranda. Yet ever since Katherine had mentioned the playhouse, his past had started to haunt him again. Picked at his nerves like buzzards on a carcass.

Maybe she'd met Miranda at one of the playhouses in Boston. Clay had no idea where the acting troupe was performing now. Perhaps Katherine had heard he was an easy target. She'd find out differently. He'd spent money on a woman once, and wouldn't do it again. He'd grown up with next to nothing, and now that his mines were successful, he enjoyed sharing the wealth, investing in things that helped others prosper, but he wasn't a fool. Once was enough. He'd learned a hard lesson.

Clay's insides recoiled. What was he thinking? Katherine wasn't after him, she was after Sam. Just because Clay couldn't get her off his mind didn't mean the opposite was true. Furthermore, he'd bought her a ticket east, and told Reggie Green she had to use it. She was probably in Denver by now.

Sam, poking a stick into the flames and sending sparks flying, glanced up with a deep frown. "Did you meet One Ear Bob?"

"That trapper who was looking for you?"

"Yeah." The youngster kept stirring up the fire. "Pa knew him."

Clay sensed there was more behind Sam's words, but knew he'd have a hell of a time getting anything more out. Sam had a shell as hard as an acorn's. Clay let out a long breath. "No, I didn't. Why, did he give you any trouble?"

"No. He just wanted to know where I was living now." Sam shook his head and then glanced up. "You thought any more about signing over the deed to this piece of land?"

A gut reaction said there was more to One Ear Bob than that, and Clay made a mental note to poke around when he got back to town. "I told you, it's not mine to give you," he answered.

"Yes, it is. This chunk of land is in the will, and you have control of it." Sam tossed another log into the flames. "It's all I want. You can keep everything else."

Clay squeezed his temples. "It doesn't work like that, Sam. I can't give it to you until you're twenty-one."

The terms of the will had shocked him. As if he didn't have enough to do, Oscar had saddled him with two underage wards. Thank goodness the other one, Kit, was back in Chicago, being looked after by Oscar's lawyer, Theodore Watson. The lawyer had traveled to Colorado a year ago to tell Clay the terms of the will. Everything Oscar Becker owned was divided in half, between Sam and Kit, and until the two grandkids turned twenty-one, Clay was in charge of investing the earnings. Once the youngsters were old enough, he could either buy them out or take them on as partners.

The whole thing was a mess he hadn't expected. Then again, Oscar's untimely death—a carriage accident in a rainstorm—had been a shock, too. Life was like that, throwing in things a person didn't expect. Like Katherine Ackerman.

"You could give it to me now," Sam said. "If you really wanted to."

Clay pulled his mind back around. "I can't. The will's ironclad. If either you or Kit attempt to claim your share early, it's to be sold to P. J. Nelson for a dollar."

"P.J.?"

Clay didn't comment. He should have stopped talking before saying the man's name. That part of the will had surprised him, too, for if it happened, it would jeopardize everything Clay owned. Oscar would have known that, and, Clay fumed, had used it to make sure he kept close tabs on Sam.

"P.J. ain't nothing but a drunk."

"Maybe, but he was Oscar's first partner, and Oscar said if there ever came a time when he no longer wanted the claim, he'd give P.J. first chance to buy it back. Guess he figured if you or Kit tried to mess with the will, it meant you don't want it." Clay didn't mention he'd written to Theodore Watson six weeks ago, asking if there were any alternative options. Four more years of arguing with Sam over a small chunk of land was useless. Made no difference in the long run, and if he had his way, he'd put Sam's name on the deed.

Up until two years ago, Sam had lived in a shack in the mountains, never coming to town. His old man, little more than a hermit, had downright despised people of any kind ever since his wife, Amelia, who was Oscar's daughter, had died. Leastwise that's what Clay had heard. He hadn't known anything about any of them until Sam had shown up at the Wanda Lou, claiming to be Oscar's grandson. Clay had wired Oscar, who'd made the trip west immediately, and spent half of the next year trying to convince Sam to move to Chicago and live with him.

"Sam," Clay started, trying not to sound repetitive. "Why don't you come to work at the mine, or the stamp mill, or even the railroad?"

"Because I don't want to work at any of those places," Sam said, puffing out his narrow chest. "I'm a trapper."

Clay's temples were now pounding. This was the same conversation he'd had with Sam for a year, and it was tiresome. Almost as wearing as Katherine had become the past two days.

Kit pushed the ticket back under the little half-moon shape in the wire cage of the train depot ticket booth. "I will say this one more time. I don't want this ticket, I want one to Nevadaville."

Smiling as if he couldn't make another facial expression, the little bald-headed man, whose shiny black string tie rubbed on his Adam's apple, pushed the ticket back toward her. "That's the ticket that was purchased for you, ma'am. And the one I was instructed you're to use."

"I don't care about that, Mr...." She paused, waiting for his response.

"Green. Reginald Green, at your service, ma'am." His grin widened, exposing a plethora of oddly angled teeth.

Kit shivered at the experience, but pushed the ticket back under the wire. "Mr. Green...Reginald," she started sweetly. "I understand Mr. Hoffman purchased that ticket for me, but you see, he didn't inquire about my plans prior to his purchase." She pressed a hand to her chest. "I must see the opera house in Nevadaville before I head back East." Stopping Mr. Green from sliding the ticket back in her direction with her fingertips, she pulled up a smile that hurt her cheeks. "I will accept this ticket after that. Until then, I need one to take me to Nevadaville."

Mr. Green had been shaking his head the entire time she'd been speaking. "I can't sell you a ticket to Nevadaville, ma'am."

Keeping the smile plastered on her lips became increasingly difficult. "Why not?"

"Because Cl—Mr. Hoffman said so. He said you might want to go to Nevadaville and I wasn't supposed to sell you a ticket to there. I was to give this one to you and see you got on the train."

"Really?" The evening before last, when he'd dropped her off at the hotel, she'd almost grown to like Clay Hoffman. Actually, for a few hours she'd pondered all the wonderful things Gramps had said about him, and confirmed they were true. However, right now she loathed him more than before she'd met him—sky-blue eyes and all. She took a moment to get her anger under control and ignore the flutters that happened inside her at the memory of those eyes. The simple thought of that man did odd things to her. In some ways it reminded her of the giddiness she experienced when opening a new book.

"Tell me, Mr. Green, is Mr. Hoffman your boss? Does he own the railroad?" she asked, ready to declare the man had no right—

Mr. Green's "Yes" stalled her thoughts.

"Yes to what?"

"Yes, he's my boss, and yes, he owns the railroad."

Startled to the point that her breathing stopped, she asked, "H-he does?"

Mr. Green was still smiling brightly, teeth and all. "Yes, he does."

"He owns the Colorado Central Railroad?" she asked for clarification.

"Yes, ma'am."

With a bout of fury, she picked up the ticket and ripped it in half. Twice. "Fine." Laying the pieces back on the counter, she lifted her chin. "I'm sure there's another way for me to get to Nevadaville."

Mr. Green's smile faded. "Not really, ma'am."

She cast a severe gaze his way.

Gulping until his Adam's apple sat on top of his tie, Mr. Green said, "Well, there's the wagon road, but there are places they gotta tie ropes around trees and stumps to keep the wagons from tumbling over the edge, and of course, the horses gotta wear blinders, especially while crossing the bridges."

It was Kit's turn to gulp.

"I wouldn't recommend traveling that way. Besides, the only wagons that traverse the road are Cl—Mr. Hoffman's, and he most likely wouldn't want you traveling on them."

She spun, huffing as she took a few steps, but then stopped and stomped back to the ticket booth. "Tell me, Mr. Green, what else does Mr. Hoffman own?"

"Here or in Nevadaville?"

Hiding the surprise rippling her spine, she crossed her arms.

As if the thought just came to him, Mr. Green pointed a shaky finger. "He doesn't own any of the saloons."

"How honorable," she spat, spinning on her heels.

"He doesn't own Miss Clarice's society house, either. She does. But he built it for her."

Kit closed her eyes, regaining her composure. Black Hawk was more than a small town, and she could only imagine Nevadaville was similar in size. It wasn't a city like Chicago or Denver, but it had several businesses, and the streets were made of cobblestones to keep the mud and dust down. She cast her gaze up and down, glancing at buildings of all sizes and shapes built on the hillside, while she waited for the traffic to clear so she could cross the road from the train station to the boardwalk that led to the two-story hotel she'd been staying at. How could one man own all this? Reginald Green must not know what he was talking about. Her grandfather had been a wealthy man, but not even he owned an entire town.

A slow-moving thought had her scanning the town again. Or did he? She'd read the will, several times, but all it said was all Gramps's holdings were to be divided equally between her and Sam. That could include a town and a railroad. Clay Hoffman was Gramps's partner. Had been for years.

Swallowing a sudden attack of sadness, wishing Grandpa was here so she could ask him, Kit squared her shoulders. Both he and Grandma had been tight-lipped about Colorado. She'd only recognized the name Black Hawk because Grandma Katie had let it slip one time. Was that because they didn't want anyone to know how wealthy they were? How wealthy Kit now was? Grandma always said it was best for women not to know their worth, for it often drew uncouth and undesirable men. Actually, in Grandma's eyes everything drew men, therefore Kit had never been allowed to do anything.

Her gaze landed on the old Indian sitting on the front porch of the mercantile. The man waved, and she fluttered a hand his way and then stepped back so a wagon hid her from other onlookers. Running Bear had confirmed that Clay lived in Nevadaville, and Sam as well. Naturally, it had cost her another package of chewing gum.

The traffic continued to flow by without the slightest break for her to cross the street. Another thought made her frown. Who was Miss Clarice and what was a society house? Kit's heart skipped a few beats. Could it be a house of ill repute? Certainly Grandpa hadn't owned one of those. He could have visited one, though, and that could be how Sam came to be. It was a disquieting thought, but over the past several months she'd thought of that possibility more than once—for ultimately, there were few other answers. Sam had to be Grandpa's son. Her uncle. And she wasn't leaving here until she met him, scandal be damned.

The curse had her sending up a silent plea for forgiveness—but if she had family, she had a right to know. More than that, she needed to know. She hated the feeling of being totally alone in the world.

The train whistle sounded, indicating that the locomotive pulling a passenger car, two freight cars and a small green caboose would soon leave the station and head for Nevadaville without her.

Kit turned, eyed the cars closely, thoughtfully, and then scanned the area for Mr. Green. The little booth was empty. Convinced her sudden idea was a good one, she hitched up her skirt and hurried past the passenger car, as well as the wooden freight cars. Steam shot out from under the wheels, forming a cloud around her as the whistle sounded again. It made her jump, but she kept her nerve.

The freight conductor, the one who sat in the little square pilothouse on top of the last car, was already there, looking over the tops of the cars and paying no attention to the ground below. Kit hurried forward, grabbing the metal sidebar and pulling herself onto the small platform at the very back of the train as the wheels creaked and shuddered. She tucked her skirt between her legs to climb over the rail, and then dashed through the doorway. Heart pounding, she glanced out the window as she closed the door, to assure no one had witnessed her unfashionable boarding.

Success made her smile, but moments later, when the little caboose shook as the wheels started to rumble, memories of her last train ride flashed in her mind. Her grin faded and a bubble formed in her throat. Pressing both hands over her eyes, she moaned, "Oh, no."

Clay caught the rail of the caboose at a run and pulled

himself onto the little platform. He paused, peering through the window, as his fingers grasped the door. She was sitting on the bench, but had her head hanging between her knees. He'd been watching, had seen her arguing with Reggie Green, and wasn't surprised when she'd sneaked on board, nor was he surprised that she stayed down, not wanting anyone to notice.

Katherine Ackerman was one determined woman.

His hand went to his front pocket, where the medicine bag he'd bought from Running Bear was tucked. This morning, after leaving Sam's cave, Clay had taken the early train to Black Hawk, claiming he needed to oversee the delivery of the new boiler, whereas in reality, though he barely admitted it to himself, he wanted to see if she had left. And again, not something he was overly willing to divulge, he was glad she hadn't. Though he still wouldn't let her get near Sam.

The train picked up speed, chugging and clanging, and the clatter disguised the sound of the door opening. Once inside, Clay closed the door, half wondering what to do next. Anger at how she'd scampered aboard was nonexistent. A hint of admiration was playing about inside him instead.

Small as it was, the caboose hosted only a tiny wood stove near the back wall and two long benches along the sides. The entire car swung left and right, rattling and shaking as the train picked up momentum.

Katherine let out a little yelp and one hand moved to the bench beside her knee, grasping tightly. He sat on the seat opposite her, their knees almost touching across the tiny aisle. Clay found himself wishing he could see more than the top of the little blue-and-white hat covering those glorious golden waves that had fluttered around her face and shoulders back on the mountainside. It was only four miles to Central City, and then another three to Nevadaville, but the train had to wind around the mountain to get there, making the ride a bit longer. The way she quivered said her nerves were already getting the best of her. Perplexing, considering the trail she'd traversed on horseback.

Maybe it was for show. Maybe she knew he was sitting across from her, and this was just another part of her act.

A clatter and clang had her jolting, and then the great clunking and banging of the wheels making a sharp turn had her snapping her head up. Clay held in a flinch at her paleness. No one was that good an actress, and his heart thudded in response. She was a beauty, no man could deny that—even with a tint of seasick-green covering her cheeks.

As if not sure what they saw, the big brown eyes staring at him closed for a moment and then opened again.

"Miss Ackerman," he said in greeting.

Her groan was accompanied with a slow and distraught headshake as she pressed a hand to her forehead. "I'd forgotten," she whispered.

Plenty of people grew sick riding the train up the mountain. The motion and altitude took some getting used to. Her head once again lowered to hang over her knees. Clay leaned across the small space, drawing back a hand moments before it could touch her knee. "Forgotten what?"

"How treacherous these train rides are."

Coupling the fear of heights he'd sensed back on the trail with the train ride, he felt compassion opening up inside him. With little thought, he moved across the aisle and sat down next to her. Resting a hand in the middle of her back, he assured her, "You're safe."

She shook her head. "If one of these cars came loose we'd plunge to the bottom of the mountain and never be found."

Clay glanced over his shoulder, out the window to where the houses, commercial buildings, even people moving about in Black Hawk looked like a miniature world. Others had made the same statement she just had, and he'd laughed it off, but the shakiness of her voice indicated real fear. Protectiveness sprang up inside him. "That won't happen," he answered. "You have my word on it."

"How could you stop it?"

She had yet to lift her head, and beneath his fingers her body trembled. There was something about this woman that got to him, and not just her unease right now. From the moment they'd met he hadn't been able to stop thinking about her, almost as if she'd had the key and opened that deeply guarded compartment inside him he'd long ago secured away.

Exposing the things long hidden there was not something he was prepared to do, so he blocked the thought from his mind and dug in one pocket. "I have something for you," he said.

"I know. A ticket to Boston."

Her groan made him chuckle. "No, Mr. Green still has that."

Opening one eye, she cast a wary gaze toward Clay, head still down, face still white.

He dangled the medicine bag by the leather strap.

A faint, wobbly smile tugged at the corners of her mouth. Inching upward, she trapped his hand on her back between her and the wall. "My amulet," she whispered. "How'd you—"

"It's not the same one you lost. But it's similar." He leaned closer and whispered, "This one doesn't stink."

As she let out an adorable half gasp, half giggle, he eased the leather strap over her head, careful of the little hat and the pins holding her thick curls in place. "There, now you're safe. I apologize for making you lose the other one."

A hint of color appeared on her cheeks as she fingered the bag gently. "Thank you."

The train rounded the hill, and the sound of the whistle announcing the upcoming depot prevented him from responding. Which was all right, since he had no idea what to say. The sincerity in her voice had sucker punched his heart.

Biting her bottom lip, she closed her eyes again as the train slowed to a crawl near the big drum of water towering over the tracks, marking Central City.

He didn't have a moment to speak then, either, because the door in the center of the roof opened and brown boots caught the first rung of the ladder.

Beneath Clay's fingers, Katherine's trembling increased, and he rubbed her back in a wide circle.

"What—" Looking dumbfounded, Ty Reins, dressed in his gray-and-white-striped bib overalls and matching hat, glanced around the small area. "Clay, I didn't know you were riding in here."

"It's not as crowded as the passenger car," he answered.

The way Katherine's eyes snapped open, and the shock on her face, said she knew he'd just covered up the fact she'd sneaked on board, and the bashful fall of her lashes had his blood moving a bit faster.

Clay, about to introduce the two, bit his tongue as she asked the man, "What do you do up there?"

"Keep a lookout for falling rocks and other things that could derail the train," Ty responded.

Clay groaned inwardly. It was what the man did, but the way Ty had said it was sure to increase her fears. "Which rarely happens," Clay said, rubbing her back again. The touch of velvet beneath his fingers, not to mention the heat of her body, was rather addictive.

Ty chuckled. "That's right. It rarely happens. Nothing to worry about, miss."

She nodded, but Clay sensed it was out of obligation, not belief.

"We'll only be here a few minutes," he assured her.

The conductor pointed toward the little overhead door. "You want to ride in the pilothouse? You can see forever up there."

Clay wanted to shake the man.

"No. No, thank you," Katherine said nervously. "The caboose is just fine." She tugged at the high, ruffled neckline of her white silk blouse. "D-down here. Down here is just fine."

"All right," Ty said, shrugging his massive shoulders and giving Clay a nod that said he'd tried. "We'll be heading out in another minute or two. Just had to drop off the mail here in Central."

"Thanks, Ty," Clay said, nodding toward the pilothouse door.

Right on cue the screeching whistle blew, and the man swung around to grasp the ladder again.

"How long will it take us to get to Nevadaville?" Katherine asked in a shaky whisper.

"It's only a couple of miles," Clay answered, as an overwhelming urge to grasp her waist and pull her closer to his side had his fingers moving over the blue velvet of her dress again.

"Course, we gotta go all the way around before we stop," Ty added, with one foot on the bottom rung of the ladder.

"Around?" she asked.

"Yeah. Nevadaville is the end of the line. The track makes a loop at the top of the mountain so we're headed back in the right direction."

"Thanks, Ty," Clay repeated, slipping his hand down to the small of her back as her shivers returned. He nodded toward the trapdoor again, half wondering how the conductor couldn't sense how deeply afraid she was.

Smiling brightly, the man said, "Some folks get scared on account of all the bridges. They're loud but they're safe. Built real solid. Ask Clay, there. He'll tell you."

"Bridges?" Her voice was a mere squeak.

"Yeah," Ty answered. "We gotta cross Clear Creek a few times and—"

"It's time you got back in the pilothouse, Ty," Clay said sternly.

With a dip of his hat, the man climbed the ladder and closed the door.

Clay scooted a bit closer, inching his arm all the way around her until his palm cupped the swell of her hip. "There isn't anything to worry about."

The whistle sounded once more, and with a bout of hissing steam floating past the windows, the train, clanging and banging, pulled away from the station. Clay waited until the chugging grew smooth again before asking, "You haven't ridden on many trains, have you?"

She shook her head. "This is my first trip anywhere."

There was more than a hint of loneliness in her tone, and that made the desire to hold her close grow stronger. Clay was a caring man; he understood that. Had to be, with Oscar's demands and Clarice's overflowing heart. Yet the immediate attraction and level of desire he felt for this woman was uncanny. His past had left him with very little trust for any woman.

A frown formed as she continued to gaze up at him. "What are you doing here?" she asked. "I thought you were in Nevadaville."

"I'm having a new boiler delivered. I came down on the morning train to look it over." The tale flowed out easy enough, after all the times he'd repeated it to himself.

A thunderous, echoing rumble signaled the start of one of the bridge crossings, and with a nervous screech Katherine burrowed into his side. "Shh," he whispered, liking the feel of her next to him probably more than he should. "There's nothing to be afraid of."

"That's what I'm afraid of," she answered timidly. "The nothingness below us."

He grinned and, holding her close, set a knuckle under her chin, intending to pull her face up and assure her the train wasn't going to derail. Yet when those big brown eyes peered up at him, a completely different thought overtook him.

Kit's heart landed in the back of her throat and the air in her lungs sat right there, unable to move, just like the rest of her body. She knew they were still on the train—the rumble beneath her said that. But Clay's hands softly holding her, and his eyes looking at her in a mesmerizing way, seemed to transport her into some kind of dreamland where thinking coherently grew impossible.

He moved then, slightly forward, and his lips brushed over her forehead, as soft as a feather. Yet they sent a hum through her body. A clump of air left her lungs and rattled in the back of her throat as his lips dropped lower, touched her eyelid, which had somehow closed.

His lips brushed her nose next, then her cheeks, and by then her entire body was humming. Instinct told her to move, and she did. She tilted her head up and pressed her lips to his. The connection was unique, and tantalizing.

It happened several times, their lips meeting. Each touch was gentle, unhurried and so tender it drew her full attention. There was excitement in those kisses, too, and they set off a spark inside her, yet even that was soothing in a fascinating way she couldn't describe. She nestled closer, not wanting the kisses to end, and gladly immersed herself in an absorbing journey that took her to a fantasyland not even books had told her about.

When he lifted his head and tucked hers beneath his chin, she was still floating in that once-upon-a-time place, and unwilling to leave, she snuggled against his broad chest, swaying with the gentle rocking beneath them. Never before could she remember feeling so content and safe, almost as if this was the one place she'd always been searching for.

It wasn't until the train rolled to a stop that Kit lifted her head, still half-dizzy or dazed in the stardust world she'd entered. Add that to the smile on the handsome face peering down at her and it was almost impossible to remember where she was. Who she was.

"That wasn't so bad, was it?" he asked.

"No, it wasn't bad at all," she answered, not quite sure what he was referring to.

With a thud, Mr. Reins seemed to drop down from the ceiling, grinning broadly. "There, now, lass," he said kindly. "I told you not to worry. The bridges are strong."

The narrow wooden bridges she'd traversed on the way to Black Hawk, crossing never-ending ravines that seemed too deep to host bridge supports, came to mind. She hadn't noticed one on this trip. Her gaze went to Clay and her mind took to wondering if they had kissed, or if it was some kind of fantasy her fear had conjured up so she wouldn't have to face the terrifying experience of crossing the bridges again.

"Come on," Clay said, taking her hand and helping her to her feet.

He led her to the door and gently guided her down a set of metal steps she hadn't noticed before. Once her feet hit solid ground, her composure returned—somewhat—as did her awareness of her state of affairs.

"I left my luggage in Black Hawk." She flinched, wondering why that had leaped to the front of her mind.

"Ty," Clay said, "collect the lady's luggage, would you? It's at the hotel."

Mr. Reins nodded. "Sure thing, boss. I'll bring it over on the six-thirteen."

"Thanks," Clay said, before leading her off the platform. "This way. Let's get you settled in The Gold Mine. It's the best hotel on the entire mountain. Mimmie Mae will have some tea she can brew up for you. How's that sound?"

A cup of hot, fortifying tea sounded downright heavenly, especially considering all the confusing thoughts popping in her head like a sinkful of soap bubbles. While many disappeared as quickly as they formed, a couple stayed, causing her to turn abruptly. "Mr. Reins," she called, stopping the man from climbing into one of the cargo cars.

"Yes, ma'am?"

She swept her gaze to the little lookout on top of the caboose. "You be careful riding up there." Thinking about the railroad man gave her mind something to do while thoughts of Clay and how he still held her arm continued to rattle and crash into one another.

Mr. Reins grinned and tipped his striped hat. "I will, ma'am. I will."

Kit returned his smile and, feeling more like herself than moments ago, turned to the man at her side. "Why are you being so nice to me?" She cringed at how that sounded. Clay had been nice to her before, but today it *felt* different. In a way she couldn't put her finger on, but it certainly was lovely.

"Nice?" he asked, steering her around a parked wagon.

The cobbled street echoed below their heels, and each footfall had her senses returning. "Yes, the amulet, the train ride…" Her mind went to the kissing, but a part of her still questioned the reality of that. She was under duress—the train had done that the minute the wheels started to turn—therefore she may have dreamed the kisses. He didn't seem to remember that. Leastwise he didn't mention it or act any differently. She didn't have any experience kissing men, but surely one who'd just kissed you would act differently from before.

"I said I was sorry for losing your first amulet," he said, with a sincere expression. "And I remembered you were quite fearful of heights."

She nodded. Had to. What he said was true. A quiver gripped the bottom of her spine and crept up until it reached her shoulders and had her gaze turning up. The smile that was still curving the corners of his lips had a lump forming in her throat. Had he discovered she was Kit and not Katherine? He was her guardian, so therefore would certainly have to be nice to her. Gramps would have insisted upon that. Leastwise until he sent her back to Chicago.

Clay nodded, toward the door he held open. "After you."

She grimaced and, feeling the weight of the world settling upon her shoulders, entered a room painted a sparkling gold color.

Chapter Four

A short time later, Kit's fortitude was fully restored. The tea served its medicinal purposes, and Mimmie Mae, a buxom woman with bright red hair and a booming voice, turned out to be an angel in disguise. Clay had barely ushered Kit through the door before he'd been summoned back to the train, and Mimmie Mae had taken over getting her settled in a room.

Room 202 to be exact, on the second floor of The Gold Mine, where there was a rust-colored starburst quilt covering a bed that had both a headboard and a footboard of tubular metal painted a sparkling gold, and a real mattress with clean sheets. Kit had checked for herself. Grandma Katie had always insisted the accommodations wouldn't be fit for the two of them—another reason they couldn't travel out here with Gramps. The diseases Grandma claimed one could obtain from dirty linens grew each time Grandpa made the trip. Kit had always felt the list was a bit exaggerated, but questioning Grandma's reasons was not something anyone did. The past few months, while attempting to discover who Sam was, Kit had wondered if perhaps Grandma hadn't wanted to come because of what she might discover.

Kit sat there on the starburst quilt, pondering that thought, just as she had for months back in Chicago. Pushing off the bed, she moved to the window. Grandma had always said there were no towns where Grandpa went. Nevadaville had been incorporated as a town only four years ago, Mimmie Mae had told her, but the mines had been there for years by then. Maybe Grandpa had been married before Grandma Katie, and Sam was his child from his first wife. Though it filled Kit with mixed emotions, it was the only other explanation she could deduce, as unlikely as it seemed.

She hadn't asked the hotel owner about Sam—mainly because she was too preoccupied with lingering thoughts of Clay—but Sam was why she was here, and if Clay had discovered her real identity, she needed to meet Sam quickly before being sent back to Chicago. If he truly was her half uncle—as all signs indicated—Sam should be her guardian instead of Clay.

Her heart did a little waltz inside, and standing there, staring down at a roadway bustling with people, she tried to make sense of things that just didn't add up. The hope of having a family again was what kept her going. The loneliness of the past year was still so overwhelming it left her aching. Yet, pressing a hand to her chest, she had to question if it was the thought of Clay that made her heart flutter. Not only had his young age surprised her, his kindness—both today and on the trail, when he had discovered her *ailment*—amazed her, and that had guilt rising up inside her. He would surely be upset to discover she was Kit Becker and not Katherine Ackerman.

Which meant she had better find Sam Edwards, fast. Spinning from the window, Kit checked her reflection in the dust-free, round mirror attached to the polished chest of drawers, and repinned a few hairs that had escaped during her travels. She adjusted the half-moon-shaped hat with its white lace trim to once again tilt slightly to the left on top of her heavy tresses, and turned her head both ways, checking for any out-of-place curls.

Her gaze caught on the amulet around her neck. Clay had kissed her. She hadn't imagined it, yet she couldn't fathom why he'd have done such a thing. But goodness, it had been amazing. Her hands smoothed her skirt and one hand rested on the spot that had been so tender two days ago. Not even a tad irritated. That salve certainly had worked wonders.

His kiss had been a lot like that salve he'd given her. Healing, calming. She could still smell the leather of his vest, the spicy scent of the soap he must use. A tremendous sigh built in her chest, then gushed out with all the force of a north wind. The way he'd delivered her to this hotel was almost identical to how he'd escorted her to the one back in Black Hawk two days ago, and each time he'd left, she'd felt a part of her mourn his absence.

A smile tugged at her lips as she recalled how Michael O'Reilly, M.D., had arrived at her hotel room back in Black Hawk and insisted on examining her backside, claiming Clay had sent him. She'd given in after he'd started talking about gangrene. As it turned out, it wasn't as bad as she'd expected—neither the examination nor his diagnosis. The salve had done its job, as had the pad Clay had provided for her to sit on the rest of the ride. Dr. O'Reilly said those two things contributed to why a boil hadn't formed. He'd left her some salve of her own, and suggested she not ride a horse for a few days.

Kit spun around. Land sakes, but this trip was turning out to be perplexing in so many ways. She gave her mind an inner shake. Sam was who she had to focus on, not Clay. Mimmie Mae would most likely know all there was to know about Sam. After a final glimpse in the mirror—during which she gave herself an encouraging nod—Kit left the room.

A niggling thought occurred as she made her way down the hall. If Mr. Reins noticed the name on her trunks, her disguise would be over for sure. She'd miss being Miss Katherine Ackerman from Boston, Massachusetts—had enjoyed playing the part of a courageous heroine. It made her forget who she really was, and the isolation she'd known most of her life. The tingling sensation in her insides as she recalled the way Clay had said "Miss Katherine Ackerman from Boston, Massachusetts" almost as if it were one word, caused a frown, which she abruptly shook off.

The alias didn't matter. He'd discover who she was soon enough—if he didn't already know. She just had to find Sam before seeing Clay again. That was the bottom line.

Clay had just overseen the unloading of the new boiler, a monstrous machine that was as expensive as she was large, but would pay for herself within a few months once they got her installed, when Ty Reins flagged him down, waving a little blue bag over his head. Now, holding the small satchel open to peer at the name embroidered in the silk, Clay felt an eerie sensation grip his spine. "This was in the caboose?"

"Yeah," Ty repeated. "I didn't know that was Oscar's

Kit sitting with you." The pilothouse conductor grinned broadly. "She sure is a cute little thing, ain't she?"

A tick tugged at Clay's brow as he shook his head, causing him to press a finger to his temple. The eerie sensation had him repeating, "Kit Becker."

"You want me to run it over to the hotel?"

Theodore Watson would have wired him if Oscar's other grandchild was on her way here—leastwise the man should have. Then again, perhaps he had. Clay ran a hand through his hair and spun on a heel, heading toward his office. "No, I'll give it to her."

"I'll bring the rest of her luggage over this evening," Ty yelled.

Clay nodded, but his mind was spinning, as was his stomach. He took the stairs leading up to his office above the Land and Claims office two at a time, and threw open the door, his heart skipping several beats. Kit was Oscar's pride and joy. The man had come to love Sam as well, but nothing could ever have compared to how Oscar and Katie felt about Kit.

Katie.

Katherine.

Kit.

Damn.

Rifling through a stack of telegrams, he came upon several marked urgent, but read only the one from Theodore Watson. It not only asked if Kit Becker had arrived, but requested an immediate response. Gritting his teeth, Clay pulled open the bottom drawer and dug until he came upon the picture of Oscar, his wife, Katie, and their granddaughter, Kit.

She was younger, since the picture was several years old, but it was her. Katherine Ackerman was Kit Becker.

"Aw, hell," Clay muttered as he fell into his desk chair. That picture was how he thought of Kit. A young girl. Not a woman. What was she up to, pretending to be someone else? A growl rumbled out of his throat. What was *he* up to? He'd kissed her. Kissed his ward. And furthermore, while holding her on the train, he'd thought about doing a whole lot more than kissing. Matter of fact, he'd imagined their next interlude the entire time he'd been unloading the boiler.

"She's a beaut. A man can't help but fall in love with that one."

"What?" Clay asked, snapping his head up and quivering from head to toe.

Raymond Walker grinned from the doorway. "The new boiler. She's twice the size of the old one."

Clay cleared his head with a shake and rose. "That she is," he responded, dropping the picture and the little satchel in the drawer and kicking it shut. Kit Becker would have to wait. "Are you ready for her?"

"Yep. By this time tomorrow she'll be working at full steam, dropping those stampers twice as fast as the old one." Raymond had a grin a mile wide on his face. The man was not only the best engineer in Colorado, he treated every load of gold as if it were his very first.

"Sounds good to me," Clay said, moving toward the doorway. "I'm amazed you kept the old one going as long as you have."

"It weren't easy, I'll give you that, but that old girl served us well. That she did. I've no doubt this new one will be just as good. Maybe better." The engineer grinned like a man in love.

"With you at the helm, I've no doubt, either." Clay unbuttoned his cuffs and rolled his sleeves up to his elbows as they walked down the stairway. Excitement zipped up his spine. There wasn't a job that had to do with mining gold he didn't love. "I can't wait to hear her hiss the first time."

"Me, either," Raymond agreed.

Hours later, long after the sun had set and a million stars twinkled overhead, they were both grinning ear to ear as the newly installed boiler was christened. Fulfilling every promise of her advertisement, the machine handled the job with ease and accuracy.

"Listen to that, boss," Raymond shouted. "She sounds sweeter than a songbird. Course, the real test will come tomorrow morning, when we hook her up to the stampers."

They stood outside the stamp mill, watching the cloud of steam rolling out of the round stack fade into the night sky. Clay grasped the man's broad shoulder. "You've done a heck of a job. There'll be a bonus in your pay at the end of the month."

The man bowed his head. "Aw, that ain't necessary, boss. You already pay me more than I ever dreamed. The missus says so every month."

"Well, you deserve it. The stamp mill wouldn't produce like she does without you." Clay glanced down the street. The rows of buildings climbing the mountainside were dark. Store owners and residents had long ago called it a night and taken to their beds. The sight caused the long day to catch up with him, and he stretched his arms overhead, arching against stinging muscles. "I hear my bed calling, and you'd better head home before the missus comes looking for you."

Raymond laughed. "Anna will have supper waiting for me. You want to come along and have some?"

The big German was married to a woman half his size, and the two, though they'd been married for years, acted like love-struck kids—something that never ceased to amaze Clay.

"Thanks, but no. I'm too tired to eat."

"Gotta eat to keep up your strength," the worker said, letting out a rough laugh. "That's what my Anna always says." A stern expression overtook his face. "Are you sure you won't come along? Anna won't mind. Matter of fact, she'll be fretting if she thinks you went to bed hungry."

"I'm sure. Tell her I'll make up for it at breakfast."

"I'll see you tomorrow, then, boss. Night."

"Good night," Clay offered as he turned to walk up the street, while Raymond went the opposite direction, toward the edge of town where a dozen mail-ordered houses sheltered miners and mill workers and their families. There were two other such clusters of homes on the other end of town, and every one of them had tenants. No, Clay thought, not tenants, owners.

It was customary for most towns like this to be completely owned by the mine. The stores, the houses…everything people needed they bought or rented from the mine. From what he'd seen, it worked all right, for most towns. But he wanted more from Nevadaville. Wanted it to be a place where people thrived, set down roots and were proud of their accomplishments. Which was why he'd invested in businesses, but only as the financier, and in housing. He'd set up payment plans so anyone willing to work was able to afford a home—their own home. Every single house he'd ordered and erected had been sold, and had people living in it.

An odd emptiness made itself known inside him,

making him pause in the street and gaze at the north end of town, where a large house stood empty. The one he'd built for Miranda. He'd thought a lot about that house the past couple of days—ever since meeting Katherine Ackerman.

Clay dropped his gaze and walked toward his office, which doubled as his sleeping quarters. It was all he needed. Thinking of Katherine was just as irrelevant as thinking about Miranda. Both women had been fragments of his imagination—actresses pretending to be people they weren't. The most frustrating piece of it all was how he'd fallen into that trap again so quickly.

Kit, snuggled in the comfortable bed in room 202, listened as the muffled noise faded. She waited for another sound. Something louder, for the hiss hadn't been startling enough to wake her. When nothing came, she slipped out of bed and went to the window. The moon and stars were so bright her breath caught. She'd been in the mountains for several days, but until this moment hadn't noticed how close to the heavens she truly was.

A sigh slipped from her lips as she leaned forward, resting her elbows on the sill and her chin on her fists. Perhaps it was the people. She'd lived in Chicago her entire life, but never felt the camaraderie this town possessed. Everyone she'd met today was friendly and welcoming, and seemed overjoyed to meet her. That may have been because of Jonathan Owens. "Oscar's Kit" was how he'd introduced her. He was a very charming man. Handsome, too, though not as handsome as Clay. Then again, there probably weren't many men that handsome. She'd never really noticed such things before, but ever since she'd met him, her mind seemed to stay focused on Clay—in a way, compared everyone else to him. To his handsome face, solid chest, strong arms and deep voice, which even now seemed to echo in her ears.

Jonathan was slender, wiry, a build that matched his pale blue eyes and blond hair. He was sophisticated and, well, attractive. Whereas Clay, with his dark blue eyes that could look almost black at times, and hair so dark brown each strand reflected the sun's rays, looked… Kit sighed, searching for the description she wanted.

Powerful came, but that wasn't quite right. He was authoritative and commanding, but she'd seen a gentle and caring side to him, too. Reliable? Trustworthy? Respectable? They all fit, but weren't quite right. She frowned. When had she started to think of him in that way? He was a foe, not a friend.

It was the town's doing. Every person she'd encountered in Nevadaville today thought highly of him. She'd asked several people if they knew Sam, and most said yes, they knew him, but then told her to talk to Clay. That was it. End of conversation.

What troubled her most was they all said it with respect, and would go on about how wonderful Clay was, to the point she'd started to agree, thinking of how he'd already come to her aid, more than once. If it wasn't for him, she might still be roaming the hillsides.

Heroic, that was a good word for him. Like the hero in a book.

A falling star caught her attention, and she smiled. What should she wish for? It could be to meet Sam, but she'd manage that on her own, didn't need to waste the lucky chance of a falling star on it. No, this wish should be for her, for something she dreamed of obtaining.

Her gaze went to the north end of town, where the

large house stood. It had caught her attention as soon as she'd stepped onto the boardwalk outside the hotel this afternoon. Though large and stately, it wasn't too formal, and fit nicely with the rest of the town. The large front pillars looked welcoming, yet in a peculiar way, lonesome.

A need to know who lived there built inside her. The interior must be beautiful. Perhaps she could stop by and introduce herself, or maybe Jonathan could take her there, make the introductions for her. He'd invited her to lunch with him tomorrow.

She turned back to the sky. The falling star was long gone, leaving no trail. Nonetheless, she closed her eyes and wished. Fancied living in that house, sheltered by the tall trees as fluffy flakes of snow fell upon the roof and piled up on the walkway leading from the end of the road. Christmastime—her favorite time of the year— would be enchanting in that house, and of course, it would be filled with family. Her family.

The image grew so real in her mind, her heart skipped a beat. She smiled and let the air flow slowly from her lungs. After fluffing the curtains, arranging each panel so it fell evenly over the glass panes, she made her way back to bed and let her imagination be the guide that led the way to more dreams of the big house.

Hours later Kit awoke gently, easing from dreamland like a bubble floating on a breeze. A smile still curved her lips, and it increased as she accepted how tranquil the dreams had left her. The inside of that house was as beautiful as the outside. She'd seen herself floating down a wide staircase dressed in a red velvet dress— no, the dress had been burgundy, with lots of white lace. And below, at the bottom of the stairs, had been a large Christmas tree, fully decorated with pinecones, snowflakes made from white lace and candles, dozens of candles.

She closed her eyes, remembering the dream she'd had moments ago. But for the life of her she couldn't picture the man who'd stood next to the tree. Her heart started to thud, and she tried harder to recall his image. In the dream, she'd been ecstatic to see him, had been holding her hand out for him to guide her down the last few steps.

Opening her eyes, Kit stared at the ceiling. It was no use; the dream was gone, along with the mystery man. She sat up, accepting the fate of dreams. They rarely came true, not without a lot of work, and she had other, more pressing dreams, too, things to do to make them come true.

Drawing a cleansing breath, she climbed from the bed and proceeded with her morning routine. Half an hour later, she searched the contents of the armoire. As promised, Mr. Reins had delivered her trunks to the hotel, and just as she'd guessed, he'd referred to her as Kit Becker. Not that it mattered by then, as she'd already told Mimmie Mae her real name, as well as Jonathan. She'd encountered him shortly after she'd left the hotel yesterday. He'd introduced himself and, upon learning she was Oscar's granddaughter, immediately invited her to join him for a cup of tea at the Gilded Parlor.

She giggled at the name. The residents of Nevadaville certainly enjoyed their gold. Practically everything in town was named after it in some way or another. Her wandering mind returned to the wardrobe. Though she loved velvet, could wear it every day and never tire of it, she chose a green twill skirt with a matching jacket and yellow blouse. By noon the sun would be high, and she had learned yesterday how stifling velvet could become in the heat.

Dressed and ready to face the day, she checked the room one last time before pulling open the door. Hungry this morning, as if she hadn't eaten for weeks, she decided upon steak and eggs for breakfast. The meal would give her the energy to search out Clay. Jonathan had said he was installing a new boiler—that monstrous piece of machinery she'd seen.

Locking the door to her room, she pocketed the key and marched down the hall. It appeared the only way to meet Sam was through Clay, so that's what she'd have to do.

The center of the stairs leading to the ground floor was covered with a thick, dark green carpet that boasted red and pink roses. Watching the pretty petals disappear beneath her skirt, she heard Mimmie Mae's voice.

"There she is now," the woman said.

Kit's fingers tightened on the banister. She took a breath and secretly told her nerves to settle down. The look on Clay's face was fierce, a mixture of civility and annoyance, and that had her swallowing hard. "Good morning, Mr. Hoffman," she greeted him, but didn't descend the final three steps.

"Miss Becker." His tone didn't hold an ounce of humor.

What had she expected—that he'd be happy to hear she had lied to him? Her toes trembled. This was new for her. She'd never flat-out lied to someone before. Well, she had told several people she was Katherine Ackerman, but that was mainly so Mr. Watson wouldn't learn she'd left Chicago. Not that that mattered anymore; by now he'd probably discovered where she'd gone. And sent a wire to Clay. She gulped.

He left the desk to move closer to the stairs. Mimmie Mae, after casting a wide smile, exited through the little door behind the chest-high registration desk. Kit wished she could call the woman back. She really didn't want to be alone with Clay. Not with the way he was glaring at her right now.

"Katherine Ackerman is Kit Becker?" he asked, resting one hand on the large post at the end of the railing.

His tone made her stomach flutter. She gripped the banister until her fingers throbbed. "Yes, she is. I am."

"I see." He stretched his opposite hand toward her, palm up.

The picture of him standing there, arm out, was remarkably close to her dream. Enough to make her breath catch. She forced the air to continue to flow, chiding herself for having such fanciful thoughts. The man in her dream had been smiling, and Clay was not smiling. He gestured to her again. Knowing her options were nil, she laid her fingers upon his, then almost pulled them back at the way the heat of his palm shot up her arm.

He helped her down the steps, and his hand, firm and fiery, continued to hold her fingers even after she had stepped off the final stair. Now she had to look up to see him, an act that left her feeling vulnerable. Shame heated her cheeks.

"Where does that leave Henry?" he asked.

His eyes were scrutinizing, and his very presence encompassing, making the air flowing in her lungs thin and ineffectual. The man in her dream appeared, floating around his image until the two merged into one.

"Who?" she asked, growing woozy.

"Don't tell me you've forgotten Henry?" The sound of Clay's voice tickled her eardrums as he whispered, "The stinking kid with a boil on his backside."

The words hit her like a thunderbolt, sending her back to earth with a shattering crack. Her cheeks blazed. "There was no boil," she insisted.

He turned and led her toward the dining room. "What a relief." His tone was definitely sarcastic.

Her fortitude returned with vigor. She picked up her pace. Clay didn't falter as he strolled beside her, still holding her hand, which by now probably had blisters on every finger. He stopped near a table and pulled out a chair with his free arm. Gesturing with a nod, he indicated she was to sit. A part of her, a large part, didn't want to, but she did. Not because he said so, or because she didn't want to make a scene in front of the dozen or so people who were gawking as if they'd just seen a circus bear, but because she had to, and not just to meet Sam. She'd lied to Clay and had to find a way to make him understand why. Gramps would expect that of her.

Clay let go of her hand and sat on the chair adjacent to hers.

She fidgeted, repositioning her skirt and tugging on the cuffs of her jacket. Why didn't he sit across from her, as Jonathan had last night? It would seem less personal, and give her more space. A part of her wanted to bolt for the door. Not because she was scared, but because there was something about Clay that had her insides doing somersaults.

"Two orders of steak and eggs, Mimmie Mae, and coffee," he said.

Kit turned to the woman, who'd magically appeared beside the table. "No," she said, finding it difficult to speak over her rough throat. "I'll just have toast and tea." Actually, even that might come right back up, the way her stomach was performing.

Clay cast an insufferable gaze toward Mimmie Mae as he repeated, "Two orders of steak and eggs." Turning the gaze upon Kit, he added, "One coffee and one tea."

She opened her mouth, but the woman was already moving away. "Coming right up."

His attitude had ire attempting to gain rank among Kit's jumbled nerves. "How do you know if I like steak and eggs?"

One of his dark brows arched. "Oscar's granddaughter loves steak and eggs."

"How would you know that?"

"She also loves reading books, kittens, peach pie and sweet potatoes." He held up a finger. "And climbing trees."

He'd named her favorite things, in almost the exact order—from when she'd been twelve. "How would you know any of that?"

"I knew Oscar. And if there was one thing Oscar did, it was talk about his granddaughter, *Kit*." He emphasized her name with a mocking tone.

"Perhaps I've changed since he died."

His eyes dimmed, took on an almost bored expression. He sat back and crossed his arms. "Perhaps."

Mimmie Mae returned, with coffee and tea, as well as cream and sugar. "How'd you sleep last night, darling? Find the room to your liking? The bed soft enough?"

Kit couldn't be rude. The woman was so sweet, and her friendly demeanor alone made one want to smile. "Oh, yes, Mimmie Mae, everything is just perfect. Very comfortable. Thank you. I may settle in and never want to leave."

"Good." The hotel owner patted her shoulder. "That would be wonderful. Oscar would like that." She turned to Clay. "Your breakfast will be out in a minute."

He took a sip of his coffee. "Thanks." Nodding toward his cup, he added, "This hits the spot already."

"A man your size can't keep skipping meals. Anna told me you refused to come home with Raymond and eat after working most of the night. I've half a mind to mention it to Clarice."

The dollop of cream Kit intended to pour into her tea turned into a half a cup. Would have overflowed the rim of her teacup if Clay hadn't reached over and taken the little kitty-shaped pitcher from her fingers. He set the creamer on the table and looked at Mimmie Mae with a devilish smile. "What Clarice doesn't know won't hurt her."

The woman giggled and walked away, while Kit, insides and mind racing in all directions, wound her hands into her skirt. He'd be much easier to deal with if he was as homely as a flea-bitten stray dog—actually, she'd always had a soft spot for stray dogs. But hearing the name Clarice had her thinking about the house of ill repute again. She'd forgotten to ask about that yesterday, and the image of Clay visiting the house was more disturbing than the thought of Gramps visiting it.

"Is the tea not to your liking?" Clay's gaze was serious, yet she swore there was a hint of mischief glittering in those blue eyes.

The cup rattled upon the saucer as she picked it up. The tea tasted like warm milk, but she nodded, licking her lips. "It's fine. Just how I like it."

He glanced around, as if wondering what to say next. Kit knew the feeling. This encounter was not happening as she'd expected, and the courage to apologize was diminishing. But she had to find Sam before being sent back to Chicago. That was the reason she was here. Afterward, she'd go home gladly—get as far away from Clay as possible. Sitting next to him made it hard to concentrate. It was a struggle not to remember how he'd kissed her yesterday. How warm and fuzzy that had left her feeling, and how she wanted to experience it again.

Kit cleared the roughness from her throat and wet her lips.

Chapter Five

Kit's tiny cough made the muscles in his neck tighten. Assuming she was about to say something, Clay cut her off at the pass. "What are you playing at?"

Watching her walk down the steps this morning had been like seeing an angel descending from heaven, complete with golden curls flowing in her wake. She was something, he just couldn't quite figure out what. She was up to something, too, and he'd best figure out what that was—quick. Before both he and Sam were in too deep.

Her brows drew together above her startled eyes. "What do you mean, what I'm playing at?"

Downing the last drop of his coffee, he set the cup down. "Why didn't you just tell me who you were? There was no need to pretend to be someone else."

"I—" She stopped, eyeing Mimmie Mae approaching their table.

"I'll be right back to refill your cups," the woman offered, after setting two plates holding thick beefsteaks and perfectly cooked eggs on the table.

Sitting stiff in her chair, with arms folded across her

chest, Kit waited until Mimmie Mae walked away before saying, "I had to pretend to be those other people."

Clay bit back the mirth tickling the corners of his mouth, caused by her obvious irritation, and picked up his knife and fork. "Why?" Cutting into the steak, he watched the pink center ooze red juice onto his plate. He kept staring at it, hoping it would quell his desire to gaze upon her blushing face. Oscar's Kit had grown into a very pretty woman, and when her cheeks flushed, she was downright gorgeous.

Her gaze darted nervously as she quietly answered, "I have my reasons."

With damn near as much force as he drove a pickax, he stabbed the meat with his fork and popped it in his mouth. Charming or not, she was Kit, his ward, and appeared to be as bullheaded as Sam.

Mimmie Mae returned, filled his coffee cup and set the teapot on the table, since Kit's cup was still full. "Can I get you two anything else?"

"I don't believe so." He glanced across the table.

Kit offered a slight smile to the woman and shook her head.

"Well, just holler if you think of something," the hotel owner insisted as she walked away.

Clay took another bite of steak and nodded toward Kit's plate. "Best eat while it's hot. Eggs lose their flavor as they cool."

"They do not," she retorted. "Besides, I'm not hungry. I already told you that."

"Suit yourself," Clay said, scooping up eggs with his fork and doing his best to act natural. "The Kit Oscar always talked about was forever hungry. He said she had a hollow leg. Said it took every ounce of gold the Wanda Lou produced just to feed her."

"He did not."

"That's how I remember it."

She cut into her steak with vigor, noticeably miffed, but soon her pace slowed and she began to eat as if sincerely enjoying the food. Clay found pleasure in the meal as well, not from the food—though Mimmie Mae's fare was always tasty—but from the company. The way she looked up, gazed at him with those soft and teasing eyes every once in a while, had his blood heating up—enjoyably so.

He finished his meal and leaned back, sipping his coffee.

She patted her napkin against her pert lips before repositioning it upon her lap. "Mr. Hoffman," she started, glancing around as if what she was about to say would reveal a highly prized secret. "Would you please tell me where Sam Edwards lives?"

An intense churning in his stomach caused his breakfast to sour and sent an aftertaste bubbling up his throat. For a moment there, he'd imagined he was sitting across from Katherine, a woman he still wanted to get to know better. Knowing that was impossible was still playing havoc on him. "Sam lives a few miles out of town."

"Which direction?"

Oscar's wish had been for the two grandchildren to meet, but Clay felt he had to uphold Sam's interests first, and her aliases had him questioning her true reason for being here. "Why didn't you wire that you were coming? Or just arrive as yourself?"

She sighed heavily, yet met his gaze square on. "I

couldn't," she said. "Sam inherited half of everything my grandfather had."

The hint of anticipation sparkling in her eyes made Clay frown and stiffen at the same time. "Yes, he did. But why couldn't you wire him?"

"Because he doesn't know me. I don't know him."

Outwardly, Clay remained calm. Inside, clicking along like the revolutions of train wheels, a dozen scenarios rolled across his mind. Lord knew, after the way she'd already tried to fool him into believing she was someone else, what type of ideas she might put in Sam's mind. If the two of them got together and decided to challenge the will, not only would Oscar's shares of his companies be in jeopardy, so would Clay's shares—the entire town, for that matter.

His ears buzzed as the scenarios kept coming. "Oscar tried to convince Sam to move to Chicago, but he refused. What makes you think you'll convince him?"

She frowned. "I'm not here to ask him to move to Chicago."

Just when he thought he knew what he was doing, Clay's instincts proved wrong. Her confusion stabbed him dead center. "Then why are you here?"

"I just want to meet him." She shrugged. "Find out who he is."

An eerie sensation crept up Clay's spine. "Find out who he is?"

"Yes. I don't understand why the will includes a complete stranger." Her facade was gone, and nothing but honesty glimmered in her sad eyes.

Clay tried telling himself to remember just how cunning women were, but something inside him said she wasn't being deceitful. She truly didn't know who Sam was.

Clay pushed away from the table. "I'll send a message to him and let you know when I hear back from him." After placing two bills on the front desk, for both meals, he strolled out the door.

"Damn you, Oscar," he growled. "How could you not have told her?"

An echo in his ears sent a shudder up his spine, and a heavy sigh left his chest as his name was repeated. Rubbing at the tension burning his neck muscles, he turned. "Hello, Clarice."

"Didn't you see my note?" she asked, barreling down the boardwalk as if on a mission—which was as normal as the sunshine. "I left it on your desk."

"Yes, I saw it."

Without missing a step she hooked his elbow with hers, forcing him to walk beside her as her heels clip-clopped a rhythmic beat on the wooden walkway. "Did you read it?" The humorous glint shimmering in her eyes said she knew he hadn't.

"No," he admitted. "I haven't had a chance to yet."

Clarice shook her head in the way that reminded him so much of their mother, he had to smile, and felt a twinge of guilt. If Kit didn't know about Sam, she might not know about her mother, either. Clay had assumed Oscar had told her, after finding Sam.

Reaching over, Clay flicked the floppy black lace dangling from the brim of Clarice's huge pink hat. "Where are we going?" His glance had gone down the hill to the telegraph office, as he wondered if Mr. Watson had sent a message yet. If Oscar hadn't told Kit, the solicitor must have upon reading the will. How else would she know Sam's name?

"To see Mr. Mason," Clarice said.

He cringed, not really knowing if it was for him or Mr. Mason. "Why?" There were so many other things he needed to see to.

She turned the corner, tugging him with her, and together they climbed the stairs built into the hill that led to the row of buildings above. One of those being the school.

Being prepared was the most he could hope for. He forced Kit and Sam to the back of his mind, or as far back as he could before he drew in a solid breath seeking fortitude. He'd need it. When it came to Clarice, one was best to pack a good supply of staying power. A side iron never hurt, either. "Tell me what's happened, so I have some idea what to expect."

She let out a hiss that made him cringe. Normally, his sister was a gentle and kind person, one everyone loved, but get her dander up and a grizzly would cower. They topped the twenty or more steps, and Clay brought their hurried pace to a dead stop.

"He's the fourth teacher you've hired in less than two years."

"Clayton Hoffman—"

His neck muscles tightened. He was in for an earful when she used his full name.

"—the children of this town deserve a quality education, and as the proprietor of the town, it's your job to see they do. I..."

He could have interrupted to say he'd spent a small fortune on the school building, the home for the teacher to live in and the salary he paid those brave enough to take on the job—especially after their first nose to nose encounter with Clarice—but he didn't. Instead, he listened as she prattled on about the importance of an education. How that was the only way the children would have the opportunity to leave Nevadaville and the mining community—as if it were the worst place on earth to live.

When she did finally take a breath, he jumped in. "What's happened?" He didn't have all day. It was time for him to know what he was in for.

Her hands balled into fists, her lips puckered, but what caught his full attention was how her voice grew soft, almost despondent. "He used a switch on Liza Rose."

As hot and swift as the flame on a fuse, vehemence raced up Clay's spine. "Liza Rose?" The little girl, only six, would never do anything to deserve a switch. Last Christmas Clay had helped pass out gifts to the children. Liza Rose had received a doll, one with glasses just like hers. She'd named the doll Mrs. Smith and carried her everywhere.

He'd never told Clarice, but he'd seen the doll in a catalog and ordered it several months in advance for Liza Rose. Her father had worked at the stamp mill, but an accident had taken his life going on two years ago, and her mother, a thin, quiet woman, worked at the society house with Clarice. Men lost their lives in a mining community. That was common knowledge. But Clay felt responsible for every life lost in Nevadaville, and the families left behind, especially the children. Not so different from Sam and now Kit.

He grasped Clarice's arm. "Come on." Each step

along the carved pathway brought his temperature higher, like steam building inside his new boiler.

"Don't you want to know what happened?" Clarice asked, skipping every now and again to keep up with him as they made their way toward the schoolhouse.

"No," he admitted. It didn't matter. Anyone so callous they'd take a switch to a six-year-old shouldn't be teaching. And wouldn't be. Not in his town. Neither he nor Clarice had had the chance to attend an actual school, and the opportunity for a formal education was just one of the things they both were proud to offer the residents of Nevadaville.

Kit watched as the man and woman walked into a building she assumed, by the bell hanging in the tower, was the school, wondering who the woman was Clay had smiled so fondly upon.

"Excuse me?"

The soft voice, along with the tug on her skirt, had Kit glancing down. A tiny girl with bright red hair, and green eyes that looked overly large behind gold-framed glasses, cast a wary glance about.

Captured by the distress in those eyes, Kit knelt down. "Hello there."

"Hello," the girl responded somewhat timidly.

Kit tapped the head of the little doll hanging over the girl's arm. "Who is this?"

"Mrs. Smith."

"Well, hello, Mrs. Smith," Kit said, shaking the doll's miniature hand. "My name is Kit."

"Kit?"

"Yes. Kit. What's your name?"

"Liza Rose."

"Hello, Liza Rose."

The girl, as if just remembering something, asked, "Have you seen Miss Clarice?"

Kit bit her lip. She really had to meet this Clarice woman. Shaking her head, she admitted, "I'm afraid I don't know who that is. Why are you looking for her?"

Liza Rose's eyes turned watery. "Because I'm afraid Frenchie's gonna eat the babies."

"Oh, my," Kit replied, understanding the child's fear was real. "Tell me, who is Frenchie?"

"Miss Clarice's cat. He ran out the door behind Miss Clarice. I tried to stop him, but couldn't catch him." She took Kit's hand. "Can you help me catch him?"

Since she had nothing to fill her time with until Clay heard back from Sam, Kit answered, "I'd love to help." She couldn't remember the last time someone had asked for her assistance. "Where did you see him last?"

"In the front yard," the girl said, already pulling on her hand.

At the end of the road, where it curved to glide down the hill, a two-story house with big pillars fit neatly onto a small grassy plateau. A fence, made of wooden slates and painted white, encircled the entire property. Liza Rose pushed open the gate, and when she released it, the big spring recoiled, almost catching the hem of Kit's skirt as she followed the child.

Now running, Liza Rose shouted, "I know he's after the babies. I just know it."

"What babies?" The house had a huge front porch, and a brass plaque hung beside the door. Kit peered closer, reading the raised print as Liza Rose shot around the corner of the house. Children's Society House. So not exactly a brothel, then.

Kit stuck the knowledge in the back of her mind, focusing instead on keeping up with the child. At the side of the house, where the edge of the mountain rose a few yards beyond the white fence, stood a large tree. The leafy branches stretched out to dangle in front of a second-story window, and two ropes hung from one thick limb, holding a long swing, the type usually found on porches. It was quite enchanting, this big swing painted a glossy white and large enough for two adults, or three or four children, to sit and swing while telling secrets or sharing laughs.

Liza Rose had stopped at the base of the tree. "I know he's after the babies."

"What babies?" Kit asked again.

"The birds." The girl pointed into the branches. "Miss Clarice can see them from her bedroom window. She showed me."

Kit scanned the tree. Several branches up, a long white tail flicked back and forth among the leaves. "Is that Frenchie?"

Liza Rose twisted and squinted, gazing up into the tree.

Bending down and wrapping an arm around tiny shoulders, Kit pointed to the spot. "Right there? See his tail?"

"Yes! Yes, that's Frenchie." Anxious, the girl shook her head. "He's gonna eat the babies. I just know it."

"We'll get him, don't worry." Kit glanced around for something to throw into the branches. The thick grass was well manicured. Not even a pebble let itself be shown, which proved she had little choice. "You stay here. Right here."

Liza Rose nodded, eyes glued on Frenchie's tail, and clutched her doll with both hands.

Kit checked the strength of the ropes. They looked new, and the knots held tight as she pulled. If she stood on the back of the swing, she'd be able to reach the branch the ropes were tied to. It had been a long time, but climbing a tree was not something one forgot. Thankful she'd left her jacket at the hotel, she unbuttoned her cuffs, and after rolling her sleeves to her elbows, rubbed her hands together in preparation. Confidence built within. This was something she'd done a hundred times. Maybe a thousand. With an inner nod of assurance, she climbed onto the swing.

"Kit, Momma says we can't stand on the swing."

"And your momma is right. You must never stand on the swing. You could fall and get hurt." Kit wrapped both hands around the thick branch and dug her nails into the bark, securing her grip. "I'm a grown-up, so I can stand on it, but only because it's an emergency. Now, you stay right there, like I told you to."

Liza Rose nodded, and Kit took a deep breath. As she exhaled, she jumped and swung her legs upward, hooking her ankles over the branch and pulling herself up until the bark bit through her pantaloons and into her thighs. While her momentum was still flowing, she swung her hips, hoisting herself up and over. With a thud, her chest and stomach hit the branch.

She pushed herself up, to sit straddling the limb. Triumph filled her insides as brightly as it had years ago. At one time, there'd been nothing she'd enjoyed more than finding a tree to sit in and pass the hours, devouring the pages of a book on a summer afternoon back in Illinois.

"Stay there," she repeated to Liza Rose, and began inching her way along the branch. Once she had the solid trunk to aid her, she rose to her feet and assessed the best path upward. The tree was a perfect climber. The branches spread out from the base like staircases, inviting any who dared to roost in the inspirational serenity to hide behind the veil of delicate green leaves. Kit drew a breath as childhood memories settled over her. She was once again ten, shimmying as agile as any four-legged creature that considered the tree its home.

A silly notion occurred to her. The tiniest wish that Clay could see her skimming along the branches. Silly, yes, but it had cheered her insides when he'd said Gramps had talked about her when he was out here. The thought, mingling with the almost forgotten pleasure of tree climbing, increased her confidence, and she scrambled through the leaves as if she was on a Sunday walk in the park.

Several branches later, easing toward the far reaches of one particular limb, she cooed, "Frenchie? Kitty. Kitty."

"What are you doing up there?"

Startled by the male voice, she grabbed the branch, securing her balance as a lump formed in her throat. Of all the wishes she'd made in her life, this would have to be the one that came true, wouldn't it? She rustled up a smile. "Hello, Mr. Hoffman," she said in greeting. "What are you doing here?"

He blocked the sun with one hand as he peered up at her. "I think I asked you first," he said. "What are you doing up *there?*"

There may have been a slight bit of humor in his tone, but she couldn't be sure. "I'm catching Frenchie," she explained, inching her way toward the cat.

"Frenchie doesn't need your help. Get down before you fall and break your neck," he insisted.

No, there was no humor in his tone. A groan rattled against the back of her throat as Kit glanced to Liza Rose, who was tugging on Clay's shirtsleeve.

"He'll eat the babies if Kit doesn't get him, Mr. Hoffman," the girl explained.

"What babies?"

"Baby birds, of course," Kit said. "What else do cats eat?"

"Just about anything they want," he said, talking up into the tree. "Mice, fish, bugs, whatever they find."

"I suspect you're right," Kit answered. "Now, please be quiet. I don't want him to go any higher." Frenchie had turned around, as if following the conversation. Sitting in a V of two branches, he eyed her curiously with a pair of light gray eyes.

"Haven't you ever seen a person climb a tree before?" she asked the cat as she scooted along the branch. With Clay watching, her courage was waning, and getting back to the ground was becoming imperative.

Frenchie meowed.

"Yes, well, I can't say I do it very often anymore," she whispered to the cat. "But if my gramps was here, he'd lay a bet that I've climbed as many trees as you."

The cat cocked his head and then, as if bored, lifted a paw, licked it and wiped it along his cheek.

She giggled softly, and scooted close enough to hold out a hand for him to sniff. His little nose, pink and cold, touched the back of her hand. "Are you going to let me carry you down? Or are you going to scratch me?"

Slowly, as if he was quite exhausted, Frenchie stood, stretched and then walked straight to her, brushing her cheek with his upon his arrival. Gathering him into one arm, she noticed the nest beyond the V of branches. The empty nest. "Oh, you naughty, naughty boy," she whispered into the cat's ear.

He meowed and then started to purr while snuggling closer. "Oh, you are a precious one, trying to sweet-talk me into not being angry." She nudged his head with her chin. "I must warn you, it won't work. I'm very upset with you."

He purred louder, quite unaffected by her sentiments, which was just as well, since she held no ill will toward the cat. It was his instinct. Nature's law. A natural principle Gramps had explained to her years ago. Cats eat birds, birds eat butterflies and so on. Everything had a predator, no matter how beautiful.

"Are you going to sit up there conversing with a cat, or are you going to climb down before you both fall?" Clay asked.

"Don't worry, cats always land on their feet," she assured him. Another one of Grandpa Oscar's insightful teachings.

"Yes, but do women?"

Kit stiffened. For a moment she'd forgotten her age. Forgotten how inappropriate it must be for her to be climbing trees—in a new dress at that. Sucking up her dismay, for there truly was nothing she could do about it, she inched her way along her former path. It wasn't until she reached the lowest branch, the one holding the swing, that she wondered how she would get down with Frenchie snuggled in the crook of one arm.

"Stand back, Liza Rose," Clay said, guiding the child farther away from the swing with both hands. "You stay right there."

Still contemplating her options, Kit watched as Liza Rose nodded, and Clay returned to the tree. He climbed onto the seat of the swing, keeping his balance with a grip on one rope. His nose was even with her knees, and the slight glimmer of amusement in his blue eyes sent Kit's heart racing to the point she wobbled.

His reactions were swift. Before she really comprehended what was happening, his hands had grasped her waist and he was jumping off the swing. The next instant her feet were on the ground, but thankfully, his hands still held her waist, because the world around her was spinning. Not so unlike when he'd lifted her off the horse a couple days ago.

"Are you all right?" he asked.

Though her legs felt almost useless, she nodded. This man certainly had a knack of showing up just when she needed him.

"Good, then give Frenchie to Liza Rose," he said.

Nodding again, she managed to whisper, "Thank you," as his hands twisted her about. Before kneeling down, she placed a kiss upon Frenchie's head. "You silly old cat," she whispered, though in some ways she was talking to herself. Then she held the animal out. "Here you are, Liza Rose."

As the child took Frenchie, Clay knelt down beside them, patting the cat's head.

The frown on his face may have appeared stern, but there was no anger in his eyes. "You could have broken your neck," he whispered in Kit's ear as one hand rubbed her back, as he had yesterday.

"Nonsense." His concern had her insides flipping, and she had to concentrate to keep from toppling against him. "I think you should take Frenchie into the house, don't you, Liza Rose?" Draped over the child's folded arms, sharing the space with Mrs. Smith, the cat looked fully content. "He's had quite a day already." Fingers crossed, Kit hoped the child wouldn't ask about the bird's nest. "He'd probably like a saucer of cream and to curl up someplace with the sun shining on his back."

"Liza Rose!"

A slender, tall woman had the hem of her paisley print dress and a long white apron hitched above her ankles as she rushed around the corner of the house. Kit stood, bracing to finally meet the highly esteemed Clarice.

With little more than a shy nod toward Kit, the woman knelt down in front of Liza Rose. "I looked all over for you, young lady." Though her words were harsh, her tone was soft and held a hint of relief as she cupped the girl's tiny shoulders with both hands. "Where have you been?"

"Frenchie followed Miss Clarice out the door this morning, Momma. I had to find him." Liza Rose turned her magnified eyes toward Kit. "She got him out of the tree, Momma. Kit got him so he couldn't eat the babies."

Dread rose in her stomach, and though she tried, Kit couldn't keep it off her face.

"Hello, Mrs. Wurm," Clay said. "May I introduce you to Kit Becker?"

"Kit Becker?" the woman questioned. "As in Oscar's Kit?"

"Yes," Kit replied. "Oscar Becker was my grandfather."

"Kit, this is Adeline Wurm." Clay completed the introduction.

Recalling the name, Kit reached out a hand. "It's nice to meet you, Mrs. Wurm. My grandfather was very saddened to hear of your husband's death."

Adeline Wurm took her hand in a gentle grasp, and the flash of pain in her eyes made Kit wish she hadn't mentioned the terrible accident Gramps had been informed of not long before his own death. She folded the woman's hand between both of hers. "My grandfather thought highly of your husband."

Adeline bowed her head shyly. "Thank you, and it's nice to meet you, too." She lifted her face as she added, "The entire town was filled with grief when we heard of Oscar's passing, and his wife's. The carriage accident."

Maybe the shimmer of sadness that swirled around her heart was intensified by Adeline's words, or maybe because Clay squeezed her elbow with understanding. Either way, Kit took a moment, acknowledged the angst her grandparents' passing had created inside her. The shock of their deaths—a spooked horse had toppled their carriage while they were returning from an engagement—had been sudden and left her numb for weeks. The pain had lessened over the months, but she doubted it would ever go completely away. Hoped it wouldn't in some ways. It reminded her how precious they had been, how important family was.

"Thank you, Mrs. Wurm," Kit managed to reply. "Your sympathies are sincerely appreciated." Gramps's voice appeared in her head, telling her once again how nothing was gained from wallowing in the past. A smile forced upon her lips, and a glance at Liza Rose and the notorious Frenchie brightened Kit's heart considerably. "I'm sorry you were worried about Liza Rose. I assure you she was never in danger."

Adeline turned to her daughter, and though she shook her head, affection shone in her gaze. "The other children have already finished their chores. You'll have to hurry to get yours done if you want to attend the matinee."

"I'll see to them right now, Momma." Liza Rose turned toward the house, and then swung around and rushed toward Kit.

Kit knelt down to accept her one-arm hug. The other arm held both the cat and the doll. "Thank you for rescuing the birds, Kit," the child whispered.

Pinching her lips together, holding in the truth about the empty nest, Kit planted a little kiss upon the girl's head. "You're welcome." When she stepped back, Kit gave Frenchie's head a little scratch. "You see he stays in the house the rest of the day."

"I will," Liza Rose promised. With the cat and the doll bobbing, the child ran for the house.

Warmth pooled in her stomach as Kit stood. The innocent affection from the child was like none she'd ever experienced. Glancing toward the tree, she swallowed. "I'm sorry, Mrs. Wurm, but I'm afraid I was too late. The nest was empty." Grief hovered in her throat. "I didn't have the heart to tell Liza Rose."

"Oh, goodness. That will upset her." Adeline shook her head. "She's such a caring child and has already had a difficult week."

"Why's that?" Kit asked.

Adeline shook her head sadly. "She was punished at school and lost Mrs. Smith's glasses." The woman gestured toward the house then. "I need to get inside and see to the children. It was nice to meet you, Miss Becker. Mr. Hoffman," she added with a nod.

"Nice meeting you, too," Kit replied, but her attention was drawn back to Clay. His hold on her elbow had tightened.

She had to take a fortifying breath before turning to peer up at him.

Clay's insides were slamming together with the power of stampers back at the smelter. Those big brown eyes, looking somewhat sheepish as she stared up at him, had him wanting to give her a smile a mile wide. Now that she was safely on the ground, that was. After leaving the schoolhouse, he'd remembered the satchel in his pocket. Mimmie Mae had said she'd seen Kit following Liza Rose up the street. He'd found Mrs. Smith's glasses in the trash can beside the teacher's desk, and they were now in his pocket, but he needed to repair them before giving them to the child. Not that he'd recalled them until now. Seeing Kit in the tree had made him forget just about everything else. "I thought you were afraid of heights," he finally said.

"Not trees," she said with a grimace. "I've climbed them my whole life."

He dug in his pocket. "Here," he said, pulling out the satchel. "Ty Reins found it in the caboose."

"Oh, goodness, I didn't even realize I'd lost it. Thank you."

His jaw was hardening, even while his heart was softening. If Oscar had told her about Joseph Wurm, surely he'd told her about Sam and her mother.

"Did you hear back from Sam?" she asked. "Will he meet me?"

"No, not yet," Clay replied. There were too many questions he needed answered before he was going to arrange that. "Did you run away from Chicago?"

The dread in her eyes said he'd hit the nail on the head, as did the way his stomach hit the ground.

Chapter Six

Back in his office, after stopping to check on the new boiler, Clay repaired and cleaned the tiny glasses until they sparkled as brightly as the day Liza Rose had received Mrs. Smith. Then he wrapped the spectacles in a soft cloth and tucked them in his breast pocket. He'd deliver them at supper, since he usually dined with Clarice and the children on Saturday nights.

A stitch built in his chest and he forced the air out, cleansing his lungs, and hopefully his mind. It didn't work. The sting was still there. Smack-dab in the center of his torso, where his heart all of a sudden had appeared again. The past couple of years it had pumped his blood, and on some occasions, such as while he was thinking of little Liza Rose or even Clarice, it warmed, let him know he wasn't completely without feelings. But for the most part, it had been just an organ, kept him alive. That's what happened when you gave it away. You got it back damaged. Too destroyed ever to work properly again.

But today it had kicked back in—with full force, and he really didn't like it. His gaze went to the window, and beyond, to the bright blue sky. He pushed back from his desk and walked across the room. From this side of his office, he could see most of Nevadaville. The other window, the one behind his desk, displayed the stamping mill, where the steady pounding of the crushers echoed over the hills. At regular intervals they pulsed, stamping the ore into pebbles and sand, the sounds as familiar as his own breathing. He no longer heard them, which was how his feelings had been—so habitual they really didn't matter.

Kit had done this to him, and that was the problem. He should have marched her straight to the train station from Clarice's, but he hadn't, and didn't exactly know why. She claimed Mr. Watson wouldn't tell her who Sam was and that's why she'd run away. That was what bothered him. Would she run away again? As soon as she had met Sam? Women were known for that—running away—and he didn't have time to be chasing after one. Especially one that was making him feel things he hadn't felt in years.

It had been the woman—Katherine, the one she'd pretended to be—that had started things flowing again, and for some reason, his heart couldn't grasp the difference between Katherine and Kit. Not the way his mind could. Yet even there, it was all such a twisted tale he felt as tightly braided as a new rope. When he looked at her, he saw Kit—but he also saw Katherine.

He gave his head a shake and told himself she was here to see Sam, and that's what he needed to be concerned about. The kid had had enough losses. Meeting Kit, only to have her up and disappear, wouldn't be right, yet there wasn't a whole lot Clay could do. He couldn't keep them apart.

There was still no word from the Chicago solicitor,

and Clay was now thoroughly questioning her tale of wanting to meet Sam. The will stated the lawyer had to approve any man she chose to marry, and Clay had to wonder if that's what had happened. That Watson had disapproved of a man she had her heart set on, so Kit was here to gain approval, and would use Sam in her scheme. She was forbidden by the will to marry before she was twenty-one, and, if Clay recalled right, that was still several months away.

He shifted, bearing more weight on the palms he'd planted on the windowsill, wondering where the man she'd chosen was, and if he was the one who had put her up to all this.

A knock sounded, and before he could respond the door opened.

"I see the new boiler's up and running." Jonathan Owens, the land agent whose office was below, strolled into the room. "She looks good, too."

Clay moved to his desk, sat casually on one corner, glad to engage in a conversation that would take his mind off Kit. "You stopped by, had a look at her?"

"Sure enough did." The man took a seat in one of the padded-leather seats along the wall. His gaze grew thoughtful, a bit furrowed. "You never mentioned Oscar's granddaughter was coming to town."

Tension landed on the back of Clay's neck like a hawk on a field mouse. He stood, twisting his shoulders at the tightness. "You've met her?"

"Yes, I had supper with her last night."

Clay rotated his head, making his neck pop, and then rubbed at the spot. "You did?" Jonathan was a close friend, apt at his job, and he was a gentleman.

Most every woman in town considered the man a dear friend—including Clarice.

"She's as adorable as Oscar always claimed."

Clay's back molars met, and it took a conscious effort to relax his jaw. Adorable and conniving, no doubt. Rounding his desk, he took a seat and shuffled a stack of papers. "Did you have something you needed? I've a lot of work to get to."

"Here." Jonathan stood and handed a folded slip of paper across the desktop. "Ted Musgrove stopped me, asked me to deliver this to you. He said it just came in."

Clay ripped open the telegram, hoping it was from Watson. Frustrated, seeing it was from the mint, he absently stuffed the paper on top of several others beneath a chunk of fool's gold. The pile was growing, but his assistant, James Otto, would go through them. Both the Denver smelter and the mint sent telegrams regularly confirming the arrival of the latest load of ore or a deposit, and James entered each receipt. His bookwork was meticulous, and something Clay grew more grateful for every day.

Jonathan frowned, but then a smug smile creased his lips. He rested an elbow on the arm of the chair and scratched his temple. "Is there something I should know about?"

Clay ignored the tingles on his spine. "No, not that I know of."

Rubbing his chin, as if contemplating the greatness of the world, the man said, "I mean between you and Kit."

His first instinct was to tell the man to stay the hell away from her, yet Clay couldn't. If there was one man in town Kit would be safe seeing, it was Jonathan. The man was head over heels in love with Clarice; the entire town knew that. Clarice was in love with her society house, and even Clay found himself rooting for Jonathan to be able one day to make her see that wouldn't always be enough. An odd thing, a man who didn't believe in love wanting others to find it.

The air left Clay's chest with a huff as he shoved himself to his feet. "I have to go check on the new boiler." He grabbed the stack of telegrams off his desk. "As soon as I drop these off to James downstairs."

"Kit was asking a lot of questions about Sam."

Clay nodded.

"She was asking other people, too. You don't think Oscar never told her he's her brother, do you?"

Without responding, Clay pulled open the door. He was going to have to get to the bottom of it, that's all there was to it. Putting things off was not normal for him, but every time he started to talk to her, all he could think about was kissing her, and that had made him cut short both of their meetings today.

Jonathan followed him out the door. "She's going to the matinee with us today."

Clay paused on the narrow steps and tossed a look of disdain over his shoulder. "Why would you want to see *The Three Little Pigs?*"

"It's not that I *want* to see it. I promised Clarice I'd help her with the children. Keeping ten of them corralled isn't easy."

Arriving at the base of the steps, where one door led into Jonathan's land office and the other into James's accounting space, Clay paused. "Kit asked to join you?"

"No, I invited her to join us." Jonathan pushed open the door to his office. "I'd ask you to join us, too, but I don't think you'd enjoy it."

The man disappeared before Clay had the chance to tell him, no, he wouldn't enjoy the play. Opening the door to the accountant's office, he found a thought taunting him. He wouldn't enjoy a performance created for children, so why did he have the sudden urge to go?

"The new boiler's a dandy," James said, climbing off the high stool behind the counter. Young, not quite twenty, the accountant was ramrod thin, with knobby wrists and elbows and permanent ink stains between two fingers on his right hand.

"Yes, she is," Clay answered, glad to talk about the boiler. "I'm counting on her to pay for herself quickly. It was quite an investment." He laid the telegrams on the counter.

James slid the papers closer, arranging them into a neat stack. "If my calculations are correct, she will in three months' time. I'd say that's a good investment for something you'll get at least five years' use out of."

"Five years?"

"Yes, that's how long you had the last one," the accountant said. "Twenty-four hours a day, seven days a week takes its toll."

"Yes, it does," Clay agreed. That's why he ran three eight-hour shifts a day, with rotating days. He didn't want tired mill workers any more than he wanted tired machinery. He smacked a hand on the counter. "I'm going out to take a look at the boiler, and then I have some things to take care of. I may be gone awhile."

James laid a hand on the telegrams. "If I see anything out of the ordinary in these I'll leave a note on your desk." His cheeks turned red. "I, uh, I promised Caroline I'd take her to see *The Three Little Pigs* today."

Clay bit back a smile, knowing James was embarrassed enough. "All right, anything else?"

"There was a trapper to see you. Said he'd be back later this afternoon."

"Did he tell you his name?"

"No, just that he had to talk to you."

There was no doubt it was One Ear Bob. Clay had often wondered if someday Sam's father would show up, wanting a piece of Sam's share, but now it seemed the man may have sent a friend instead. "I'll let you get to work, then, so you can get out of here by noon," he said.

"I'll see you on Monday, sir."

Clay nodded and left. On the front walkway, he turned toward the stamp mill, but something had him pivoting, looking down the road.

He wasn't going to get much work done until he got things settled with Kit, so he might as well do it now.

Huffing out a sigh, he headed toward the hotel.

The bell jingled overhead as he shoved the door open, and the sound mingled with a lilting giggle, one he instantly recognized as Kit's.

"Well, Clayton Hoffman," Mimmie Mae said in greeting. "I declare, I simply don't recall the last time you were here twice in one day."

The hotel owner, as jolly as she was round, always made him grin, and today was no different. He gave her a nod before admitting, "I need to speak with Miss Becker." His gaze went through the open doorway, and his grin faded at the way his heart decided to throb against his rib cage.

"Go on in," Mimmie Mae said. "There's no one else in the dining room. I have to get back to the kitchen.

Once those trains start rolling in for the matinee it'll be so crowded you won't be able to walk through here."

A muffled thud said the hotel owner had slipped through the door behind the front desk. Clay's eyes had never left those of the woman staring at him from the dining room. She certainly looked more like a Kit than a Katherine. He didn't know what that came down to, but was glad one thing had settled in his mind.

"Mr. Hoffman," she said, moving to the doorway, probably because he hadn't walked into the room. His feet had grown roots upon seeing her. He hadn't wanted to admit it before, but even while dripping wet, she'd had that heart-stopping beauty few women ever achieved naturally.

He gave a nod of his head, indicating a table behind her. "Shall we sit for a moment? I'd like to speak with you."

"You're sending me back to Chicago, aren't you?"

"Why do you say that?" he asked. The gloom on her face had him stepping forward, taking her hand.

"Just assuming, I guess," she answered. "You look upset."

"I'm not upset," he said. "I'm, well, I'm confused." The scent of summer flowers floated in the air, made him recall the train ride, and kissing her, and that, of course, sent his desires reeling. Trying to get past the effects she had on him was becoming useless, yet he had to remember he was her guardian. Oscar had entrusted him with her livelihood, and that had to come before his emotions, no matter how tangled they became each time he looked at her.

"Shall we?" he asked. When she nodded, he led her to a table and pulled out a chair. Once she sat, he took the seat beside her. "Did you run away from Chicago because Mr. Watson didn't approve of a beau?"

"A beau?" She shook her head. "I've never had a beau. Grandma refused to allow me to encourage gentlemen callers."

A sigh of relief much larger than appropriate eased out of Clay's lungs. Pulling his mind back to Sam helped him gain control of his wayward thoughts. "I need to protect Sam's interests, Kit. Therefore, I need to know why, out of the blue, you ran away from Chicago and showed up here, looking for him."

She wrung her hands in her lap as her face filled with sadness. Clay wanted to reach out in comfort. Instead, he laid both of his hands on the table, where he could watch them, control them. "I'd like the truth, Kit. Why'd you pretend to be someone you aren't?"

Her sigh was so long and heavy it hung in the air for several moments before she spoke. "I was named after my grandma Katie. Her real name was Katherine, but Gramps always called me Kitten, and shortened it to Kit as I got older."

Clay nodded. Oscar had told him all that, and he sensed she was trying to find a way to explain everything—to herself as much as to him.

"My birth name was Ackerman, but both my parents died shortly after I was born. I went to live with my grandparents, and since everyone assumed my last name was Becker, when I was ten Gramps had my name legally changed. That's why I used Katherine Ackerman as an alias."

A frown formed as Clay listened, but he held in another thought to ask, "Why did you need an alias?"

She bit her lip as she glanced around the room. When

her gaze, worried and sad, met his, she softly said, "Because Mr. Watson refused to allow me to travel out here, and I was afraid you wouldn't tell me the truth, either, if you knew who I was."

"The truth about what?"

With a slight shrug, she said, "Everything. Mr. Watson says you're in charge of everything. He gave me a copy of Grandpa's will. Your name is listed as the overseer, but other than that, all it says is everything is to be divided equally between Grandpa's heirs." Confusion filled her face as she held up two fingers. "Two heirs. Me and a man named Sam Edwards."

Clay's stomach churned as he asked, "So, Oscar never told you about Sam?"

She shook her head. "I'm an only child, and I thought my mother was, too, but..." Sighing again, she asked, "Is Sam Edwards my uncle?"

"Your uncle?"

She nodded.

A chill ran over Clay. He had to think this through before he could explain everything. "No, Sam's not your uncle."

"Then who is he?" she asked. "I came out here to..." She blinked several times, as if holding in tears. "Why doesn't anyone want me to know if I have a family?"

An urge to fold her in his arms overtook him, but Clay settled for reaching out and wrapping his fingers around hers. "What did Mr. Watson tell you when Oscar died?"

"He read the will to me. Told me he'd oversee my welfare in Chicago, and that if I wanted to travel out here I had to have your permission." She sighed heavily.

Her sadness was eating at Clay, had a string tied

around his stomach and was pulling it tighter and tighter. "Why didn't you contact me? Ask me?"

"I don't know. I never really thought about that, I guess," she said. "At first I was too focused on losing Gramps and Grandma Katie, and then I saw an old ticket stub of Grandpa's and… No one would tell me the truth about this Sam Edwards." She shook her head. "I've just made a mess of everything."

Clay wanted to tell her she wasn't the one who'd made the mess, but then he'd have to tell her everything. Tell her she had a brother she never knew about. A mother who hadn't died, but had instead deserted her as an infant. Hell, Clay would rather fight off two grizzlies and a mountain lion than be the one to tell her that. All he really wanted to do was hold her close, protect her from the pain of it.

She leaned forward, as if to make sure no one would hear. "You can tell me if Sam is illegitimate. It won't shock me. I know Gramps was out here every year for as long as I can remember, and though I don't agree with what may have happened, I could understand."

Clay shook his head, half in disbelief, half in awe at her honesty. His heart was going out to this girl like it never had to another soul. "Sam's not your grandfather's illegitimate son," he assured her.

"Then who is he?"

He took one of her hands, squeezed it reassuringly. "I'll tell you, Kit," he said. And he would, but not here in the hotel dining room. She'd need some privacy afterward, and comfort. Thankful more than ever for having a sister, he said, "But right now, we need to get ready for the matinee."

"The matinee?"

"Yes, you were invited to go with Jonathan and Clarice, weren't you?"

She shook her head briefly, but then nodded. "Yes, they invited me." Looking at him keenly, she asked, "You're going, too?"

That hadn't been the plan, but it was now. Anyone in town could tell her who Sam was; it was a miracle it hadn't been accidentally blurted out already. Reaching in his pocket with his free hand, Clay pulled out the glasses. "I have to give these to Liza Rose. They're for her doll." The tips of his ears practically caught fire. "She lost them at school the other day."

For the very first time in her life, Kit was speechless, or maybe just too thrilled to talk. Her insides were erupting with happiness, though she wasn't exactly sure why. It was exciting to know she'd soon find out who Sam was—maybe he was adopted? She'd never thought of that, but that would still make him her uncle, wouldn't it? Drawing a breath, she decided to give her mind a break. She was finally going to get to hear the truth.

When Clay had left her standing outside the Children's Society House, he'd been angry. She'd seen it in his eyes, and had truly expected him to escort her to the train station. But right now, there was nothing but compassion on his face.

She and Mimmie Mae had been talking about the play when he'd entered the hotel. The woman had said three trains would roll in before one o'clock, bringing people from as far as Denver to watch the play.

Today's showing of *The Three Little Pigs and the Big Bad Wolf* was a first. Put on just for the children. Mimmie Mae said it was Clarice's idea, and all of the proceeds from the event would be used to buy clothes and such for the children at the society house.

Realizing she'd yet to respond, Kit offered an understanding smile. "Clarice told me about the teacher, that you had to fire him."

Clay gave a simple nod. "When did you meet Clarice?"

Kit stopped shy of saying after he'd left her standing by the tree. "This morning, at the society house. Jonathan was there, too. That's when they asked me to attend the matinee." She glanced down, remembering why she'd returned to the hotel. "I came back here to get my jacket. I'm supposed to join them for lunch at Clarice's."

Clay stood and grasped the back of her chair. "Well, go fetch it, then, or we'll be late."

"I'll be only a minute," she assured him. As she left the dining room, her footsteps were light as feathers, and by the time she started up the steps, the smile on her lips couldn't stretch any wider. Minutes later, when she hurried back down the stairs to see Clay standing at the bottom, waiting for her, her heart skipped a beat. Ever since meeting him, finding Sam had seemed to fade into the depths of her mind. She still wanted to meet him, discover who he was, but a stronger, more poignant desire had grown inside her, one that was focused on Clay. She kept hearing Grandpa Oscar's voice, talking about him over the years.

"Ready?" Clay asked.

She nodded and took his hand as she stepped off the stairs.

"So," he said, holding the door open for her to exit the hotel, "what else have you done this morning, besides climb a tree to rescue a cat?"

Her footsteps still felt light, and she couldn't help but grin. "Well, I had a tour of the society house, and Clarice told me all about it."

"I'm sure she did," he answered.

The grin on his face had Kit's heart jumping in her chest, and that left her so unbalanced she almost tripped over her own feet. He caught her arm, and continued to hold it as they walked toward the edge of town. She shouldn't be surprised to feel so giddy. This was probably how most every girl felt on their first outing with a man. Not that this was really an outing, but yet it was. Grandma had never allowed Kit to accept invitations from boys. She'd always said Grandpa would have to approve first, and since Grandpa was usually in Colorado, by the time he returned the boys had found someone else to court.

Kit hadn't been overly upset by it at first, but as the years had gone by, fewer and fewer boys had asked, and this past year she hadn't received a single invitation. Though she was only twenty, her friends from school were all married, and in some ways, looked upon her as a spinster who'd go on living alone in her grandparents' house forever. No friends. No family. No longer being that solitary person was enough to make her giddy in itself.

"Here we are," Clay said, pushing open the gate.

He took her arm again as the gate swung shut, and didn't let it loose until he lifted a hand to knock upon the door.

"Hi, Kit," Liza Rose said brightly, before her big eyes turned to Clay. "Hello, Mr. Hoffman."

"Good afternoon, Liza Rose," he said, kneeling down to her height. "You are just the person I came to see."

"I am?"

Kit had to grin at the brightness that glittered in the child's eyes.

"Because I found something I believe belongs to you." He tapped the doll's round head. "Or Mrs. Smith, that is."

"What is it?" the child whispered, clearly in awe.

Kit's heart swelled as she imagined the happiness the little girl would soon experience. Clarice had told her how Liza Rose had taken Mrs. Smith to school for sharing, and another child had teased her about the doll. The two had scuffled, and not only had the doll's glasses been broken, but the children had been switched for fighting. Another shower of warmth spread over Kit, and she conceded it must be pride for how swiftly Clay had acted. His sister had said he'd fired the teacher this morning, and told the man to be on the noon train.

Clay had pulled the glasses from his pocket and now held them in his open palm, and Kit watched the child closely while he folded back the protective cloth.

"These," he said.

"Mrs. Smith's spectacles!" Liza Rose grabbed the glasses and dropped the doll, which bounced once, landing on the porch with her cloth arms and legs sprawled in all directions. "She'll be able to see again, Mr. Hoffman. She'll be so happy." Falling to her knees, the child worked her chubby fingers, trying to get the little frames hooked over the doll's miniature ears.

"Here," he offered. "Allow me."

Kit knelt beside the two of them, patting Liza Rose's back as they watched Clay wrap the tiny wires around the doll's ears. When the glasses were secured, he picked the doll up and handed it to the girl.

"Oh, thank you, Mr. Hoffman." She hugged the toy closely, and then hooked her arm around his neck. "Thank you so much."

"You're welcome," he whispered, returning her hug. "You're very welcome."

Liza Rose stepped back and held out the doll. "Mrs. Smith would like to hug you, too."

Kit giggled inwardly as he glanced her way.

He took the doll, then tucked Mrs. Smith under his chin and gave her a big hug. The sight was so touching Kit wanted to hug him herself.

"She says thank you, too," Liza Rose explained.

"Aw," he said. Holding the doll out, he looked directly through the little glasses at the painted eyes. "You are most welcome, Mrs. Smith."

Liza Rose took the doll when he handed her back, and spinning on her heels, thrust it toward Kit. "Look, Kit, Mrs. Smith got her glasses back!"

"Indeed she did," Kit answered, running a finger over the tiny frames. "And I must say, they look beautiful on her."

The child hugged the doll again. "Oh, thank you, Mr. Hoffman. Thank you."

A woman's laughter had Kit glancing into the open doorway. "Hello, Kit," Clarice said, before she took hold of Clay's arm. "And you, you big lug, have to be about the nicest brother a girl could have."

When he stood at full height, his sister stretched on her tiptoes and kissed his cheek, something Kit wished she could do. Her heart was expanding so fast her chest hurt, both at how Liza Rose had reacted to her gift, and how wonderful it must be to have a family like this.

"Oh?" Clay said, giving his sister a hug. "What do you want now?"

Clarice laughed and reached over to take Kit's arm. "Nothing. That was very nice of you to repair Mrs. Smith's glasses."

He took Kit's other arm as Clarice tugged her into the house. "Then you'll be surprised to hear I'm attending the matinee with you."

Though Clarice's hair was a delightful shade of yellow, her eyes were the same dark blue as her brother's, and right now they darted between Clay and the hold he had on her arm, making Kit's toes curl inside her dress shoes.

"You are?" Clarice asked, as if she didn't believe him.

"Yes," he said, "I am." Still holding Kit's arm, he led her through the open doorway. "I believe we were invited to join you for lunch before the play begins."

"Well, then, right this way," Clarice said, waving her arm.

The meal proved to be the most delightful one Kit had ever had. Though twelve chairs sat around the table, there weren't enough for everyone, so on both sides, long planks were stretched across three chairs, making room for four or five to sit instead of three. Kit sat directly across from Clay, and every once in a while, when she'd feel his gaze upon her, a heat rose into her cheeks such as she'd never experienced before.

The meal started with an orchestra of platters, bowls and plates being passed left to right. Well-behaved, the children took a sample of everything going by, and the older ones helped the younger ones when needed. For the first few minutes, after the last platter was set back in the center of the table, a busy silence filled the room as the children enjoyed the meal with gusto. It had Kit enthralled, just being a part of it all, and shortly afterward the conversations had her laughing aloud. The children had eaten enough to take the edge off their endless hunger, and their array of questions focused on the matinee, and were mainly directed at Clay, who responded with exaggerated teasing.

By the time the meal ended Kit's cheeks hurt from laughing. When the children, well-versed on their chores, began to clear the table, she rose to help, but paused when Clay took her arm.

"Are you sure you want to attend the play?" he asked, sidestepping out of the way of rushing children.

"Yes," she answered, her insides bubbling all over again. An ounce of dread rose up, making her ask, "Don't you?"

"Sure," he said, but his eyes were reading her face again, in that way they seemed to do. "I just didn't know if you still wanted to, after seeing how wild ten kids can be."

"I think they're delightful," she answered honestly. "I always wished I'd had siblings."

"You did?"

She nodded, but her smile slipped as she caught the serious look that all of a sudden covered his face. Her skin prickled, too, as if in warning of something about to come. There wasn't time for her to reflect upon it, though, because Clarice patted her arm right then.

"Kit, would you mind helping the children for a moment?" she asked. "I need to speak with Clay for just a second."

"Of course not," Kit answered, and was immediately given instructions by a nearby Liza Rose.

The cleaning up was completed in no time, and then the entire group exited the house, gathering on the front porch for a count of heads.

Clay's fingers wrapped around her hand as he said, "I told Clarice we'd be the caboose, make sure no one gets sidetracked on the way."

Kit nodded. It was the most she could do. The fire his touch caused was growing. Now, not just the skin where his fingers touched heated up, but her insides did, too. The warmth was enough to make her sway on her feet. Well, that and the fact that as soon as he said *caboose* her mind recalled how they'd kissed.

"Are you all right?"

She blinked and took a deep breath. How could mere thoughts make a person feel as dizzy as if she'd just twisted the ropes of a swing together and spun around in tight circles?

"Yes," she said. "I'm fine. Being the caboose is a good idea."

Chapter Seven

"**O**h, goodness, that was fun, wasn't it?" Clarice asked, sitting down in the chair in the large kitchen.

"Yes, it was," Kit agreed, still as dizzy as if she'd been on a swing. Sitting next to Clay in the darkened playhouse had turned her entire body to mush. Her legs had barely managed to carry her back to the society house. Now that he was gone, a sense of normality was returning, but somehow she knew she'd never be the same.

Clarice was as kind and friendly as she was beautiful, and as if sensing Kit was still a touch off-kilter, she patted her hand. "Sometimes the children can be a bit overwhelming. Thank you, again, for helping today."

The children were not what had overwhelmed her. "I really enjoyed it," Kit replied, taking another sip from the teacup painted with blue roses and then replacing it on the matching saucer. The inside of Children's Society House was as neat and tidy as the outside. It was a cheerful home, made more so by the laughter floating through the open door. This was the kind of place she'd never tire of, including the cat that right now was rubbing against her leg. She bent down to pat his head. "I'm so happy to hear Frenchie didn't eat those baby birds."

"I should have told Liza Rose they flew away this morning, but with everything else going on, I just didn't think of it. I'm glad you didn't get hurt climbing that tree after him," Clarice said as she refilled both their cups.

Kit had thought changing the subject might help, but talk of climbing the tree made her think of Clay all over again. Hearing a male laugh mingling with the children's in the backyard, she snatched on to the distraction. "Jonathan certainly enjoyed the play."

Clarice's face grew soft and a dreamlike gleam appeared in her eyes as she gazed toward the doorway. "He's so wonderful with the children and has been such a help since I opened this place."

"How long ago was that? When you opened the society house?" Kit asked, determining that was an even safer subject.

"Almost two years ago now."

"I wonder why Gramps never mentioned it," Kit murmured. He would have known she would be interested in hearing about such a home. When she was younger she had used to beg him to bring home another child for her to play with. With that low-pitched chuckle of his he'd say she was the only child he and Grandma could handle.

"I don't believe he saw it. The last time he was in Nevadaville he spent most of the time out at the mine."

"That sounds like Gramps." Despite the tug at her heart, she grinned. "He loved to get his hands dirty, as he used to say."

Clarice looked thoughtful for a moment and then smiled with understanding while resting a hand on top of Kit's. "He was a wonderful man. I remember being little and looking forward to his visits. I used to wish he was my grandpa."

Kit nodded, blinking at the sting in her eyes. During the past couple of months, when her wondering mind had gone down dark roads, her love for her grandparents had faltered at times, which had been silly indeed. She would always love them. "He was the best."

They sat for a moment, sipping their tea, while joyous sounds continued to echo outside. After a year of living in solitude, Kit found it refreshing to be with others, to feel welcome and a part of something. Not that her home had ever been overflowing with people, but even when it had been just her and Grandma, at least she hadn't been alone. Not like the past year, when there had been times she'd feared the very walls would fall in around her. No one, unless they'd experienced it, could understand just how lonely she'd been.

"Clarice," Kit said. "Do you know Sam Edwards?"

Clarice took a sip of her tea, and then set it down on the matching saucer. "Sure, everyone does. But I want to know what you're interested in. What did you do back in Chicago?" With a wave of her hand, she added, "I always dreamed of owning a place like this, for children. What have you always wanted to do?"

Have a family, Kit almost answered, but compared to a society house, that sounded like an insignificant dream. "Well," she said, "I thought about starting a library."

"A library?"

Kit nodded. "I have rooms full of books back home. All kinds, and I have them all cataloged and arranged." Mainly because there'd been little else to fill her time with over the years. "I thought about opening a library to memorialize Grandpa and his love of books."

"How many books do you have?"

"Thousands," Kit answered. "Well, five thousand, six hundred and ninety-eight. New York and Los Angeles, as well as a few other cities, have been working at getting public libraries, and I thought Chicago might want one as well, but after talking with city officials, I realized the Oscar Becker Memorial Community Library was just a silly dream."

"You talked to the city?"

"Yes, and Grandpa's solicitor, but they both said it would be a very expensive venture. That I should just loan my books out to friends and such."

Clarice frowned, looked seriously thoughtful for several moments, but then her face brightened. "We could do it here. I could help you."

"Here?"

"Yes, here in Nevadaville. I know the city would agree to it."

Kit's heart fluttered wildly, but among the commotion a thought formed, and it was focused on Clay. Creating a library here would mean she could see him regularly, and something about that was overly appealing. She bit her lip, exploring the excitement dancing about, but ultimately shook her head. "All my books are in Chicago," she said, while her mind told her eventually she'd have to go back there. That's where she lived.

"So?" Clarice said. "We could have them shipped here."

Biting her lip again, Kit shook her head. She'd left the house empty long enough, something that was probably making Grandma Katie roll over in her grave. That had been the one thing that had kept Kit from coming out here earlier. Years ago Grandma had made her promise never to leave the house empty, and now she had. The guilt was enough to swell her throat shut.

Clay slid the piece of paper back toward the man on the other side of his desk. "This means nothing."

One Ear Bob, covered in animal skins so it was impossible to tell if he had only one ear or not, didn't take the note. "It says right there that Edwards wanted me to look out for his boy if anything happened to him. I can show you where I buried him if you don't believe he's dead."

"Whether the man is dead or not is no concern of mine," Clay said, leaning back in his chair. "Sam's been on his own for years. He doesn't need anyone to look out for him."

"That boy inherited a gold mine," the trapper said, puffing out his chest and narrowing his eyes. "Edwards would want me to help him oversee his financial responsibilities. I gave my word I would."

Sam's inheritance was well known in the local area, so Clay couldn't deny that, but very few people knew the intricacies of it all. "Sam will inherit shares in a mine when he turns twenty-one, but not before then." Pushing out of his chair, Clay continued, "If you'd like to assist Sam financially until then, by all means, go ahead. You know where he lives."

One Ear Bob glowered. "I know you're part owner in that mine, too, and that you're just stealing the kid's money."

Clay refused to be riled. "Sam's share is being overseen by the terms of his grandfather's will. No one has access to it until he's twenty-one." He picked up the paper, which was clearly a fabrication, and handed it to the man. "If you'd care to take it up with a judge, I'll be happy to give you the name of the solicitor in Chicago who is overseeing everything."

The trapper took the paper and stomped out of the office, slamming the door in his wake. On a good day, Clay would bet on never seeing the man again. On a bad day, he'd say the trapper wasn't done with trying to profit off Sam. Since this was a middling day—where things had gone fifty-fifty—he couldn't say which way it would go, so just to be safe, he wrote a note to be delivered to the mine, asking the miners to keep a closer eye on Sam and the surroundings.

The whistle from the stamp mill sounded, declaring shift change time, which also meant it was time to go and see Oscar's other grandchild. Clay rubbed his head, replaced his hat and headed for the door. Neither Sam nor Kit could turn twenty-one fast enough to suit him today.

Laughter floated through the windows as he approached his sister's house, and he wasn't sure what washed over him, delight or dread. Either one could make a person's heart race and his palms sweat. He'd asked Clarice to join him this evening in telling Kit about Sam. There was no predicting how she might react, and most likely would need another woman's support.

It was still a bit confusing, why Oscar had never told her. Clay had spent the better part of the afternoon looking through his partner's old files. Kit deserved to know the truth, and all he really had was hearsay. Most of it had come from Oscar, but even in that, the man had been sharing what he thought had happened.

Clay squared his shoulders and climbed the steps. Someone must have heard the thud of his boots because the door opened before he knocked.

"Hello, Mr. Hoffman."

The child always made him smile. "Hello, Liza Rose." He bent down to flick the end of her nose and her doll's. "And hello to you, too, Mrs. Smith."

Liza Rose giggled and darted off, leaving Clay to close the door. As he turned, he found a set of brown eyes gazing his way, and his heart, which had decided to take up permanent residency in his chest again, gave a little kick. He accepted the reaction. Kit was just like Sam. His ward. He should care about them. If reading all of Oscar's paperwork hadn't confirmed that, the visit from One Ear Bob had.

Her expression changed, went from smiling to thoughtful, as if she was trying to read his mind.

"Hi, Mr. Hoffman," a tiny voice said.

"Hi, yourself, Willie," Clay responded, and moving into the room, he patted the crown of dark curls on the boy's head. "Did you enjoy the play today?"

"Yes, sir. I especially liked the wolf."

"Really?" Clay asked, keeping one eye on the sofa, where Kit was now fidgeting with the folds of her skirt.

Clarice had ten children at the home, and it seemed to Clay as if they all started talking at once, every child explaining the part they had found particularly interesting or humorous. The chaos didn't distract his attention. It remained on the woman peeking at him from beneath her lashes. The news was going to be shocking and that tugged at his newly acquired heart with more force than anything in the past had. Oscar had told him Kit wanted a family, and that made the fact that he hadn't told her about Sam even more perplexing.

"Children, please, Mr. Hoffman can't hear anyone when everyone is talking at the same time," Clarice said above the clatter. "There, now, that's better," she added when things quieted down.

It was a standing event that he supped with her and the children every Saturday. She felt the children needed a male influence. He didn't believe he was the best person for the role. Furthermore, Jonathan was there most Saturdays as well. The man was there now, sitting in an armchair beside the sofa where Kit sat.

"Have a seat, Clay." Clarice waved a hand toward the sofa as she took the other available armchair.

He moved across the room, sidestepping a game of checkers and a rope loop full of marbles, on his way to the sofa, where he sat, leaving plenty of space between him and Kit. "How was your afternoon?"

"Fine," she answered. "How was yours?"

"Supper is almost ready," Adeline Wurm said just then from the kitchen doorway. She nodded his way, smiling. "Thank you, Mr. Hoffman, for Mrs. Smith's glasses. I didn't get a chance to tell you that earlier."

He nodded back, feeling his neck heat up, a bit tongue-tied with Kit's eyes still on him. A *bit*. The word made him want to grin, thinking of another time, another place, when she'd been talking about being a "touch" miffed when Big Ed wouldn't sell her a gun to chase down Sam. The memory brought Clay full circle.

"All right, children, pick up your games and go wash your hands," Clarice instructed.

The children responded, gathering items as they left

the room, and the next hour or so was little more than a blur to Clay. He couldn't keep his eyes off Kit, and that had a battle ensuing in his head. The things he was feeling toward her weren't the same as the ones he felt toward Sam. They should be, he kept telling himself, but nothing changed in his heart. He'd reread his copy of instructions pertaining to Oscar's will this afternoon. Not only the one about P.J., but the others, about Kit. If she married before she was twenty-one, she lost everything, and that had him pondering exactly what Oscar had been thinking when he'd added that stipulation. The next one wasn't much better. Clay had to approve any man she wanted to marry until she was twenty-five. Without his approval, she wouldn't receive her inheritance.

As the meal ended, Clarice arrived at his side, watching while Kit helped the children carry dishes into the kitchen.

"She asked about Sam several times today," his sister whispered.

"What did you tell her?"

"I just kept changing the subject." Clarice glanced toward the kitchen, where his gaze was as well. "I can't believe Oscar never told her."

"Neither can I," Clay admitted.

Kit reentered the room and looked at them quizzically.

Clarice tugged at his arm. "Clay, why don't you take Kit for a short walk, while I help get the kids settled for the night? Afterward the four of us can play a game of cards or something. Does that sound good to you, Kit?"

"Sure," she answered, still gazing at him.

Clay wasn't so sure that was a good idea, him being

alone with her. In his mind, when she wasn't near, he could think of her as his ward, but when she stood in front of him she became a woman he wanted to get to know, intimately. During the matinee, while everyone else was enthralled by the actors, he'd been consumed by the stick of dynamite that had all of a sudden planted itself between his legs. He'd never had this kind of reaction to a woman before, not even Miranda, and it wasn't right. Kit was his responsibility, and if another man was thinking the things he was about her, Clay would have him on the first train out of town.

"I'll get my jacket," Kit said, though it sounded almost like a question.

He nodded, following her out of the room, and cursing Oscar.

They exited through the front door, and as they walked down the steps she said, "Clarice said she'd talk to Alice Asher in the morning, see if she'll take over the job of teaching school until someone new can be hired."

"That's good," he replied, smiling at her obvious attempt to make small talk. He'd already witnessed her genuine concern for the children, above and beyond climbing a tree to save baby birds. "She's filled in before."

They were at the gate, but as he opened it for her to walk through, she stopped.

"This is about Sam, isn't it?" she asked. The moonlight glimmered in her eyes and enhanced the apprehension there.

Clay's insides sputtered and spit. He wasn't sure if it was because he was losing steam or gaining it. He let the gate spring closed, took her hand and didn't stop until they arrived at the swing he'd put up a few weeks before.

She sat, and when he was settled next to her, said, "That's what you and Clarice were whispering about, and why you've been so quiet tonight."

"Yes, it is," he admitted. This shouldn't be so hard. Wouldn't be if his mind wasn't so tangled up with his heart.

"Is it bad?"

"No, Kit, it's not bad." *I just wish someone else had told you,* he added to himself. He'd never been this hesitant about telling someone the truth before. The thought of putting her through more pain gnawed at him. Theodore Watson had sent messages last year about how the deaths of Oscar and his wife had left her distraught—to the point she rarely left the house. Clay had saved those telegrams, had them in the same envelope as the will, and had reread them today. No wonder the bridges had scared her; she'd probably never ridden over one before. Watson had said he checked on her once a week, made sure she had provisions. It was perplexing, because the woman sitting next to him didn't act like the same one the solicitor had described. She was more like the one Oscar had always spoken of, and that, too, left Clay confused.

Pushing the swing into a gentle rocking motion with one foot, he said, "There are several stipulations to Oscar's will. Did Mr. Watson tell you any of them?"

She sighed. "Yes, he told me the stipulations about getting married before I turn twenty-five, and if I try to challenge anything, everything will be sold to a former partner. Other than that, he said I had to talk to you."

The marriage aspects didn't seem to bother her, if the tone of her voice told him much.

As if reading his mind, she added, "My mother married young. She was only seventeen when I was born, and Grandma Katie always said they wanted to make sure I was more mature when I got married." A waning smile arrived and disappeared just as quickly. "My mother died when I was a baby, my father before I was born."

Clay couldn't stop from reaching over and curving an arm around her. As if it was the most natural thing on earth—and it did feel that way—she scooted closer and laid her head on his shoulder. He rested his chin on the top of her hair and kept the swing swaying until Clarice waved from the side of the house. During that time, he should have been thinking about how to tell Kit the truth, but he hadn't. Instead he'd just held her, not really thinking of anything other than how right it felt. How good it felt to be connected with someone. Something he hadn't had in a very long time—if ever.

The urge to kiss her, even briefly, was consuming him again, something else he hadn't experienced in a very long time. He drew in a sigh and let it out, distressed that it didn't lessen his frustration. "Are you ready to go in?"

"Not really," she answered. "But I don't suspect I have a choice."

He wanted to tell her she did, but couldn't. "Let's go."

Once inside the house, he led her to the lumpy velvet sofa the same shade of green as her skirt, and continued to hold her hand after sitting down next to her. He wanted to pull her close, have her snuggle against him as she had outside, but that wouldn't make anything easier.

"Kit," he started, once Clarice and Jonathan sat on the chairs flanking the sofa. He'd rather cut off his right arm than say this, but didn't have a choice. "Your mother didn't die when you were a baby."

A tiny frown formed between her brows as she nodded. "Yes, she did."

He took hold of her other hand, squeezing them both with his. "Oscar and Katie's daughter, your mother, *Amelia,*" he said, emphasizing the woman's name so Kit would know he knew what he was talking about, "lived not twenty miles from here until she died ten years ago."

Kit glanced to Clarice and Jonathan, who nodded sympathetically. The entire town knew about Amelia's death and how badly Oscar had tried to persuade Sam to go to Chicago with him once he'd found the boy. Once again Clay wanted to curse the man for never telling Kit.

Her troubled gaze landed on him. "My mother was alive?" Shaking her head, she pulled a hand from his hold and pressed it to her throat. "All those years, my mother was alive?"

Like when a bolt broke and a brace beam fell unexpectedly, something let loose inside Clay, spewing compassion for her pain throughout his system. He wrapped an arm around her. "I'm sorry, Kit." It was insignificant, but he couldn't come up with anything better.

"Did Gramps know?"

"Yes, he knew."

Utter disbelief shimmered in her eyes. "W-why didn't he tell me?" she asked, as if he should have all the answers.

"I don't know why."

"All these years?" The blood had drained from her face, leaving her white and her voice little more than a faint and quivering whimper. "Why?" She pressed a hand to her forehead and then pulled it off, as if she didn't know what to do with it.

"Clarice, get a glass of water," Clay said, taking the trembling hand in his.

"No…" Kit said between little huffs of air. "I—I need to return to the hotel." Tears were now dripping onto her cheeks. "Clay, I…" She squeezed her eyes shut.

"Shh," he said, guiding her to her feet. "Clarice has a place you can lie down for a minute." He held her tightly. "It's going to be all right."

"Here, I'll take her," Clarice said.

Clay found the ability to step aside, though he really didn't want to.

"We'll go right in here," Clarice said. "It's my room and you can rest for a bit."

Feeling as useless as a broken smelter hammer, he watched as the two women entered the bedroom at the end of the hallway and shut the door.

Chapter Eight

Clay waited for what seemed like hours before Clarice entered the hall, quietly closing the door behind her.

"She's sleeping," his sister whispered.

"Is she all right?"

"I'm sure she will be. It's just been a shock. Go on home. I'm sure come morning she'll want to ask you a few more questions. I told her what I could, but I don't know much."

"Neither do I," he admitted. Though he wanted to say he'd sleep on the lumpy velvet sofa, he walked to the door, with his sister gently pushing on his back. It was doubtful he'd sleep at all. There was a frustrating poison, as lethal as the eighty-pound canisters of mercury over at the stamp mill, eating at his very soul. He'd always respected Oscar—owed the man for all he had—but right now he wished he'd never met him.

Clay climbed the hill behind the house, to the second level of Nevadaville, and used that street to make his way toward his office. He'd witnessed people in pain before, stricken with disbelief, but it had never affected him this way.

"Damn it, Oscar, why hadn't you told her?" he said,

or maybe just thought it. Either way, the words echoed in his head, and then, out of the blue, he heard Oscar's voice. But the man wasn't talking about Kit. The words Clay heard were from when Oscar had told him Miranda wasn't the girl for him.

Clay paused, looking ahead to where the steady beat of the stamp mill echoed in the night air. Demons were hellish creatures, and clever. They hid, acted as if they'd moved on, whereas they never really did.

The air left his chest, leaving him empty and pitiful. Never had another person touched him in that vulnerable spot Miranda had left open, until Kit. And this time it was worse.

"Damn it to hell," he muttered. Being infatuated with a woman he could never marry—never love in that way, but had to take care of—was worse than one that had left him.

His office, straight ahead, had a back room, with a cot and a little potbellied stove, all he needed to get by. But beyond his office, up the hill, was his house, complete with all the furnishings and appliances it took to fill a place that size. He kept walking. If he was going to fight demons, he might as well fight them where they lived.

Kit took a deep breath and closed her eyes. When she opened them, the walkway to the big house still lay before her. Dawn had barely broken, yet the streaks of light made every window sparkle, almost as if they were excited at the possibility of company. It was in such contrast to the way she felt. Another shiver hiked its way up her spine, and she glanced over her shoulder. The entire town seemed to still be asleep, but she'd been awake for hours, and needed answers.

Moments later she knocked on the door, which held a piece of beveled glass etched with a scene of pine trees nestled below a mountain.

A thud sounded on the other side, and she planted her feet on the porch, refusing to allow herself to turn about. Something dark and heavy, a drape of sorts, covered the beveled window inside, making it impossible to see behind it. If indeed anyone was home.

What seemed an eternity later, the knob turned and the door opened a few inches.

"Cla—" She cleared her throat and willed her voice to remain stable. It was incredibly hard. Just looking at him made something inside her open up, begging for him to wrap his arms around her and hold her so she could release all the pain burning inside.

"Kit?" He pulled the door open wider.

She bit her lip, unable to speak. He still wore the same clothes as yesterday, a white shirt and black trousers, minus the vest he'd worn at Clarice's last night, and one suspender was dangling at his side. His dark hair was going in all directions, as if he'd just crawled out of bed. Heat rushed into her cheeks at the thought. Perhaps it was too early, but she'd been unable to lie in Clarice's bed any longer, and the hotel room had been worse.

Pulling the door all the way open, he stepped aside and waved a hand for her to enter. As she walked in, he hooked an arm through the suspender and snapped it over his shoulder, and then combed his hair flat with both hands.

"I was hoping," she said, "maybe you could answer some of my questions."

As soon as the door closed the house became so dark she couldn't see. The shock and depth of the blackness caused a startled gasp to ripple from her throat.

"Oh, um, I haven't opened the drapes." His hand wrapped around her elbow.

The heat of his touch was like fire against the numbness that had overtaken her body since last night, yet at the same time, it reminded her she was still alive.

He guided her across what she assumed was the foyer and then pushed open a door, allowing light to splay around them. With his hand still holding her elbow, he led her into a kitchen painted bright white and boasting several wide windows.

"Would you like some coffee?" he asked, releasing his hold.

It was a moment before she could speak, remember her mission. "If it's no problem, that would be nice."

"It's no problem." He ran his hands through his hair again. "It'll just take me a minute to get the fire started."

She glanced at the big stove he gestured toward. Black with shiny chrome handles and decorative swirls, it looked as if it had never been used. Actually, everything in the room looked brand-new. "It's really not necessary. I—"

"No, it's no problem. Here—" he took her hand "—have a seat while I get things going." He led her to the table and pulled out a chair. His touch once more chased aside the numbness that had been with her all night—as if she couldn't feel anything on the outside with so much happening on the inside. The fact that her mother hadn't died while she was a baby was utterly unbelievable. Kit had asked Gramps and Grandma Katie— their spirits, anyway—several times while tossing upon the bed at the society house and pacing the floor at the hotel, why they hadn't told her. Of course, they hadn't answered, and now, after hours of crying, wondering and brooding, she was no closer to understanding the whole affair than she'd been last night.

Clatters and thuds made her glance up. Clay had got a fire started and was now opening and shutting cupboard doors. After the last one, he scratched his head and then walked across the room to a door on the opposite wall. When he opened it a pantry was exposed.

He entered the space and quickly walked out again, carrying two packages. "I have both tea and coffee. Which would you prefer?"

"Either is fine, but really, I don't need—"

"I said it was no problem." He carried the bags to the stove, set them on top of the warming ovens and started looking in cupboards again.

His behavior held her attention, made the troubles overcoming her slip aside. "Do you not live here?"

"I have a cot in my office. I usually stay there." He pulled out a copper pot and, smiling as if he'd just discovered he owned the coffeepot, carried it to the sink. "I'm still getting used to where everything is. Clarice stocked it, cleans it once in a while."

"She said you built this house two years ago," Kit said, having had a conversation about the intriguing house yesterday afternoon, while visiting after the play. To her disappointment, Clarice hadn't offered additional information.

"Yes, I did." He pumped water into the pot, dumped it out and filled it up again.

"And you're just learning where things are?"

He scooped beans from one of the bags into a metal

coffee grinder, and turned the crank. The noise filled the room, and Kit's mind circled back to the reason she was here. Would he know why Gramps had never told her about her mother? She didn't know who else to ask.

Clay pulled out a chair and sat next to her, his eyes so sad they tugged at her already bruised heart.

"Kit," he said solemnly. "I'm sorry. I don't know what more to say than that."

A heavy sigh left her chest. "You know, when I was little, I used to dream she wasn't dead, and neither was my father, and that someday they'd return and I'd have the family I always wanted." Accepting a mingling of guilt welling inside her, she tried to explain, "Gramps and Grandma were wonderful to me, but I remember other kids and..."

"They loved you," he said softly.

Nodding, she kept the tears at bay. "I know. I loved them, too, and as foolish as it sounds, I'd hoped Gramps had another family out here, one that would want me."

"Aw, Kit..." Clay laid a hand on her arm.

"It was silly, I know. My imagination got away from me. And I was afraid. I kind of liked being Katherine Ackerman. She was brave. Braver than me, anyway, and she'd..." Not knowing exactly how to explain it, she let it drop, simply said, "I was just so lonesome and I thought..."

Clay's hand roamed up to rest on her shoulder. "You do have family out here."

Another burning sensation took over her throat. "I know. Clarice told me Sam is my brother." It was so hard to explain, but that almost hurt worse. "Do you know why no one ever told me?"

With deep blue eyes full of compassion, Clay shook

his head. "I thought about it all night. I can't say for sure, but I can tell you what I think."

"I'd appreciate it." Before she lost her nerve, she added, "I am sorry to put you in this spot, but I don't have anyone else to turn to."

He removed his hand from her shoulder and used it to cup her cheek. "It's all right. I'll help you in any way I can."

The sincerity in his tone warmed her heart and made her smile. "I bet there's a part of you that wishes you'd never met Oscar Becker."

He chuckled kindly as he pulled the hand from her face and shoved it through his hair again. "I owe everything I have to Oscar."

She nodded, then flinched inwardly while admitting, "But I bet you wish you'd never met Katherine Ackerman from Boston, Massachusetts. That I'd have just stayed in Chicago."

A wayward, but charming smile formed on his lips. "No, I don't wish that," he said. "But I do have to admit you and Katherine Ackerman from Boston, Massachusetts, smell a whole lot better than Henry did."

A tiny giggle tickled her throat. "Sorry about that."

He let out a brief, but nice-sounding laugh. "The more I thought about it last night, the more I realized the Kit Oscar always talked about would have dressed like a boy and pretended to be a rich woman from Boston." A glimmer sparked in his eye as he added, "He always said you were an adventurer."

A tingling wave of joy washed over her. "He did?"

"Yes, he did."

Another lump formed in her throat. "I don't know

why he would have said that. I rarely left the backyard. But thanks for telling me."

Clay's gaze roamed her face, as if he was seriously examining her features. It made her cheeks warm and had her wondering if she'd been too hasty in her morning routine. Her eyes were red-rimmed, but there hadn't been anything she could do about it. The cool cloth she'd pressed to them earlier hadn't helped.

"You're welcome, Kit." A sizzle coming from the stove had him pushing away from the table. "Looks like the coffee's boiling." He walked over and pushed the pot off the burner before going to a cupboard to retrieve cups. "I'm afraid I don't have any cream, but might be able to find some sugar."

"That's all right. I've had it black before," she admitted, glad for a second to regain her equilibrium. Her heart was wishing he was her family. Someone she could love and laugh with and share whatever the future might bring.

He carried both cups to the table. After he slid one in front of her, he sat and lifted his to his lips, but stopped before taking a sip. "You know, the last time we had coffee together, I couldn't drink it."

"You drank your coffee yesterday morning," she reminded him.

"But you had tea." He set the cup down. "The last time we both had coffee was on the trail, when you stank to high heaven."

Her cheeks caught fire this time and she glanced toward her cup. "That was awful."

"So your coffee was appalling, too?" he asked, sounding skeptical.

"Yes," she admitted. "It tasted like the amulet bag smelled."

"I thought it was just me."

She wrinkled her nose and shook her head, peering at him through her lashes.

He grinned and then picked up his cup. "Let's hope this tastes better." As she reached for hers, he added, "But I'm not promising anything."

She cringed, glancing from the cup to him.

"I've never used that pot before." He winked.

Relief oozed through her and she took a sip, though she had no idea what the coffee tasted like. Her insides were too busy bubbling for her to notice.

They both drank a small amount, and then he set his coffee on the table. "I think Oscar was afraid to tell you." He spun the cup in a circle. "About your mother, that is."

Clay's friendliness had eased the sorrow engulfing her, allowing her to question things without sadness overtaking each thought. "Why?" She set her own cup down. "For the life of me, I can't figure out why. He knew how badly I wanted…" she had to take a breath before saying "…a family."

"And I think that's why." Clay took another drink. "It's a long story," he said, as if warning her, "how I came to my conclusion."

"I have time to listen, if you have time to tell me."

He nodded, but sat quietly for a moment, as if contemplating where to start.

She took another drink of coffee, filling the time with something, anything. What she'd said was true. She would wait until the end of time to hear what he had to say. To learn why Gramps had deceived her so.

"I was just a kid the first time I saw Oscar. Maybe eight or so, I can't say for sure. My father was working a mine over by Georgetown. The war had just ended and men were pouring into Colorado in droves. We'd pretty much cleaned out our claim, all the surface gold, anyway, when I heard my parents talking outside our tent about moving across the ridge." Clay paused to take a sip of coffee. "My father said he'd met a man to partner up with. That man turned out to be Oscar."

"My grandfather," she said, mainly to assure him she was listening and wanted to know more.

"Yes. We moved and set up camp near the Wanda Lou. I didn't know at the time, but Oscar already had a partner, P. J. Nelson. But P.J. wasn't interested in mining. He was only interested in spending the gold after it was found. Oscar needed someone to buy P.J. out, and figured a man with a family to feed would be more set on mining and developing the claim than a bachelor like P.J. In the end, Oscar and P.J. parted as friends. Once in a while P.J. works at one of the mines, to earn enough to get by for a time. That was a request Oscar had right from the beginning." Clay rose from his chair to retrieve the coffeepot.

Kit quickly emptied her cup so he could refill it. "What happened to your parents?" she asked, genuinely interested.

"My mother died from mountain fever when I was twelve and Clarice eight. Clarice had it, too, but, thankfully, she survived. And my father died nine years ago. He was out checking the ice on Clear Creek and fell through. He made it back home, but pneumonia set in."

"I'm sorry," she offered, touched by Clay's losses.

He nodded, but the set of his jaw told her the deaths

of his parents still affected him. She wanted to touch him, just squeeze his arm as he had hers, but tightened her hold on the coffee cup instead, not really sure why.

"After my father died, Oscar asked if I wanted to be his partner." Clay shook his head. "He didn't have to—offer, that is. My father wasn't one for bookkeeping or legal matters. He'd never written out a will or kept track of things. My mother had kept ledgers of every ounce of gold discovered. Oscar had shown her what to record and asked her to send him a report every few months. He'd asked me to continue filling out the ledgers after she died, and he paid me for doing so each summer on his trip out, said even a boy needed some spending money in his pocket."

Kit smiled, warmed by memories of Gramps. He'd had friends wherever he went. If he didn't when he arrived, he certainly had when he'd left.

"I wired Oscar as soon as my father died, and he came out here a month or so later. That was the first time we ever really talked. Sure, he talked to both Clarice and me every year when he made his annual trip out, but that time we discussed things. The mine, the business parts of it all. My father was more concerned with the work, claiming the gold from the earth, finding that big nugget, whereas Oscar was interested in the long-term outcome. The things that could manifest from finding the gold. He didn't have to offer me a partnership. He could have claimed it all, since I didn't have a scrap of paper proving my father's investments. But Oscar being Oscar, he offered me the fifty-fifty partnership he had had with my father. And he asked me to become more involved. To work with the stamp mill over in Black Hawk, and the smelter in Denver, as

well as the mint. He also wanted me to become more
involved in creating Nevadaville."

Clay held up the coffeepot, but she shook her head.
Unable to pull her attention from his tale, she discovered her cup was still full.

"The surface mining," he continued, setting the pot
back down, "had been played out at the Wanda Lou.
She still had a good vein, still does, but we were digging deeper and deeper to pull the ore out. The silver
in it is high grade, too, and by shipping the ore to the
smelters we could double the mine's payouts, more so
if we had our own stamp mill."

"I'm afraid I don't know much about gold mining,"
she admitted, interested in learning more. "I knew
Gramps owned a mine, but other than that, neither he
nor Grandma spoke much about it."

"I'll take you on a tour of the stamp mill. We extract
a lot of gold here, and then send the rest of the ore off
to the smelters, where they refine it, separate all the
minerals. Gold, silver, quartz, zinc, lead." He paused,
looking at her. "If you're interested, that is."

She nodded. "I'd like that. Really, I would."

He smiled, and then continued thoughtfully, "Well,
about two years ago, the miners sent word I was needed
at the Wanda Lou. When I got there, they pointed out
a boy that had shown up looking for Oscar. I explained
to him that Oscar lived in Chicago, but the kid insisted
he had to talk to him, so I brought the boy to Nevadaville and had him send a wire to Oscar. I don't know
what the wire said, but Oscar sent one back almost immediately, to me. Telling me not to let the boy out of
my sight, and that he was on his way."

The timeline clicked in her mind. "Gramps was gone over six months that time."

Clay let out a sigh and nodded. "Yes, he was here for a long time."

Her spine was tingling from her hips to her shoulders. "That boy was Sam, right?"

Clay folded both his hands around hers, which were holding on to the coffee cup to keep the trembling at bay. "Yes. That was Sam."

Taking in a breath, she attempted to comprehend it all, as she had back at Clarice's. It seemed so surreal. She was prepared to hear Sam was her uncle, but a brother was still so hard to understand. "How old is he?" she asked.

Clay's insides were twisted into a jumbled mess, as they had been all night. He'd thought he was still dreaming when he'd opened the door and found her standing on his porch. Now, sitting here, holding her hands, he found other things were playing into the mix.

Pulling her hands off the coffee mug so he could wrap his fingers around her trembling ones, he said, "Seventeen." She must have a million questions zinging around in her head. "Let me finish telling you what I know. Maybe it'll help answer some of your questions."

She nodded and offered a tight-lipped little smile.

"Well…" It took a moment for him to decide where to start. "Oscar arrived and I took him out to the mine, where Sam insisted on staying. Sam had a necklace, the kind you carry pictures in. One of the pictures was of Oscar and Katie, the other of…" He paused to swallow. "You."

"Me?"

"Yes, as a baby. Sam said the necklace was his mother's. Oscar confirmed it. The way Oscar told the story was that your mother had married a Union soldier who died in a battle shortly before you were born."

Kit nodded.

Clay sighed, relieved she'd known at least that much. "Oscar said your mother was grief stricken, and then one day just disappeared. Somehow he learned she was in Denver, and started searching for her. I don't exactly know how it all happened, but that's where he met P.J. and they partnered up on the Wanda Lou. Oscar said the mine was his excuse to come looking for Amelia every year."

"Did Grandma Katie know?" Kit's fingers, entwined with Clay's, clutched tighter.

"Yes," he said, "she knew. Oscar hated leaving her each fall, knowing when he got to Chicago he'd have to tell her he hadn't found their daughter…again."

Kit sniffled, and a single tear dropped on her cheek, unraveling all sorts of things inside him. He wiped the droplet away and then folded his fingers around hers again. There was nothing more he could give other than compassion, and he hoped it was enough.

"They always told me my mother went East, to tell him about me, and took sick and died out there. That's why she didn't have a grave in Chicago." Kit shook her head slowly and met Clay's gaze with beseeching eyes. "Where'd they live? Why didn't Grandpa find them before…?"

He squeezed her hand again. "When Oscar arrived, he spent most of his time with Sam, asking those same questions. From what he told me, Amelia met Harry Edwards in Denver and they moved out here to mine gold, but that didn't pan out and Harry took to trapping for furs. They lived about fifteen miles from the Wanda Lou."

"She'd been that close all those years and Gramps never found her?"

Clay offered what he hoped was an understanding smile. "That's what Oscar said. But you have to understand what these mountains are like. There are no roads, no trails, just miles of ridges, gullies, creek beds and unclaimed land. So much it's impossible to search it all. Sam said he'd never been in a town before I brought him to Nevadaville to send that message to Oscar."

"But surely my mother—"

"Don't, Kit," Clay interrupted. "Don't try to understand the whys and why-nots. Oscar did that, and never found an answer." Clay rubbed the soft skin on the backs of her hands with his fingertips. "Sam told Oscar that Amelia had died a few years before, and that Harry had gone out trapping a few weeks prior to him coming to the mine, and never came back. He said Harry told him if something ever happened to him, Sam was to go to the Wanda Lou and find Oscar, that he was Sam's grandfather." Clay didn't know how else to say it. Sam had actually said his father had told him to go to the mine and claim his share of the Wanda Lou. Harry Edwards had known who his wife's father was. That had been a bur under Oscar's saddle, as well as Clay's. Everyone had known how Oscar had searched for Amelia, and Clay felt certain Harry had known. Amelia, too.

He took a breath, drawing fortitude from the belief that Oscar had only wanted to protect Kit. Clay believed that, and hoped, in time, she'd understand. "When Oscar learned of Amelia's death, he was heartbroken, yet said he was glad the search was over. He said not knowing was worse than knowing. I think that's why he was afraid to tell you. Because he knew the frustration of looking for someone he never found, he knew how hard it was for Katie, and he didn't want you to experience that pain. The yearly cycle of hope and disappointment. But he did try to convince Sam to go with him to Chicago. Worked at it for months."

"Where is he?"

Clay looked up. "Sam?"

A wobbly little smile formed on her lips. "Yes, Sam."

"He lives out by the mine."

"I can't believe I have a brother," she whispered, so tenderly Clay all of a sudden wanted to slay every dragon in her past.

A series of flashes went through his mind. He couldn't remember life without Clarice, and had to admit it would be boring without his sister. He loved her deeply, in that special way dedicated to brothers and sisters. If he was in Kit's shoes, he'd have set out to find his family, too.

"I'll go and get him," he said.

"Can't I go with you? Out to the mine."

Denying her request was impossible, but he felt inclined to warn, "Sam can be a bit prickly."

The tiny giggle she emitted brightened the entire room, or possibly the world. "So can I." She settled her sparkling gaze on his face. "At times." Shrugging, she added, "It must be a family trait."

Allowing himself to embrace her humor was easier than he'd thought. Letting out a chuckle, he answered, "It must be."

"You'll take me?"

"Yes, I'll take you."

"Right now?"

He slipped his hands from hers and stood. "Yes, right now. I just have to go saddle some horses." The outcome of her last ride came to mind. "I'm afraid it's too far to walk, and the trail is too rough for a buggy."

"I figured that." A tiny frown appeared between her brows, as if she was puzzled about his caution.

He knew the moment she figured it out.

Lifting her chin in that adorable way she had, she said, "Don't worry. I'm healed, and Dr. O'Reilly gave me my very own tin of salve." Her cheeks grew pink. "In case of future outbreaks."

She had so many charming and endearing qualities, and every one of them caught him just a bit off guard. Like bursts of southerly winds hitting the frozen mountain lakes. The warmth thawed the frozen water and renewed life after the inert days of winter. That's what she'd done to his heart. Clay paused for a brief moment, wondering what that meant. But he'd spent the night contemplating his feelings, and didn't need to go down that road again. The bottom line was she was his ward, not a woman he could love, and nothing was going to change that. He couldn't give up everything he had for her, which was what would happen if he went against Oscar's will. Too many people depended on him.

Silently, he cursed the will, then said, "I'll be back in a few minutes."

"I'll go with you." She pushed away from the table.

"No, we'll have to ride past here again. There's no need for you to trek up and down the hill. It won't take me long." He moved to the doorway. "I just have to get my hat. Have some more coffee." He offered the last bit as an afterthought, before the door to the foyer swung shut behind him.

Chapter Nine

Too overwhelmed to do much else, Kit stared at the swinging door. Her mind and nerves were swirling faster than fireflies in a mason jar, sparking light and fading just as quickly. Not only had her mother been alive, she'd remarried and had a son. Kit's brother. Sam Edwards.

Add all that to the way her hands still tingled from how tenderly Clay had held them while he explained it all to her, and there was too much to contemplate. She just couldn't. Not all at the same time. The same day.

The door swung open, and Clay, with his hat on his head and one arm in his vest, said, "I'll be right back. Stay here." This time he left the kitchen using the door near the stove, the one that led outside, while slipping his other arm through an armhole of the black vest he'd worn the night before. He'd come and gone so fast she barely had time to react.

He popped his head back around the door, looking at her expectantly.

"I—I will," she stuttered, remembering his request.

He smiled, pulling the door shut, and her mind flipped about, questioning how easily she'd responded.

She'd always done as she was told. Not that she was ever *told* a lot. Such as the fact that her mother hadn't died when Kit was a baby. She winced at the direction of her thoughts, and the bitterness she felt. Yes, she'd always wanted a family, but at the same time, she'd never doubted being loved. Gramps and Grandma Katie had seen to that. Yet right now, she felt about as empty as a discarded can.

Kit stood and scanned the kitchen, wanting something to combat the jitters attempting to overtake her. After circling the room, in which everything was brand-new and unused, she walked to the swinging door that led to the foyer, and pushed it open. The darkness on the other side made her pause. It was such a disparity, the bright cheeriness of the kitchen compared to the other rooms shrouded in darkness. Holding the door wide, she walked as far as her arm would stretch. Beyond the front foyer, through a wide archway, there looked to be a parlor of sorts. Tiny rays of light shot up to the ceiling from behind the heavy drapes, proving windows graced two walls of the room.

Curiosity got the best of her, and she found a piece of kindling to use as a wedge under the door. With it propped open, light from the kitchen flowed across the foyer and into the large room adjacent. She maneuvered around furniture to the windows in the front wall. The drapes were heavy and several layers thick. Hooking one behind a nearby chair to let in sunlight, she turned to inspect the room.

White sheets draped the furnishings, and dust motes floated in the shaft of light as if they'd been sleeping for years and just awakened. In the center of the room was a long couch, and the impressions in the sheet said someone had lain upon it, perhaps slept there.

Why would Clay sleep here, when the upstairs had to contain bedrooms? She walked to the far end of the room, to a wide staircase hugging the wall. No light brightened the landing, making her assume all the windows upstairs were covered as well. She turned and made her way back across the room. The house had an oppressed, empty feeling. Pushing the chair back where it belonged, she let out a sigh as the curtain fell back into place, shrouding the area in darkness once more. Or maybe it was just her that felt empty. Though she wanted to meet Sam—after all, her greatest wish in life had been to have brothers and sisters—she felt browbeaten.

If someone had told her that her grandparents had lied to her her whole life, she'd have called him a liar. Yet that's what Clay had told her, and she knew he wasn't fibbing. It all made sense. Gramps's trips to Colorado. How highly strung Grandma was during his absences, how excited she would grow, anticipating his return, and then how sad she'd be for weeks after he finally arrived.

Kit left the big front room, released the wedge beneath the kitchen door and dropped it in the wood box, and then, feeling fidgety, gathered the cups and pot from the table. After depositing the cups in the sink, she carried the pot to the back door, and discovered it led to a porch that ran along the entire side of the house, complete with railings. She walked to the far edge, where the mountain continued to climb upward several yards away, and dumped the contents over the rail. After taking several deep breaths to calm the crusade going on in her head, as well as fuel her dwindling spirits a touch, she turned.

This side of the house faced the stamp mill, and on a narrow path that curved around a few large boulders, she spotted Clay. He was hurrying—not running, but not walking casually, either. The trail went from the mill to the house, with a little offshoot that led to the back of his office. There was a paddock, too, behind his office, and that's where he stopped. She watched him open the gate and cross the corral, patting horses as he went. When he entered the barn on the far side, she carried the coffeepot back into the house.

There were a thousand things she could be thinking about, yet wasn't. Her mind was focused on one thing. Why didn't Clay live in this house? Why would he "usually stay at his office" when he had all this just a short walk up the hill?

She washed the coffeepot and cups, dried them and returned everything to the places she'd seen him take them from. Her fingers lingered on the cupboard doors. The cabinets, finished with a thick coat of glossy white paint, ran along one entire wall. She spun, taking in the room in a long, thoughtful gaze. The room was full of furnishings, everything needed for preparing meals, yet it gave off an untouched feeling. Kit shook her head, partly to dispel the loneliness of the room, partly in confusion. A house like this needed to be lived in. It cried out for love, for a family.

A wave of sentiment stopped in her throat. It wasn't the house crying out for a family, it was her. She always had been. Ever since she was a child, it was all she'd ever wanted. A real family. With a mother and father and brothers and sisters. The hole inside her hadn't come about when Gramps and Grandma died, it had always been there. Their love had just kept it from consuming her.

One would think that when she finally discovered something deep and profound about herself, she would feel a sense of relief, because now she could set about making changes to obtain what she had always wanted. But that wasn't how it was for Kit.

Not at all. The more she thought about it, the sadder she grew.

Needing air, she walked out the back door and moved to the stairs, breathing deeply. She sat on the top step and covered her face with her hands. What if Sam hated her, wanted nothing to do with her? That might be worse than never meeting him. Tired and confused, she found her mind grew more jumbled with each breath she took.

"Ready?"

When she lifted her head, her insides seemed to burst open at the gentle concern on Clay's face.

"Hey," he said, climbing off the horse. "What's happened?"

"Nothing. Everything." She wiped her cheeks with both hands, sniffling and swallowing, trying to block another wave of sadness from engulfing her. It all seemed so useless. Her. Her life.

"Kit." He sat down next to her. "I know this has been a lot to take in."

She nodded, unable to speak.

His arm slid around her shoulders. "Come here," he whispered, tugging her closer.

She leaned against him, gladly accepting the comfort his arms offered. It was like a blanket, warm and protective, a shield against all the pain bearing down on her.

He twisted, tucking her into his chest. "Let it out, honey. Bottling it all inside isn't good for you."

His gentle tone, and the way he rocked her, slowly, soothingly, broke through the final inner obstacle. With a shudder, she let the sob out, and then cried, burying her face in his shoulder. She wept for it all—her mother. Gramps and Grandma Katie. The not knowing. The knowing.

Clay held her the entire time, rocking her and whispering little words of comfort she didn't hear, but felt. They helped, as did the way he shifted slightly and folded his arms all the way around her. The pain eased, slowly but surely, and when the storm inside her settled, dissolved into little more than a mingling ache, she let out a deep sigh and twisted her face, fitting her cheek against the solidness of his shoulder.

They sat there a while longer, as if he knew her spirit needed time to rebuild. It did, and when she finally had the strength to lift her head, Clay's flower-blue eyes were there to meet hers.

Filled with understanding, his gaze never wavered from hers. "Better?" he asked.

She nodded.

"Good." He leaned closer and pressed a kiss to her forehead.

The action touched her deeply, set off a gentle flood of contentment. Crying so should embarrass her, but his compassion alleviated any shame.

He sat back then, rubbing her shoulders. "Did you still want to go see Sam? We can wait for another day."

"No." She shook her head. "I mean yes, I want to go see him. I don't want to wait."

One of Clay's hands went to her cheek. "You know,

Kit, sometimes we can't understand why people do what they do. We can't comprehend what they were thinking or feeling."

Closing her eyes, she nodded.

His lips touched her forehead again. "So don't go blaming yourself for any of this," he whispered.

His strength, his benevolence and generosity must have somehow transferred themselves to her, because willpower seemed to grow inside her. Or maybe she just didn't want to disappoint him. Either way, it made the gloom dissipate. Glancing at him, she nodded. "I won't."

"Good." Smiling, he said, "Then let's go see Sam."

The warmth of Clay's palm and the gentleness of his voice were so precious. "Thank you," she whispered. The gratitude she felt was beyond compare. Feeling renewed, refreshed even, like the air smelled after a rain, she lifted her face to the sky. She might not have had the family she dreamed of, but at least she'd had a family. Gramps and Grandma had loved her so much, and it was more than many orphans had. She wouldn't resent it. Nor them for the choices they'd made.

Holding both her elbows, Clay assisted her to her feet, and with a nod, gestured toward the horses standing in the grassy area near the railing. "You remember Andrew?"

The smile on her face was genuine. "Yes. Hello, Andrew." She greeted the big, red-brown horse as she walked down the stairs.

The animal tossed his head and let out a little nicker. She patted his neck and then moved toward the silver-colored horse next to him. "And who do we have here?" Holding up one hand, she turned to Clay. "No, don't tell me. Martin. After Martin Van Buren, the eighth president of the United States."

Clay grabbed her hand, tugging her around Andrew. "No, this is Rachel." Leaning close, he whispered, "She's a mare."

"Forgive me," she said to the animal. Patting the horse's silky mane, she asked, "Rachel? Andrew Jackson's wife's name?"

"Yep." Clay patted a blanket rolled up behind the saddle. "The seat's padded, but I brought a blanket just in case you get, uh, tender. Let me know and I'll strap it to your saddle."

"Thank you," she said. "But I think I'll be fine. It was the wool britches I had on that caused the problem last time." Since his gaze was on her brown velvet skirt, she added, "This dress will be fine."

"You sure? We can stop at the hotel if you want to change."

She grabbed the saddle horn. "I'm sure."

He bent over, cupping his hands. "Here, step in and I'll hoist you up."

Unsure exactly how he would do that, she lifted a foot. He caught it with both hands, and it was as if she flew right into the saddle, landing with a plop that caused her to emit a tiny squeal.

"You all right?" He touched her knee as worry filled his eyes.

"Yes," she assured him, while adjusting her skirt around her legs. "I'm fine. I just didn't expect it to be that easy."

He looked as if he was contemplating something deep and hard, holding her gaze the entire time. "Not everything in life should be difficult, Kit." He reached down and grabbed the reins. Flipping them over Rachel's head, he handed Kit the ends. "Some things should be easy. Just fall into place as they're meant to be."

She took the reins, but before he pulled his hand away, he squeezed her fingers. "No worries?"

Kit shook her head. With him beside her, it was easy to believe the world was a wonderful place. "No worries."

"All right, then." A second later he mounted Andrew. "The trail's not too bad, but it's slow going in some spots. I'll warn you before we get to those."

She nodded, following his lead.

They traversed the narrow space between the back of the house and the mountainside, and then met up with a well-worn trail. Rachel's gait was smooth and Kit found herself relaxing in the saddle, even when the trail went straight up in places and sloped downward in others. "Why do you name your horses after presidents? And their wives?"

Riding beside her, Clay shrugged. "Named the first one George just for the heck of it. From there, it just kind of happened. Rachel was the first wife, though."

"She's pretty." Kit ran her fingers through the horse's long mane. It was nice, talking about inconsequential things that gave her mind a reprieve. "Did you know Rachel Jackson had been married before she and Andrew wed?"

"Yep," Clay replied. "And I know they thought her divorce was final when they got married, but it turned out it wasn't. Three years later, they got married again." Giving her a wink that made her breath catch, he added, "Makes you wonder about those three years, doesn't it?"

When the silliness inside her slowed, Kit asked, "How do you know that?"

"I read it."

"You like to read?"

"Yes, very much." He propped one hand on a knee as the horses plodded along. "Oscar encouraged that. Every visit he'd bring both Clarice and me a book or two. We'd look forward to them all year."

Happy to recall good things about Gramps, and be thankful for them, Kit nodded. "Books were his favorite gifts. He always brought them home for me, too. From his trips out here."

"Did you really talk to the city about starting a library in Chicago?" Clay shrugged and glanced aside as he added, "Jonathan mentioned it while you and Clarice were in the bedroom last night."

She felt a twinge in her heart, and willed herself not to focus on it. The library wasn't the bright spot it once had been. "It's…" She paused, not understanding what she felt. "It was just a silly dream."

Andrew stopped, as did Rachel. Kit glanced around, wondering why, until she caught the way Clay looked at her. Her heart skipped a dozen beats all at once.

He shook his head. "Dreams aren't silly, Kit. We wouldn't have the world we do if people hadn't had dreams and pursued them."

Another dream flooded her mind. The one she'd had upon arriving in Nevadaville, about her living in the house she now knew was his. The staircase leading off that dark front room was exactly like the one in her dream had been.

He clicked his tongue, urging Andrew forward, and she kneed Rachel, staying beside him. They rode in silence, which only gave her more time to contemplate things.

When he glanced her way, her mouth opened. "Why don't you live in your house, Clay?" She bit her tongue, but it was too late; the thought had already voiced itself.

Air lodged in his chest. He knew she'd eventually ask, yet he still hadn't figured out what he'd say. No one knew, not the whole story, and he liked it that way. However, there was a part of him that wanted to tell someone, knew it would be the final step to putting it all behind him.

He took a chance and glanced her way. Her brown eyes, what he now saw as windows to her soul, looked at him gallantly, yet he noted the hint of apprehension, as if she hadn't wanted to say what she had. It was then he realized she was the one he wanted to tell his story to.

"I didn't build it for me," he said, looking back at the trail ahead of them. It was rocky, and though the horses were surefooted, he needed to pay attention to every step.

"Who'd you build it for?"

He scratched at the hairs on the back of his neck, now standing at attention, irritating him. "For a woman."

"Oh."

That was it. All she said. What had he expected her to say? Tell me about her? Who was she? He let out a sigh, wishing he'd never said anything. Should have just kept his mouth shut. Holding her while she'd wept had made him think of things he hadn't thought of in a long time—mainly, how empty his life really was.

"Who was she?"

He'd let his guard down, that's what had happened, and that was a foolish mistake. The desire to talk left him. "Just a woman." Pointing ahead, he said, "The trail gets rough up there. You'll have to follow behind me. Plant your feet deep in the stirrups and hold on to the horn."

"All right," she said.

He nudged Andrew, getting ahead of her, even though the trail was plenty wide enough for a ways yet. There was no rhyme or reason to how his insides were reacting. Nor his mind. Last night, when he'd arrived at his house, he'd expected Miranda memories to meet him at the door. But they hadn't. All he'd thought about all night was Kit, and the confusing things she stirred up inside him. Plus how badly he wished things were different...

Over the past two years, he'd spent a lot of time thinking about Miranda while traversing back and forth to the mine. Yet right now, he couldn't recall why. He knew she had long black hair and blue eyes, yet no image of her formed. Then again, everyone knew her hair and eye color, because that's how papers described her when reporting a show she'd been in the night before. Until last year, he'd had a stack of those papers, each one proclaiming the outstanding performances of Miranda McCoy. Actress extraordinaire. Now performing with a troupe in Paris. Not even the thought of that, her departure, wrangled up old feelings.

The treacherous section of trail he'd mentioned appeared. It went straight down, barely wide enough for a horse to traverse, with perpendicular cliffs stretching straight up on both sides.

"You doing all right back there?" he asked without turning around.

"Yes." Kit's answer sounded solid, and moments later she asked, "How long is it like this?"

"Not far. Just keep your seat in the saddle. I don't want you flipping over Rachel's head." He pinched his lips, wishing he hadn't said that last sentence.

"Yeah, well, you keep in your seat, too. I don't want to have to pick you up off the ground after these horses trample you."

Her gruffness tickled him. "Anyone ever tell you you sound like your grandfather?"

"Yep. Grandpa himself."

"You're made of tough stock, Kit Becker."

"And you best remember that, Clay Hoffman."

He laughed, enjoying the banter and the sound of humor in her voice. "There's a couple rough spots ahead. Hang on."

"I am."

He planted his feet deeper in the stirrups and leaned back as Andrew headed down the steepest point. It was a tedious ride, but the last piece of this trail was the worst. A three-foot dropoff left only a small chunk of flat terrain for the horses to land on, and it was edged by a cliff that ended miles below. Once they made that final corner the hilltop evened out into a long plateau that led almost all the way to the Wanda Lou.

"Kit, coming up is a dropoff. I have to be all the way through before you step off it." He glanced over his shoulder. "I'll tell you when, all right?"

"All right." With a nod, she added, "Turn around and watch where you're going."

"Yes, ma'am," he teased. The tricky spot was just ahead, and he patted Andrew's neck. "You've done it a hundred times, boy," he whispered. The words were as much for him as they were for the horse. Normally the jump didn't faze him, but the thought of Kit doing it made his heart thud.

Less than a minute later, he instructed, "Pull Rachel to a stop."

"Here?"

"Yes." He brought Andrew to a halt so she had to stop. "The dropoff is just ahead. I'm going to jump down and then come back for you." There was no reason to take a chance when it wasn't necessary.

"I thought you said we'd *step* off it."

The trepidation in her eyes was enough to confirm he'd made the right decision, and gazing at her heart-shaped face made a smile tug at his lips. Oscar had aptly named her. "Kit" fit her in so many ways. Clay could understand why the man had never told her about Amelia. Her grandfather hadn't wanted to see her hurt, and he didn't, either.

"I did. But it's a really big step." A crick was forming in Clay's neck from twisting around so often. "I'm going down, and I'll get Andrew out of the way before I come back. Don't move."

She agreed with a nod. "I won't. But you be careful."

The concern in her voice wasn't wasted on him. He gave her a wink and watched her blush. "It's not that bad. I just don't want a greenhorn getting hurt on my watch." With that, he turned and kneed Andrew.

The dropoff appeared, and there was a moment of being airborne, but as usual, the horse didn't miss a step. Within seconds Clay reined the animal in at the widest spot of the curve and dismounted.

Kit still sat in the exact spot he'd left her. The rock walls were tight, but there was enough room for her to climb out of the saddle when he asked her to. He stopped near Rachel's nose, rubbing the horse between the eyes.

"I see you made it," she said.

His heart knocked against his ribs. Between her smile, the glimmer in her eyes and the teasing in her voice, it didn't have a choice not to, not with the way his blood raced. "Were you worried?"

"Yes." Her cheeks reddened. "I don't know if I could find my way back without you."

Time stopped for a moment as they looked at one another. Not staring, or gaping, but simply looking. She was one beautiful and determined woman. Oscar would be proud of how she'd embraced the wilderness. Clay was, too.

The chirp of a bird flying overhead broke the silence, and his trance. He blinked and cleared his throat. "I want you to climb down and wait here. I'll ride Rachel down and come back to help you."

She flipped a leg over the back of the saddle and lowered herself to the ground, gathering the yards of her dress out of the way as she moved. Then she flattened herself against the rock as he shimmied along the wall to hoist himself into the saddle.

"I'll be right back," he said.

"I'll be waiting."

"You'd better be," he said, and smiled at her tiny laugh.

Rachel handled the landing fine, and Clay swung out of the saddle, patting the horse on the rump to send her next to Andrew, a few feet ahead.

"That was a rather large step."

Clay spun around. Though his heart lurched, he

couldn't help but shake his head at the grin on Kit's face. "I told you to wait."

"I didn't need any help climbing down." Her gaze went to the dropoff a few feet away. "But I'm glad I didn't have to ride a horse over it." Tapping her cheek with one finger, as if deep in thought, she said, "You know, I never felt queasy about heights until...well, until I left Denver."

"Denver's not in the mountains."

She cast an impish sideways glance his way. "You don't have to tell me that."

He chuckled, and the desire to pull her close was too strong to ignore. When he did drop his arm around her and rub her upper arm, she tilted her head to glance up at him.

"Are you afraid now?" he asked.

An affectionate twinkle appeared in her eyes. "No."

It was a moment he'd never forget, and his breath stalled. It was as if they spoke to each other silently, and not kissing her was one of the hardest things he'd ever done.

She grinned and leaned against him.

His blood heated up ten degrees and bubbled through his veins. He patted her arm again and then gave it a squeeze, pulling her more firmly against him. "It's pretty, isn't it?" he said, gazing over the edge, at the mountain ridge on the other side of the gully.

Nestled in the bright blue sky, the sun cast its rays across the white-tipped peaks, leaving a splattering of miniature rainbows, and down the slope, foliage grew thick and lush.

"Yes, it is." She let out a sigh. "It kinda reminds me

of a row of Christmas trees, all decorated with stars on top."

"Oscar said you loved Christmastime."

"I do. Always have. It's, well, enchanting. Makes one remember miracles do happen." She twisted, glanced back up at him with a thoughtful gaze. "She left you, didn't she? The woman you built the house for."

Clay stiffened and glanced back over the mountain peaks. "Yeah," he admitted.

"I know all about being left." Kit's heavy sigh had him squeezing her upper arm again. She spun then, glancing back toward the rocky path they'd traversed. "The horses can climb back up that?"

Thankful for the change in subject, he turned them both around so they could view the trail. "Nope."

"No?" Her expression was adorable, a mixture of confusion and mockery.

"No," he repeated. "They can come down, but it's too steep going up."

"Then how do we get back?"

"We'll follow the rail tracks that haul the ore from the mine to the stamp mill."

"Why didn't we come that way?"

"Because this way is shorter and closer to Sam's camp." He gave her a final squeeze. "No worries." Taking her hand, he led her to the horses and hoisted her into the saddle. "It's not much farther now."

Her hand wrapped around his as he passed her the reins. "Thanks, Clay. Thanks for bringing me."

"You're welcome, Kit. There's nowhere else I'd rather be." He snapped his lips together. His mouth had a mind of its own today. As did his heart, which was hammering inside his chest so hard it might explode at any moment.

"I'm sure there're a million places you'd rather be," she said. "But I'm glad you're here. And thanks for saying it."

He gave her knee a pat and then moved to Andrew, wondering if he'd lost his mind. Or at least half of it. By the time they rounded the last boulder, bringing them within sight of Sam's camp, Clay figured he hadn't lost his mind, but a sizable chunk of his heart. He understood why Oscar had talked nonstop about Kit. She was unforgettable.

He held up a hand, signaling her to stop. When she did, he gestured toward the hillside. "We're here."

"Here?"

He nodded and, knowing they were being watched, shouted, "Sam!" The single word bounced, repeating several times.

Almost immediately a response came. "Who's with you, Hoffman?" Sam's voice started to echo before he finished his sentence, making the words mingle together as they floated about the hills.

Clay waited until the sounds faded. "Someone who wants to meet you." The anticipation inside him was akin to watching the first load of ore fall beneath the stampers back at the mill. There he waited to see the flecks of gold. Here he hoped he hadn't set Kit up for more disappointment. Sam was a good kid, but not overly open to visitors. He most likely already knew it was the woman they'd discussed a few days ago, but he just didn't know *who* she was. Holding his breath, Clay nodded toward Kit.

"My—" She cleared her throat and started again,

louder and stronger this time. "My name's Kit Becker, Sam. I'm Oscar's granddaughter."

Once the echoes died away, the silence that fell hammered the insides of Clay's ears. He wanted to shout, tell Sam he'd better show himself, but at the end of the day, it wasn't his choice. He couldn't take that away from the kid. It was hard to say how Sam would react to Kit. He and Oscar had finally developed a kinship, but it had taken time and hard work, most of it on Oscar's part.

Seconds seemed to stretch into minutes.

Clay was just about to tell Kit to stay put while he went closer, when a figure walked out from behind a boulder up the hillside.

"You know the way," Sam shouted.

The tension in Clay's chest released itself with a long breath. "Let's go meet your brother."

The expression on Kit's face teetered between apprehension and joy. A grimace appeared as she asked, "Is he always this friendly?"

Chapter Ten

Kit's insides gurgled, but she kept her shoulders squared. Life hadn't prepared her for all she'd encountered lately, and right now she was about as unsure as she'd ever been. It was unnerving and her chest grew so heavy that breathing hurt.

Clay's hand falling on top of hers—which was clutched to the saddle horn—was just what she needed. The gentle touch gave her fortitude and snapped her out of her disheartened stupor. She wasn't alone in this. Clay was by her side, and that helped. Immensely. Since arriving in Colorado he'd continued to be at her side just when she needed someone.

"All right?" he asked.

A simple question, yet an encompassing one, and comprehending that, she nodded. When he was near she was all right.

They followed a narrow path uphill, around boulders and between clusters of evergreens and aspens that filled the air with a freshness she'd never known. The sky overhead was blue as blazes, as Gramps used to say, and allowed her once again to appreciate the beauty of the mountains. The trail led to a flat overhang that acted as an entrance to a cave. Near the half-moon-shaped opening stood a tall and lanky young man. He was so thin she wondered if he ate regularly, but more than that he reminded her of some of the street urchins back home.

A powerful ache filled her. This was her brother, not some unwanted orphan. Or was he an orphan? A soul begotten by this world, left to his own devices by no fault of his, abandoned by his family. Not so unlike herself. Her stomach knotted so tightly she flinched.

"Kit?"

She twisted, surprised to find Clay standing next to her horse. The question on his face was clear, but her answer wasn't. She couldn't assure him she was fine. It would be a lie. He caught her waist with both hands and once again spoke to her with his eyes, this time asking if she was ready to dismount. She put her hands on his shoulders, wishing he could fill her with hope and assurance once again.

He lowered her slowly, as if giving her knees time to prepare to hold her weight. When her feet did touch the ground, he held her for a moment longer, gazing down at her the entire time. His blue eyes were so perceptive, and the connection she felt—a silent communication between them—was supportive, and went deep, entered her soul in a unique and unusual way. In the past she'd had people she could rely on, Gramps and Grandma, a few friends in school, but never had she experienced this exceptional companionship. This trust that had formed so quickly and felt so strong.

His fingers squeezed her waist, as if he completely understood her deliberations. She took a deep breath and then used a nod to signal she could stand on her own, as her gaze went around his shoulder to Sam. A wave of shame washed over her. When she'd lost her parents, she'd had Gramps and Grandma. But when Sam had lost his parents, he'd been left completely alone.

Clay stepped aside, but slid one hand around her back, holding her steady as she came face-to-face with her brother.

He was tall—not as tall as Clay, but a good six inches taller than her. His clothes were worn ragged in places, but looked clean, and his boots didn't have holes in the toes.

"Wow," Sam muttered.

Meeting the startled look blazing in his emerald eyes, she said, "Hello, Sam." Her mind skipped to the kids she'd seen in Chicago and then the ones at the society house. Orphans were a proud lot and normally didn't care much for strangers. She could understand that.

Sam ran his hand through his hair, the color of carrots and growing about as thick and wild as the vegetable did. The thought made her grin. That's how Grandma Katie would have described the tousled mane upon his head. Warmth filled Kit, as if Grandma was beside her right now.

"Wow," he repeated.

Clay's fingers, hooked on her waist, gave a gentle squeeze. When Sam turned around in a circle and then opened his mouth as if to mutter "wow" again, Clay interrupted him.

"You already said that, Sam." He then made a formal introduction. "Kit, this is your brother, Sam Edwards. Sam, this is your sister, Kit Becker."

Sam pointed a finger at her. "You really, really look like my ma."

Kit's insides fluttered. "I do?" Grandma Katie had said that often, and Kit had a picture of her mother, but never saw the resemblance. Hearing Sam say it, she felt a bubble of joy form around her heart.

"Yeah, you do." He leaned forward and peered closer. "Her hair was different, had more red in it, but your eyes look just like hers."

Kit didn't know what to say. Part of her was excited. What Sam said gave her that longed-for connection to her mother, yet did it matter? She couldn't remember her. The warmth inside her seeped away, and an odd paradox took its place. The irony of who she was and what she was doing. Her legs began to tremble.

Clay's fingers tightened and he took hold of her elbow with his other hand. "Sam, are you going to make your guests stand out here in the sun, or are you going to invite us inside?"

Sam's neck reddened. "Sorry, I don't get much company." He waved an arm toward the cave. "Come on in."

Kit had no choice but to follow Clay's lead. He had ahold of her and expected her to move. On her second or third step, her ankle turned, folding her foot beneath her.

Clay caught her before there was any real pain, and long before she went down. "Are you all right?"

Uncertain about everything, she shrugged. "Just nervous, I guess."

"You have a right to be," he said softly. "But I'm not going anywhere, so there's nothing for you to be nervous about."

She dug the tips of her boots deeper into the worn dirt below, mainly a reaction to the authenticity in his tone. Due to everything—last night, today, the past year— her emotions were a tangled web of things she couldn't put her finger on. Feelings she'd never encountered before, and confusion about what they meant. And right now, what she experienced looking up at Clay's concerned and intense eyes had something balmy and tender swirling around everything else. It was more than trust, what she felt for him.

"I won't leave you, Kit," he said.

She wanted to believe that, but everyone she'd ever known had left her, and that set off an explosion of sorts inside her, leaving her skin tingling and a surreal mist clouding her thoughts. His eyes had the ability to draw her in, make her world stop. Or maybe it made it spin faster. Either way, she found it hard to think when he looked at her like that. As if they were the only two people on earth. Maybe the world had spun out of control, tossing the earth's population into the great span of space and leaving just the two of them in the here and now.

"Promise?" she asked.

His gaze bored deeper as he whispered, "I promise."

Her heart thudded, drummed in her ears as a new intuition overshadowed everything else going on inside her. She wanted him to kiss her, like he had on the train. The longing grew all encompassing. Her lips tingled, her pulse beat faster and her entire body took on a heated energy. He'd kissed her forehead back at his house, and though that had been comforting, it wasn't what she wanted right now.

She searched her mind, trying to remember what she'd done on the train for him to kiss her then. Nothing formed. Staring into the crystal-clear depths of his blue eyes was too absorbing.

"Are you two coming or not?"

Clay moved, glanced over his shoulder.

The air Kit had been holding in her lungs left with a rush, as if she'd just been knocked to the ground. Her own shoulders drooped, and a rush of awkwardness burned her cheeks. What had she been thinking? They stood on a mountainside, where she was meeting her brother for the first time. Kissing was probably the last thing Clay had been contemplating. It was the last thing she should be thinking about, too, even with the blood in her veins literally gushing, leaving her flushed from head to toe.

"Give us a minute, Sam," Clay said.

The sound of his voice echoed in her ears, and had her going back to contemplating all the ins and outs of kissing. Including how badly she wanted it to happen. Her gaze roamed to his lips. They were thicker than hers, fuller, and—

"Kit?" His lips parted as he spoke.

"Yes," she whispered. The craving inside her grew agonizing, stealing her breath and making her insides tremble. She closed her eyes. It was enticing, yet powerful and confusing. Finding her breath, she drew in air until her lungs stretched.

"Kit, are you all right?"

Clay's voice, somewhat urgent, pulled her back, almost as his hands had in the pool of water the first day they'd met. Her eyes snapped open, and the buzzing left her ears. Letting the air out of her chest, she nodded. "Yes. Yes, I'm fine."

"You sure?"

Breathing was easy now, the air flowing as it should. Accepting that, she answered, "Yes, I'm sure."

Engrossed in her own body, she hadn't noticed he'd

been holding his breath, not until he let out a long sigh. "Good," he whispered, bending his face downward.

Her heart leaped, sent her blood gushing. Goodness gracious, it was going to happen. He was going to kiss her. She licked her lips, anticipating the moment they'd meet his. She would remember this moment forever. The taste, the feel, the—

Disappointment cooled her faster than her dunk in the pond had. Clay was kissing her; his lips, warm and gentle, were pressed against her forehead. The action was full of affection and it warmed her shivering heart, but it was not what she wanted. Not at all what she wanted. Again.

He lifted his face, and after gracing her with a gentle smile, turned her toward the cave. "Sam's waiting."

She took a breath, not only to brace herself, but to release pent-up frustration. He may not have kissed her on the lips, but he'd wanted to. A commanding bout of intuition told her that. It also said one day he would. Kiss her like she wanted. She just had to be patient. It was impossible to know what told her that, but she believed it. The air left her chest slowly, sending out the last bits of dissatisfaction until her lungs were completely empty and ready for a fresh breath. Patience was not something she had a lot of.

However, the world took on a brighter hue, and her life didn't seem so dismal. As a matter of fact, happiness attacked her soul, spewing a rainbow of joy from her heart to her mind. She might not be Katherine Ackerman, a brave woman from Boston, but she was Kit Becker, and she was starting a new chapter in her life. As a smile formed, she approached the cave with an entirely different attitude than she'd had a few minutes ago.

Reaching out a hand toward her brother, she said, "Hello, Sam. I'm very excited to meet you."

He looked perplexed for a moment, but then took her hand and gave it a friendly shake. "I heard a lot about you from Oscar."

"Well," she admitted, without a touch of animosity, "I can't say the same. I only learned I had a brother a few hours ago, but I hope to have one for the rest of my life." She trusted he saw the sincerity in her smile.

Sam shuffled his feet and wiped the back of his hand over his nose. "Come on in, out of the sun," he said, turning into the cave. "It's not much, but I call it home."

What had she anticipated he'd do? Jump for joy? Hug her and declare he'd always wanted a sister? That was downright silly, yet it would have been nice. Accepting what he did offer—an invitation into his home— as a positive step, she readily followed, telling herself to give him time. One day they'd be the best of family and friends.

Blinking, she was a bit surprised by the inside of the cave. It smelled of lingering smoke, and was very dark, but she made out a table, two chairs, several boxes and crates, and in the back there was a bed, complete with pillows and a patchwork quilt.

With his hand in the center of her back, Clay guided her all the way to the table, where Sam was lighting a lamp to brighten the area a bit more.

"Clay keeps hauling furniture out here. Thinks I can't take care of myself," Sam said, with a nod toward the bed as he put the glass chimney back on the lamp.

"I never said you couldn't take care of yourself, but

I promised Oscar I'd watch out for you." Clay held the back of a chair and gestured for Kit to sit.

A smile tickled her lips. Clay might tell others, or even himself, that he watched out for Sam because of Oscar, but she knew differently. She'd witnessed how readily he'd stepped in to take care of "Henry," and how he'd returned Mrs. Smith's glasses, and how he provided for Clarice, and—

"Ma talked a lot about you, too," Sam said.

Kit's spine tingled, causing her to pause in the process of settling in the chair Clay held. Shaking off the tingling, she sat. "She did?"

Clay laid a hand on her shoulder.

"Yeah, she did." Sam shifted slightly. "She cried at times, missing you. Said her folks wouldn't let her bring you to Colorado. She had a jar she put money in for a trip to Chicago to get you."

Kit lifted a hand and wrapped her fingers around Clay's on her shoulder, as if that would ground her. "Really?"

"Yeah," Sam said. "She got sick, though, real sick, and my pa spent the money."

If only there was a way to change the past, to meet her mother. Kit had to swallow, knowing there wasn't, but Clay's touch helped ease the pain. "Can you tell me about her, Sam?"

He stared at her, not really acknowledging he'd heard her, and the minutes seemed to drag on before he shrugged. "Sure. What I remember, that is."

She chewed her lip, wondering what to say next. There were a number of things she wanted to know, but also realized Sam would have been only seven when their mother died.

As if he was as unsure as she, Sam gestured toward a crate in the corner. "You folks hungry? I got peaches and beans." He nodded toward Clay. "He brought them out last time he came. I can warm the beans up, but they're good right out of the can, too."

Kit bit her lips together, to hold in a grin at his hospitality and explanation. It was understandable that he was as nervous as she. "That sounds wonderful." Right now she'd eat anything Sam offered. Not because she was hungry, but because she really wanted to get to know him. He was her brother. More so, she was his sister. Something she'd always wanted to be.

"You want 'em hot or cold?" he asked, already digging in the crate.

"Sam, I think you should heat the beans up for your guest, don't you?" Clay responded, squeezing her fingers.

A clattering of cans hitting against each other sounded as Sam answered, "Uh, yeah. I reckon so."

Kit glanced up, and the smile on Clay's face sent her heart tumbling about in her chest. She returned the smile and wondered if she'd ever experienced the happiness clattering inside her right now.

Carrying six cans at once, Sam dropped them on the table, catching them as they began to roll in all directions.

"What can I do to help, Sam?" she asked.

Once he had the cans standing side by side, he nodded toward the stacked crates. "There's plates and forks in the top, under the cloth. I gotta go start the fire."

Clay stepped aside for her to stand, but when she started to move, his fingers wrapped around her arm. He held her in place, not saying anything as he watched

Sam scurry out of the cave's arched opening. When her brother had disappeared in the sunlight, Clay asked, "You sure about this?"

"Yes," she answered without hesitation. "I'm sure."

His eyes held respect, and that touched her. Significantly.

"All right." He let go of her arm. "I'll go see to the horses."

She couldn't ask him not to see to the horses, and she wasn't afraid to be in the cave alone, so why didn't she want him to leave? Kit reached out and took his hand before it fell to his side. Searching for something, anything to keep him near for a moment longer, she squeezed his fingers. "Thank you."

He took her hand in his, and then folded his other one around it as well. "You've said that enough already today."

"I'll never be able to thank you enough. I want you to know that. Bringing me here, introducing me to Sam…" A lump formed in her throat. She licked her lips and took a breath. It was true. He'd done so much for her. No wonder Gramps had thought so highly of Clay.

He leaned forward and once again kissed her, this time brushing his lips to her temple. "It's my job," he said. "I promised Oscar I'd watch out for both of you."

It was a moment before Kit could move or drag her eyes from Clay as he strolled through the cave opening. A sickening lump had formed in her stomach.

"Hey, Hoffman," Sam shouted as Clay walked out the doorway. "You got a dog?"

"Nope," he answered, moving to where Andrew and Rachel stood, patiently waiting to be led out of the sun. The first meeting between siblings had gone well. Not that he'd been worried. Sam was a good kid, just a little lost, and Kit… Well, everyone who met Kit liked her. His insides bucked, reigniting the fire that had flared when he'd wanted to kiss her before. Not on the forehead as he'd done, but on the lips. A full man-to-woman kiss. Shaking his shoulders, hoping that would help distract him from his thoughts, he loosened the cinch on Rachel, then pulled the saddle and blanket from her back. Carrying them over to set on a rock, and still needing a diversion, he asked, "Why's that, Sam?"

"Just wondering," the youth answered, building a tripod of sticks to start a fire in the well-used pit outside the cave door. "If you named your horses after presidents, you'd probably name a dog after the states or something." He struck a match on his boot heel and held the flame near the bits of dried grass he'd sprinkled at the base of the sticks. "A dog wouldn't know how to act if his name was Massachusetts."

"If I ever get a dog, I'll take that into consideration." Clay walked to Andrew and undid the cinch of his saddle. Massachusetts. Interesting choice. He'd never wondered about the state before meeting Katherine Ackerman from Boston, Massachusetts.

The leather straps hung to the ground, and he grabbed the saddle, but didn't lift it off Andrew. His mind was divided. Even though one side knew who Kit was, the other side kept thinking about how he'd kissed Katherine on the train, and how he wanted to do that again. Downright craved it.

Clay cursed silently, not wanting anyone to hear. He spun around, staring toward the cave opening. Though she looked like a woman, a lovely one, Kit was Oscar's granddaughter, and Katherine didn't exist.

No amount of pondering the ins and outs could ever change that. With a heavy sigh, he turned back to Andrew and took his time unsaddling the horse. Afterward he led both mounts to the side of the cave, where the creek trickled by and trees provided them shade and a nice patch of grass to graze. He could have led a dozen animals to that spot and it still wouldn't have given him enough time to figure out his thoughts. Flummoxed, that's what he was, through and through. How different things could have been if Katherine hadn't turned out to be Kit.

That thought certainly didn't help—it set flames scorching specific parts of his body. Parts that, just like his heart, had regained full consciousness lately.

"You looking for something?"

He spun around. "No."

Sam frowned. "You just standing there staring at the ground, then?"

Clay shrugged, but experienced an ounce of gratitude when his confused mind found an excuse. "I figured you and Kit might like some time alone. Get to know each other."

Sam shook his head. "She seems nice and all, but she also seems like the kind that wants to take me to Nevadaville, or even Chicago, just like Oscar. I ain't going, Clay."

He nodded, accepting how Sam recognized Kit had inherited Oscar's determination, but he had to ask. "Why not?"

Sam threw out an arm, gesturing toward the hills. "And leave all this?" He shook his head. "These hills are my home. I can't figure out why folks think I should leave them."

Clay walked over to stand next to Sam and gaze out at the vista of peaks and valleys. "What about when you get your full inheritance? You'll leave then."

"No, I won't," Sam insisted. "I'll live right here. Might build a cabin. Probably a barn, too." He leaned over and punched Clay in the arm. "Maybe even get me a dog named Massachusetts."

Clay had to grin at that, but still he wondered. "You want your inheritance so you can go on living right here?"

"Well, yeah. All I really want is the deed to this here land. Then I'll have a place I'll never have to leave. I'll get me a few more traps." Sam drew a deep breath. "At one time Pa and me made a good living trapping. Course, Pa liked gambling a bit too much. With the right traps and a good line, I could do just fine. Might even set up a spring rendezvous. What would you think of that?"

Clay took off his hat to scratch at his tingling scalp. He'd never asked Sam what he'd do with his inheritance. He had assumed the kid just wanted the money to go and waste on some frivolous dream.

Clay's gaze went back to the horizon, and he stuck his hat back on his head. He'd admitted to Kit that dreaming was a good thing, so that should apply to Sam, too, shouldn't it? "A rendezvous?"

"Yep," Sam answered with stars in his eyes.

"For trappers?" Clay clarified.

"Yep. These hills are still full of them. More and more furs are needed for all the folks mining. They need good coats, you know."

Clay gave a nod.

"One Ear Bob was just saying your mining towns don't cater to the trappers. Gotta go all the way to Den-

ver to get a good price on a hide. With my inheritance
as backing money—" Sam kicked at a rock "—and your
train to get the supplies here, I could set up a rendezvous
that would bring trappers from all over. They don't take
good to trading with city folks, you know."

A nerve had snapped when he'd heard One Ear Bob's
name, but for now, Clay didn't want to overshadow Kit
and Sam's meeting with more of his own worries. "I
think that's a fine idea, Sam. I've never been to a rendezvous. I might have to check that out."

"I'll send you an invite." Sam planted his hands on
his hips and gazed around the hillside like a man overseeing his kingdom.

Clay stood silently, giving the kid his moment of
glory.

"Well," Sam said a short time later, while glancing
at the cave. "I'd best get back in there. She'll probably
never figure out how to open those cans." He took a
step, then paused. "You coming?"

"Yeah, I'm coming."

"Good," Sam said. "'Cause I don't want to be left
alone with her."

Shaking his head, Clay assured him, "She doesn't
bite."

"How do you know?"

Sam had a way of bringing out the kid hidden in everyone. Clay hooked him around the neck and knuckled
his mop of red hair. "She's your sister."

"So?"

"So, there's nothing to be afraid of. She won't hurt
you."

Sam stiffened. "I may have lived in the hills my
whole life, but there's one thing I know."

"What's that?" Clay asked. The serious glint in Sam's eyes sent a tiny shiver racing along his spine.

"That a man's better off being leery of women. All women. There ain't a one of them that's not out to change him."

The shiver caught the top Clay's spine with a death grip.

"Every one of them has a plan," Sam continued, "whether they act like it or not. And usually they need a man to fulfill it. They'll do anything to get the means to their ends."

"Where'd you learn that?" Clay asked, rubbing his neck, which had started to stiffen.

"Don't you read any of those books you keep hauling up here?" Sam asked.

"Yes—"

"Well, there you have it," Sam said.

"There I have what?"

"Where I learned so much about women."

Clay ignored the urge to keep scratching his head. "Those books are—"

"I know, adventure stories, about men sailing the seas and trekking across unknown territories, but in every one of them there's a woman making up a list of chores for him." Sam, evidently satisfied with his explanation, began walking toward the cave.

Clay followed, his mind making a list of the books he'd brought to Sam over the past year. He'd read them all, but he'd never picked out what Sam had. Perhaps he'd have to reread a few of them.

"Even the Bible's full of stories about women getting what they want," Sam added, moments before he entered the cave.

His screeched "I'll open those!" had Clay picking up his pace. He turned the corner just in time to see Sam pull a long knife from Kit's hand as the kid repeated, "I'll open those."

Clay stopped in the archway and leaned against the wooden frame built on the inside, where Sam attached a door during the winter months. How had a kid of seventeen figured out more about life and women than Clay had in his twenty-eight years? Sam lived in a cave, but knew exactly what he wanted.

Whereas Clay didn't *live* anywhere. He slept in his office, because he'd believed a woman when she said if he built an opera house she'd move to Nevadaville. At first Miranda had wanted him to move to Denver. Convincing her he couldn't and still run his mines and mills, she'd finally conceded to moving—with conditions. And then, after he'd built the opera house, and a home he thought she'd be infatuated with, she'd told him she was going to Paris. That was it. Going to Paris to perform with the Royal Troupe, without ever seeing the opera house or the home he'd built for them—him and her.

"You growing roots there, Hoffman?"

Clay glanced up. "No," he answered. Keeping his gaze off Kit, he turned and followed Sam to the fire. Sam had an account Oscar had set up for him, and it held more than enough money to buy traps and supplies, build a cabin, too, if that's what he wanted.

"Sam," Clay started. "I've told you before, about the money Oscar left you. There's enough—"

"Nope," Sam interrupted.

"You could—"

"No." Sam kicked down the fire and set an iron grate

across the coals. "I've told you before. I don't want it that way." He placed the pan of beans on the grate. "Right now you have to oversee every dime I spend. I don't want a partner. When I set up my rendezvous, I want it my way. Then there's no one to blame if it don't pan out, and no one to divvy up the profits when it does."

Clay held in the sigh building in his chest. The account was set up so every transaction had to be approved by him, and the will was ironclad.

"Why's she here?" Sam asked, stirring the beans with a long spoon as thoroughly as his words invaded Clay's ponderings.

"She wanted to meet you," he answered, crouching down beside the kid.

"Is she gonna move out here?"

Once more, Clay's heart took to racing. He had no idea what her plans were now that she knew the truth. The thought of her leaving had something coiling inside his stomach. "You'll have to ask her," he finally said.

"Me?" Sam shook his head. "Didn't you?"

"No."

"Why not?"

Clay dug deep, but couldn't come up with an excuse. "It's none of my business," he finally said halfheartedly.

Sam laughed. "There's nothing in Nevadaville that ain't your business. You own the entire town, and a good portion of Center City and Black Hawk to boot."

He couldn't deny his ownership of many businesses and properties, but could refute his interest in nonpublic issues. "I don't involve myself with people's private affairs."

The look Sam shot his way said more than any words

could, and the kid knew it. "You're her guardian, same as mine."

Clay's teeth clamped together. "Yeah. I know," he admitted. "I know."

Chapter Eleven

Lunch went well. The siblings talked between themselves. Kit asked Sam about his home and with unique pride Sam shared his trials and errors of building the cave into a dwelling. When the conversation turned to Sam's childhood. Clay excused himself, giving the siblings time to share things privately.

He walked up the hill as his thoughts tumbled and churned. It was exasperating, all that was going on under his scalp. Kit and Sam were his concern, made so by Oscar's will, but also by Oscar's friendship. That part Clay understood. What swam about uncontrollably, and had him somewhat off center, was the growing desire he felt. It was deeper now than when he'd wanted to kiss her, and had grown soft and gentle as he'd watched her with Sam.

Every time Kit spoke, his heart fluttered, and when she giggled that adorable little laugh she had, his heart thudded. Pounded like he'd never known it could. And the excitement in his stomach…what was that? Oh, he'd experienced it before. Would never forget the first time, when he'd seen the massive vein of gold running along the wall in the Wanda Lou. He still felt a rush when he saw veins, but nothing like that first one. It had been life changing, and he'd known that from the moment he saw it.

The hairs on the back of his neck stood up as he returned to the cave. He stopped near the opening, leaned against the rock. Life changing?

She'd done that, all right. Turned his life upside down since arriving in Colorado. The question Sam had asked earlier reappeared, and had Clay leaning harder against the rock. He'd already grown attached to her, and certainly didn't want her to go back to Chicago. That drew up more questions, namely, about what he did want.

"Riders coming in," Sam said, appearing at the cave entrance.

"I don't hear anything," Kit said, stepping out beside her brother.

"Listen," he instructed.

She held her breath, listening with all she had, but it wasn't until she closed her eyes that a very faint tinkle merged with the dead silence.

"Hear that?"

She nodded.

Sam pointed toward the back of the cave. "Tunnels lead off this room in all directions. Dirt falls when the ground trembles. And the ground trembles when something runs over it." He turned to Clay. "They're coming from the Wanda Lou."

Clay pushed away from the rock wall, and the look on his face had Kit moving as well, rushing forward.

His smile instantly calmed the slight tremor of fear that had formed in her stomach, even before he said, "There's nothing to worry about." His hand settled on her back. "Should we go see who it is?"

She nodded, able to face anything when he was near.

"Did you enjoy your lunch?" he asked as they walked to the side of the hill.

"Yes."

He lifted a brow.

She giggled. "To be perfectly honest, I love peaches. Always have."

He gave a single nod. "Peach pie."

That he remembered such insignificant details about her sent something in her whirling with enchantment. "Yes." Shadows stretched across the ground, making her realize how long she and Sam had talked. Glancing around, she asked, "Where'd he go?"

Clay turned and pointed to the rocks jutting out of the mountain above the cave. "Up there."

She scanned for a figure among the boulders and trees, but was still searching when Sam's voice said, "It's the land agent."

A deep frown appeared on Clay's face. "Did you tell Clarice you were coming to my house this morning?"

"No," she answered. "Why?"

"Then that would be Jonathan looking for you."

"Me?" She shook her head. "Why?"

"I didn't tell anyone you were with me. They've probably been looking for you all day."

"Why?"

"You want me to let him in?" Sam asked from above them.

"Yes," Clay yelled. "He's here to take Kit home."

Sam hollered down the hill, but Kit wasn't listening. "I'm not ready to leave," she said.

"You can come back and visit Sam another day," Clay said, taking her arm.

During the past few hours, even while talking about her mother and grandparents, she hadn't forgotten what Clay had said—that he'd promised Oscar he'd take care of her, of them, her and Sam—and it had stewed inside her until her stomach ached. Somehow along the way, she'd thought Clay was there because he liked her, but listening to Sam talk about how Clay had to oversee even his spending money, she'd started to wonder about other things.

"Did you know who I was from the beginning?" she asked.

"What?"

"When did you know I was Oscar's granddaughter?"

A deep frown sat between Clay's brows. "Why?"

"Because I want to know."

"Shortly after we arrived in Nevadaville."

The pounding of horse hooves sounded, along with a shout. "Kit! Thank goodness you're all right."

She turned to see Jonathan jumping off a big bay horse. "I've been looking all over for you," he continued, rushing forward.

"Of course—" The words stopped as her mouth was pressed into Jonathan's shirt when he grasped her shoulders and pulled her against him, hugging her hard. She liked Jonathan, but his hold made her uncomfortable. There was only one man she wanted hugging her. Yet that couldn't be because she was a job to him, something she only comprehended now—after hearing Sam describe how seriously Clay took the task of being Sam's guardian, how rigidly he upheld the terms of Grandpa's will. Pulling out of the embrace, she took a step away. "Of course I'm all right. I'm perfectly fine."

Jonathan kept one hand on her shoulder. "Clarice

and I went to see how you were doing, after church this morning, and Mimmie Mae didn't know where you were. No one did." He turned to Clay. "Half the town is looking for her."

"I should have thought of that," Clay said. "I'll get her horse."

A spell of panic gripped Kit and she moved, didn't stop until she'd caught up with Clay. "Aren't you coming?"

"No, I'm going to stay and talk to Sam." Clay untied Rachel's reins and started leading the horse back toward the cave.

"Why?"

He had yet to meet Kit's gaze. "I need to talk to him."

"About what?" she asked.

"Several things." He stepped around her.

She twirled and took long strides to stay beside him. "Then I'll stay, too."

"No, you go on back with Jonathan." He stopped near the saddles and threw the blanket over Rachel's back. "The ride home takes longer. I probably won't make it back before dark."

"I'm not afraid of the dark," she insisted.

His back stiffened, and Kit watched as he drew in a deep breath, as if he was holding it in frustration. She could relate. Annoyance zipped around inside her faster than bumblebees gathering nectar. There were still things she wanted to ask Sam, but more than that, she didn't want to return with anyone but Clay.

"Just ride home with Jonathan, Kit," he said.

She held in yet another protest, but it was hard. In some ways Clay reminded her of Gramps, and how he'd always insisted she and Grandma couldn't go with him to Colorado, no matter how hard Kit had begged. Even though she now understood Grandpa's reason, the pain of being left was gurgling inside her like it had all those years ago. She told herself that was silly, that Clay wasn't leaving her behind, yet the sense of being on her own again wouldn't ease.

"It was good seeing you, Kit. Maybe you can stop out again before you head back to Chicago. I'm always around, lest I'm tracking a critter," Sam said, stepping up beside her.

The mention of returning to Chicago sent her thoughts in another direction. She wouldn't be returning anytime soon, not now that she'd met Sam, but she couldn't overstep her welcome, either. Drawing a breath, she braced inwardly, as she used to when Gramps left, telling herself she'd see both Sam and Clay soon.

"I'd like that, Sam," she said. "Thank you for the offer. And thank you for lunch. I enjoyed it very much."

Sam's cheeks grew pink and he shuffled his feet. "It's kinda nice, meeting my kin."

Kit took a chance, a big one, and leaned forward to give him a quick hug. "I agree. It's very nice."

His shoulders and spine were stiff as a board, but he did pat her back once before he stepped away, and then took off for the cave as if something was chasing him.

When she turned, Jonathan was at her side, ready to help her onto Rachel's back. Clay had moved, now stood near the cave entrance, and there was a peculiar pulling sensation inside her when he tipped his hat her way. She climbed in the saddle and waved as the horse started forward.

The journey home was long. Jonathan was full of questions at first, but after frowning at her few clipped answers, he stopped making small talk, and they simply rode. The terrain wasn't as treacherous as the way she and Clay had taken. The rail tracks provided a well-worn trail, used by the mules to pull the ore carts from the mine to Nevadaville. It was only a few miles, but the trail had to wind its way down the side of the mountain to keep the grade from being too steep.

Kit didn't mind. It gave her time to reflect and eventually stew—mainly because with all that had happened, the thing still foremost in her mind was kissing Clay. Absurd, that's what it was. Yet it was there, smack-dab in the center of her mind, as was the fact that he'd called her a job. Well, he'd said it was his job—watching out for her and Sam.

Steam built up inside her, burning her chest and eyes. If that wasn't about the finest how-do ever. Being someone's job.

There was no need for someone to watch over her. She'd got along just fine back in Chicago, and would do so out here as well.

The churning in her stomach increased. She'd been fine, but it had been so terribly lonely, and deep down, that's the part that was hurting. Eventually, she'd have to go back to Chicago. Face Mr. Watson, who was not going to be happy. He'd been kind to her, checking on her as he had, and she should have told him she was going, even though he'd never told her about Sam.

All of that didn't play around in her mind as deeply as Clay continued to, however.

A shout sounded from somewhere, making her scan the hillside.

"Yes!" Jonathan replied, yelling down the mountain to where several people stood. "I found her."

It was as if a dozen people stepped forward then, rushing up the trail to meet them where the tracks curved toward the stamping mill.

Mimmie Mae practically tugged her from the saddle. "Oh, girl, girl, girl. We have been so worried about you."

Kit opened her mouth, but little more than a short squeak emitted as Ty Reins grabbed her waist and finished pulling her off Rachel.

He gave her a solid hug. "We got half the town out looking for you." When he let her loose, he yelled, "Raymond, go tell Chet to sound the whistle to let the others know we found her."

A big man with a heavy stock of blond hair waved before he swung around and barreled down the hill.

"You come with me, now," Mimmie Mae said, pulling her forward. "Where'd you find her?" the woman asked, looking at Jonathan.

"She was with Clay up at Sam's cave."

"Where's Clayton now?"

The fury in Mimmie Mae's voice sent a shiver slicing through Kit. Her head was spinning from all the commotion, and without thought—other than that Clay wasn't to blame for her absence—she answered, "He's still up at Sam's. I wanted to meet—"

"Well, I'll give that man a talking to. That I will," Mimmie Mae insisted, pulling her down the hill.

"Why?"

"For taking you off and not telling anyone. Miss Clarice was downright frantic when she didn't find you in your room."

Kit's stomach gurgled. She hadn't meant to cause such turmoil, and certainly hadn't wanted to upset Clarice. The guilt grew, making her insist, "It's not Clay's fault. I asked him to take me to see Sam."

"Yes, well, he should never have done that without telling someone." Even the screeching whistle splitting the air didn't lessen the fury lacing Mimmie Mae's voice.

"Oh, Kit!" Clarice shoved her way through the growing crowd. "I was so worried about you."

This kind of concern for her welfare was uncanny. These people barely knew her. "I'm sorry," Kit said. Her apology seemed insignificant compared to the size of the crowd. "Truly," she repeated, glancing around at the horde of people. "I'm very sorry. I never expected—"

"You're part of the community, Kit. Family," Clarice said, hugging her. "We had to go looking for you, but as long as you're safe, that's all that matters."

Family?

"I'm fine," she assured her, too stunned to grasp all she was feeling inside. "I really am. I wanted to meet Sam and Clay offered to take me."

"Let's get her to the hotel," Mimmie Mae said. "Are you hungry, child?"

"Did you see Sam?" Clarice asked at the same time.

"No," Kit said to Mimmie Mae, before turning to Clarice. "Yes, I did."

"How is he?" Clarice asked, concern and affection filling her voice.

"Why that boy doesn't move to town is beyond me," Mimmie Mae muttered, still marching forward as if on a crusade.

"He's fine," Kit assured Clarice, before she responded to Mimmie Mae. A growing need had her defending Sam. "Because he doesn't want to. He likes his place."

"But it's a cave," the hotel owner insisted.

Kit was growing short-winded keeping up with the fast pace, but there was no suggestion the older woman would slow down. "Maybe it's a cave to us, but to Sam it's his home. And he's proud of it." The truth in her words had Kit's mind connecting with her heart. Sam was proud of his home, and she was proud of him.

The crowd dispersed as they walked along the street. People she barely remembered seeing before, and several she knew she'd never met, said goodbye and expressed their happiness that she was home safe and sound, as they put it, before moving along to attend other tasks. Mimmie Mae and Clarice continued to lead her to the hotel, where they insisted she eat and then sent her upstairs for a bath and bed.

Kit, thankful for the time alone, gathered a clean set of clothes and made her way into the bathing chamber at the end of the hall. She'd lived in Chicago her entire life, and knew many people, but if she was gone for a day, no one would have come looking for her. Then again, any of her neighbors could have been gone for a day and she wouldn't have bothered looking for them, either. They were nice people, and had been kind and generous upon Grandpa's and Grandma's deaths. It was just different here. As if the entire town was one big family.

And they considered her a part of that.

Kit contemplated the concept. The entire day, actually. The way the town went looking for her. Meeting her brother for the first time. His somewhat unorthodox home. When her mind shifted to Clay, she shook her head. The bathwater would be ice-cold by the time she was done contemplating him. And she wouldn't be any closer than she was right now to understanding why she was so infatuated with him. They'd known each other barely a week, yet the way she missed him, one would have thought they'd known each other their entire lives.

The town was dark, barely a light flickered in a window, yet Clay stood on the boardwalk outside his office, staring at the houses and businesses where people, whole families, were already dozing. Was Kit sleeping? Mimmie Mae had most likely taken control, had her fed, bathed and sent to bed shortly after Jonathan brought her home.

He should go check. Mimmie Mae could be overwhelming. She'd probably give him a what-for the next time he saw her. He should have told someone, anyone, before leaving town this morning, but the thought simply hadn't crossed his mind.

Clay turned. His house stood on top of the hill, as dark, if not darker, than the rest of town. The weight of the world seemed to descend upon his shoulders, so heavy he had to shift his feet.

Kit knocking on his front door, sitting at the table, crying on his back steps—the images kept coming, and they were harder to face than the ones that had kept him from the house prior to last night.

He rolled his shoulders at the tension and turned, walked up the flight of steps to his office, where piles of papers sat on his desk. Things he needed to see to.

Pulling off his hat, he ran a hand over his forehead. Not even when Miranda had informed him she was leaving for Europe had he let things stack up like this. Yet that's what had been happening ever since Kit had arrived. The most work he'd completed was installing the new boiler. The physical labor forced him not to think about other things, but when he sat behind the desk, pushing around paper, his mind had a tendency to wander. He'd barely accomplished daily tasks the past week.

It wouldn't happen tonight, either, so there was no sense in standing here contemplating it. He made his way into the side room that doubled as his living quarters, and stretched out on the bed.

The weight on his shoulders shifted, moved to sit on his chest with suffocating heaviness. He could curse Jonathan for arriving when he had, but that wouldn't change anything. Especially not the glow that appeared inside Clay whenever Kit's image formed in his mind. It didn't take much. A remembrance of something she'd said or did. The way she tilted her head or her lifting giggle. The shimmer in those big brown eyes.

Truth be told, it was a good thing Jonathan had shown up, otherwise something might have happened. Something that could never happen—kissing her again. A real, deep and fulfilling kiss.

His heartbeat picked up. It was annoying, the way he had no control over his body when it came to her. The best thing to do would be to send her back to Chicago. Send Sam with her, for that matter.

As if that would solve all Clay's problems.

It would if she stayed away another five years. He could marry her then. The stipulations of the will would be fulfilled when she turned twenty-five. A sigh built in his chest. Marry her? That was a hell of a thought. He had no intention of marrying. Not Kit or any other woman. It was all her talk about wanting a family that had his heart going out to her.

He blew the air out of his lungs and set his gaze on the stars out the window. Kit just wanted a family. He understood that. Though he had Clarice, and for the past few years had told himself differently, he wanted a family, too. Heirs. Someone to whom he could pass down all he'd worked so hard to acquire.

Fully frustrated, Clay shot off the cot, grabbed clean clothes and made his way down the stairs. He had a house, complete with a bathing room and soft feather mattresses, and it was time he started using it.

An hour later, clean and lying in a bed as soft as a cloud, he found his mind was still on Kit. Trouble was, now he was wishing she was in the bed beside him. Not only that, he actually missed her, which was ridiculous, considering he'd seen her just a few hours ago.

The hairs on his arms rose, tingling as if issuing a warning, just as a faint knock sounded on his front door.

Kit squeezed her hand tighter and pulled it back. Glancing down the hill to the quiet, dark town below, she once again questioned her sanity. It was the middle of the night. What would people think? It was doubtful, but someone could have seen her sneak up the hill. Would they think she was trying to rob Clay's house?

Maybe he wasn't home. He might have stayed out at Sam's. There were no lights in the windows, but with the heavy draperies, she wouldn't be able to see any even if they were lit.

Would she ever learn? Hadn't her impulses caused her enough problems already? The trip to Colorado. Chasing after Sam. Being tossed in a pond. Stowing away on a train. Climbing a tree to rescue birds that weren't even there. Kissing Clay.

She spun around and laid a hand on the rail to guide

her way back down the porch stairway. The sound of the door opening froze her steps, had her fingers gripping the rail tighter.

"Kit?"

Blood pounded so hard in her veins she could hardly hear around the echoing in her ears. He was home. She should never have come here. Back at the hotel it had seemed like a good idea, but now it most certainly didn't.

A gentle but firm hand wrapped around her elbow.

"Kit," he repeated, while turning her about.

Seeing him had her heart missing so many beats she was growing light-headed.

Oh, good heavens, was this what it felt like to faint? Light-headed, dizzy, heart racing, knees weak. She gulped for air, not wanting to land on his porch in a haphazard pile.

He pulled her forward. "Come inside before someone sees you." Once over the threshold, he let go of her elbows to push a lit lamp into the center of the table near the door. It had been sitting on the edge, as if someone had hastily set it aside.

The flickering light bounced off his arm and chest, which was where her eyes stalled. He didn't have on a shirt. She'd never have imagined a man's chest could be so sculpted. Full of refined curves and notable bulges of muscle that made her think of the drawings of historic Greek gods she'd seen long ago in a book.

"Kit."

Her gaze wandered upward, caught the confusion in his face. "I couldn't sleep," she blurted, trying to explain her reason for being there, while doing her best to keep her eyes from moving back down to his bare chest.

"You couldn't sleep?" he repeated skeptically.

A flood happened inside her head, as all the thoughts and fears she'd been battling and scrutinizing back at the hotel hit her in one solid blast. "I don't need a guardian."

"You don't need a guardian?" he repeated, before saying, "You don't have a choice in the matter, Kit."

Anxiety burst in her stomach, and she quickly started to explain. "I know the will says you are, but I don't want you to be my guardian. I'm perfectly capable of taking care of myself. Plenty of women my age are married or running businesses. Clarice, for instance. Even my mother, by the time she was my age—" Kit let out a huff of frustration. "I don't understand why Gramps made this all so complicated."

Feeling cramped and needing space, she spun around, took a few steps along the foyer wall. "I can understand why he didn't want Grandma and me to come to Colorado with him, but I can't…" She stopped pacing. "Have you ever been lonely, Clay? Really, really lonely?" she asked. "To the point where you don't even want to get out of bed in the morning because there was no one to talk to, no one to see?" She shrugged. "No one would have even known if I hadn't gotten out of bed, other than Mr. Watson, who stopped by every Wednesday morning to see if I needed anything."

"You didn't have any friends or…" His voice trailed off as she shook her head.

"I have acquaintances, people from the stores I frequent, or church." The hollow, empty feeling of the past year was growing inside her again. "I was never allowed to socialize, and about the time I was grown up enough to ask, well, that's when Grandpa and Grandma had their carriage accident. They were on their way for another engagement, to pick me up."

"You can't blame yourself for that," he said.

"I did for a long time," she admitted. "Maybe I still do, but I figured out it wouldn't change anything. Then, while I was cataloging the books in Grandpa's office, I found a letter he'd been writing to Sam, and the ticket stub. Mr. Watson wouldn't tell me anything, and I was so tired of being alone. I thought if Sam was my uncle, I'd have a family again. That's when I imagined being Katherine Ackerman. I didn't add the accent and being from Boston until I met a lady on the train." The words were gushing out of her mouth, and she couldn't stop them. "Gramps talked about you all the time, but I was afraid you'd send me home. You're a good person. You care about others and children. Like Sam, and Liza Rose with Mrs. Smith's glasses. And Henry. You even took care of Henry. But I'm not a child and I don't need a guardian. I'm—"

The tips of Clay's fingers landed on her lips. "Stop," he whispered.

It was kind of a relief. She was winded, and barely recalled what she'd said.

His gaze grew intense and a somewhat cynical glimmer appeared before he asked, "Did Mimmie Mae give you some medicine? A little brown bottle that—"

"No," she said. "I didn't take any medicine."

"Some wine, perhaps?"

"No." Flustered, she spun about and walked as far as the lamp cast light before stopping to stare at the dark wall. There were just so many confusing things inside her. She'd somehow thought seeing him would solve them all. "I shouldn't have come here tonight. I just wanted you to know I told everyone it wasn't your fault. That I asked you to take me to Sam's. No one except Grandma and Grandpa has ever cared what happened to me before, and I don't want everyone mad at you. I like you too much for that. You make me not feel lonely anymore." The air in her lungs grew thick. She let it go by sighing heavily as hopelessness filled her. "I should have just stayed at the hotel. Sitting there feeling lonely all over again, and wishing you were there kissing me."

"Kissing you?"

The whisper was so close the hairs on her neck tingled.

A sickening realization sent a groan rumbling from her lips while she buried her face in her hands. Humiliation burned her cheeks and she mentally saw herself running for the door.

His hands clasped her upper arms, forced her to turn around. "Kit."

Half groaning, half sighing, and swallowing the last bits of pride she had left, she faced him, knowing there was no way to put that cat back in the bag.

The tender smile on his lips and the compassionate shimmer in his eyes were almost more than she could take. But it was the way his hand cupped her cheek that had her insides sparking like the fuse on a Chinese lantern—though she was still mortified by the outbreak of thoughts that should have remained private. This was all new to her, and so confusing. She'd never had *feelings* for someone like this before.

His free hand grasped her other cheek and he lifted her face, held it directly in front of his. "I don't feel lonely when I'm with you, either. And I was sitting here thinking about kissing you, too," he said.

Her heart might have quit working. Leastwise it would never, ever be the same. "You were?"

"Yes." His eyes were still locked on hers as his face came closer. "I was."

Soft and warm, his lips touched hers, so perfectly the connection went all the way to her toes. Then, like a rubber ball, the feeling rebounded, racing back up her body, igniting little sparks along the way.

Her breath caught and then his lips moved, playfully coaxing hers to join the fun. She did, and it was magical. Like a great wonder that was more spectacular than anything she'd ever imagined, and teased every sense she had.

An alluring temptation erupted inside her and an overpowering instinct told her lips to part. Clay's tongue ran along her bottom lip, igniting sweet sensations, before it slid into her mouth. Her tongue twisted and twirled with his in a mystifying dance that had her spellbound.

Her hands found the bare skin of his chest, and her fingertips skimmed over the hot, smooth expanse, pausing to inspect the contours she'd admired earlier. Good gracious heavens above, kissing him had her entire body singing, and it wasn't a sweet poetic song. No, siree, this was a fast, jaunty tune like the ones that filtered out of saloon doors back in Black Hawk, and would have had Grandma Katie slapping her hands over her ears.

Kit wrapped her arms around his bare torso, amazed at how wonderful it was to touch him, feel his body against hers. It was just the two of them in the world again. A wonderful, lovely place.

He moaned as his mouth slid off hers. She let out a lighter version of the sound—several times—as his lips kissed a line down one side of her neck and back up the other, before settling on hers again, at which point she eagerly met him kiss for kiss, swirl for swirl.

"Kit, Kit," Clay mumbled, unable to express all he was feeling as he broke the kiss long enough to catch a breath of air. Pulling her body, every delectable inch of it, to lightly glide against his, he took her mouth again, fully, completely, and exactly how he'd imagined doing while lying in his lonely bed upstairs.

Someone could have knocked him over with a feather when he'd opened the door and seen her standing there. Matter of fact, it wasn't until he'd touched her that he'd known for certain she was real and not a figment of his imagination.

Her lips were so perfect. Met and curled around his as if they were specifically made for him to taste. And taste them he did. Over and over.

Her fingers played havoc on his skin as they caressed and kneaded his back, generating enough chaos inside him to make him as unstable as a bottle of old nitroglycerin. He grabbed her shoulders—as if that could stop her hands. It didn't, of course, but as he tugged her forward her breasts pressed harder against his bare chest, creating a torment so excruciating he wondered if the material separating her skin from his had scorched his flesh.

He'd never imagined desire could be this strong, this consuming, but he did know himself well enough to recognize that soon, kissing wouldn't be enough. It wouldn't be long and he'd snap—carry her up the stairs and show her exactly how much he loved her.

The silent admission shocked him, and he pulled out of the kiss.

Kit, gasping for air, collapsed against him. As she

clung to him, he folded his arms around her and tucked her head beneath his chin, wondering what he was going to do now.

It could have been minutes or hours they stood like that, cradled in each other's arms. It felt so right. So perfect and authentic.

Her breathing had returned to normal, but though he was more composed than he'd been before breaking the kiss, his desire for her was as strong as ever. He stepped back, waited for her to lift her head. The serene smile on her face and the passion still glimmering in her eyes almost made him rethink what he was about to do.

Almost.

He leaned down and kissed the tip of her nose while grasping one of her hands. "Come on."

Her fingers folded around his easily and she fell in step beside him. "Where are we going?"

He paused long enough to pick up the shirt that had fallen from his hand when he'd opened the door. "I'm taking you back to the hotel."

She planted her free hand on the doorframe. "I don't want to go back to the hotel."

This was going to be a test of his willpower. "It's late, and you shouldn't be here."

"But I want to be here."

He reached out and pried her fingers off the wood. "You," he said, kissing the tip of her index finger, "could tempt the devil out of hell."

She bowed her head bashfully, but then snapped it up, gazing at him with a touch of bewilderment. "Is that a compliment or an insult?"

Clay took a moment to shrug into the shirt before he took her hand again and pulled her over the threshold.

"A compliment." Reaching back, he closed the door behind them. "Definitely a compliment."

She walked down the steps beside him, but paused once they'd stepped onto the trail.

"You don't have to walk me back. I know the way," she said, as her hold on his hand tightened.

The gesture wasn't lost on him—neither his heart nor his mind. He stepped closer, so her shoulder rubbed against his arm as they walked. "I know you know the way. But it's dark, and it's late, and I want to walk you back."

"Because you're my guardian," she said quietly.

He had to bide his time, give her the opportunity to get to know him, decide if Colorado was a place she could live. If it was, he'd have a serious decision to make. A life-changing one. "No," he said, "because I like you."

"You do?"

"Yes, I do."

Her hair brushed his shoulder as she tilted her head up and smiled at him. "I like you, too."

Maybe it was the little man in the bright full moon overhead serenading them, or simply the night noises of crickets and a gentle breeze fluttering the spring leaves, but Clay swore he heard music. A sweet romantic tune that lulled his heart into perfect rhythm. "Good," he whispered, planting a little kiss on the top of her head.

They walked in silence until the hill leveled out on the upper layer of town. The path wasn't too steep, but now, walking beside her, he wondered if he should have steps carved in the rock. The trail could be hazardous come winter.

"Clay," Kit said, sounding a bit hesitant.

He squeezed her hand. "Yeah?"

"I don't think I want to go back to Chicago, ever."

The jolting of his heart stole Clay's ability to move, right there at the top of the stairs that would take them down to the next level, where the hotel stood. Light from the million stars overhead reflected in her eyes, making them sparkle despite the uncertainty he saw in them. The fact that anyone who might be awake and looking out a window would be able to see them didn't stop him. He took her face in both hands and held it as he brought his lips down upon hers.

The kiss remained chaste, just the mingling of lips, and he took his time. Kissing her until he hoped the last ounce of trepidation had disappeared from her unforgettable eyes and precious mind.

When their lips parted and she opened her eyes, they shone as brightly as the stars overhead. Satisfied in more ways than one, he looped his arm around her shoulders and guided her down the steps.

At the front of the hotel, he asked, "Which room is yours?"

"That one," she said, pointing to the window at the corner of the building.

"Then go on," he said, easing his arm off her shoulders. "And light your lamp so I know you're in there."

She looked at him, clearly full of questions, as was he. But now wasn't the time.

He lifted a clump of hair off her shoulder and let the silky strands glide through his fingers as it fell back in place. "Come to my office tomorrow. We'll talk there." It was the safest place, once he hauled away the cot from the back room. He'd see to that first thing.

"What time?" she asked.

"Whenever you want."

She nodded, but didn't make any attempt to move toward the door. He bit back a smile. She wanted another kiss. The knowledge was stirring, exciting, and he wanted the same thing. But the fact that anyone could be watching from a window held him back. He'd already given in to temptation once—on top of the stairs—and wouldn't do it again. Nevadaville was a good town, his town, full of kindhearted people, but that didn't mean he could behave scandalously. Besides that, he protected what was his. Kit and her reputation were worth all the protection he could supply.

"Go on, now." He gestured toward the building. "And light your lamp."

She went, glancing back as she opened the front door slowly, so the bell wouldn't ring, and then again as she waved before pulling the door closed just as gently.

He stood on the street, right below the window she'd indicated, waiting and watching, even after a glow filled the room. His heart rumbled as the sash lifted and Kit stuck her head out the window.

"Good night," she whispered.

"Good night," he answered, and then, not really wanting to, but knowing she wouldn't pull her head back in until he did, he left. The distance to his house seemed shorter, merely a few feet. Maybe it was because his steps were lighter than they'd ever been in his life, allowing him to practically float all the way home. Until he heard a snap, like someone stepping on a branch.

The sensation of being watched had the hairs on his neck standing up, and his stomach sank. He'd been so engrossed with Kit, and all the once-dead feelings she'd revived inside him, that he'd forgotten about the trapper. Sam had said he hadn't seen the man since Black Hawk, and Clay had dropped the conversation, although he had told the boy to be on alert. One Ear Bob wouldn't injure Sam, but who knew what the man might attempt, believing he could somehow gain access to the boy's inheritance?

Clay made his way onto the porch of his house, opened the door and shut it again without entering, staying hidden in the porch shadows. Eventually, when no other sounds occurred and his inner vibrations had returned to normal, making it clear that whoever had been there was gone, he entered the house.

Chapter Twelve

Kit had never, ever felt so good. Her insides were singing, her heart was filled with joy and her mind, well, it thought of only one thing. Mr. Clayton Hoffman if you please. She did please, all the way through putting on a lightweight cotton dress with short puffy sleeves and a square neckline. It was dusty-blue with tiny white flowers and trimmed with delicate lace—one of her utmost favorites she saved for special occasions. "Such as today," she said to her reflection, followed by a giggle that just couldn't be contained.

While she pulled the sides of her hair to the back of her head and secured them with combs, leaving the rest hanging down her back, she hummed a tune. A jaunty one she must have heard somewhere along the line, but had never recalled before.

She skipped down the stairs and was fully prepared to bypass breakfast until a flittering bout of guilt caught her when Mimmie Mae waved.

"I have your breakfast ready, Kit," the woman called.

Strolling into the dining room, she told herself she was a fast eater, and probably should give Clay time to get to his office.

The hotel owner was busy with other guests, so it didn't take Kit long to eat the eggs and toast, nor drink the little pot of tea. "That was wonderful, Mimmie Mae. Thank you," she said, floating toward the front door.

"Where are you off to in such a rush this morning?" the woman asked, balancing four plates in her hands.

"I have to talk to Clay." Kit couldn't wipe the smile from her face, so she quickly added, "About some of Grandpa's affairs."

Mimmie Mae lifted an eyebrow. "I still need to have a word with that man." A genuine smile formed on her lips. "Tell him I said that."

"I will."

"Oh, and Kit?"

She turned back. If anything, Mimmie Mae's smile had grown. Her eyes twinkled, like a kid who held a secret she couldn't wait to share. "Have fun."

"I will," Kit assured her, skipping out the doorway as a whistle blew, signaling the first train arrival of the day.

Nothing had really changed since yesterday, except for the fact that Clay had kissed her again, and said he liked her. *Liked her.* Those had to be the sweetest words anyone had ever spoken to her.

The brilliant sun, shining down with all the glory it held, filled her already blossoming insides with more radiant light than one could possibly hold, to the point she wanted to hug everyone and everything in sight. Instead, she lifted her arms over her head to absorb more of the wonderful sunlight for a moment, and then started up the street.

People were already out on the walkways, sweeping their sections and carrying supplies in and out. She'd met a goodly number of townsfolk at the matinee, and yesterday, when Jonathan brought her back from Sam's, so she returned waves from across the street, including Ty Reins's, from his spot atop the train, in the pilothouse.

"Morning, Kit," the mercantile owner called as she passed his shop a block up the road from the hotel.

"Good morning, Mr. Glasso," she responded.

"Beautiful day," he said, propping the door open with a chair.

"That it is," she agreed, strolling along.

"Hello, Kit. Lovely morning," the next shop owner said before she even got near the door.

"Yes, it is, Mrs. Williams."

"And that's a lovely dress you have on. I believe I have a hat that would match it perfectly," the woman responded.

Kit paused. She was in a hurry to see Clay, but she did want to look her best when she arrived at his office. "You do?"

"Yes, I do. Come in and I'll show you."

It was the better part of an hour before Kit was out the door, sporting a straw hat with blue silk ribbons and white flowers. She continued her route toward Clay's office, greeting shopkeepers and customers along the way as if she'd lived in Nevadaville her whole life. Giddy, her feet barely touching the ground, she felt her smile grow as she came closer and closer to the steady pounding of the stampers.

"Good morning, Kit," Jonathan said, opening the land office door as she arrived at the building. "You look extraordinarily lovely today."

"Thank you," she said, nodding her head. "It's the new hat. I just bought it from Mrs. Williams."

"The hat is lovely as well," he said.

Her cheeks warmed, and a gnawing feeling started in her stomach. "Jonathan, I'm sorry if I was rude yesterday. I—"

"Think nothing of it." He reached out and squeezed her hand briefly. "I'm glad you were all right. Actually, from the looks of things I'd say you're better than all right."

"I am," she readily agreed.

"Meeting your brother must have been exciting," he said.

"Yes," she replied. Meeting Sam had been wonderful, but nothing could compare to what had happened last night. Her gaze went to the door she knew led to Clay's office.

Jonathan patted her shoulder. "He's in. Been here since early this morning."

She couldn't think of a response, so remained quiet.

"Go on," Jonathan said. "His eyes were as bright as yours are this morning."

A tiny giggle escaped as she all but bolted toward the open door. The staircase was narrow and steep and rather dark near the top, since the only light was from the doorway behind her. A splattering of nervousness raced over her, but she shook it off, hitched up her skirt and began to climb.

At the top she let out the air in her lungs, took a fresh breath and then paused. Should she knock or just walk in? Questioning herself, she turned around, and glanced toward the bottom of the stairs, where Jonathan stood.

He grinned and waved a hand, as if to say go on. She spun back around, grabbed the doorknob and pushed open the door.

Her heart pitter-pattered so hard she swore her dress moved in response as she caught sight of Clay sitting behind his desk.

He smiled and rose to his feet, but his gaze didn't stay on her; instead, it moved to one side. She followed it, to a man sitting in one of the chairs in front of Clay's desk. Her heart fell. Landed in her stomach right next to where the gnawing started up again.

The man in a three-piece suit, with graying hair, rose to his feet. "Miss Becker."

"M-Mr. Watson." Half fearing his answer, she asked, "What are you doing here?"

"Well," he said, in that drawn-out way he always spoke to her. "When you unexpectedly left town without a word, I took it upon myself to find you."

"Oh." She swallowed the lump forming in her throat before glancing toward Clay. His expression wasn't far from Mr. Watson's frown. Feeling thwarted, she still found the gumption to say, "That really wasn't necessary."

Clay maneuvered around his desk and took her arm, leading her to the chair beside Mr. Watson. "He was worried about you. Rightfully so. He is your guardian."

She sat. Was actually very thankful for the sturdy chair, since her legs were no longer of much use. Returning to Chicago was not what she wanted, no matter who was her guardian.

Mr. Watson cleared his throat. "Well, I was your guardian as long as you lived in Chicago. Now that you are out here, and if you intend to stay, Mr. Hoffman will take over my role."

Kit could have sworn she heard relief in the man's

tone, but the look on Clay's face didn't give her a clue as to how he felt about it—or her—this morning.

Clay lowered himself onto the chair behind the desk and rubbed his chin thoughtfully before he said, "Perhaps it would be best if you returned to Chicago, Kit."

A clash of sorts happened inside her, quite painfully. "But I don't want to return."

"This may all be a wonderful adventure right now, Kit," Clay said solemnly, "but you'll soon grow tired of the remoteness, want the things Chicago has."

"Where do you plan on living, Kit?" Mr. Watson asked. "Staying at the hotel will soon grow costly. You'll need Mr. Hoffman's permission to increase your living allowance."

Clay's jaw had taken on a stern set and didn't relax as he stared at her, and all of a sudden she was reminded of the woman who had left him. Had she grown tired of the remoteness? Clay was comparing the two of them?

"I'm not leaving," she insisted. "I'll ask Sam if I can move in with him."

"You're not living in a cave, Kit," Clay said.

"Why not? Sam does. It didn't appear to be too uncomfortable."

"Kit," Mr. Watson started. "Neither of your grandparents would want you living in such conditions. You can return to—"

A knock sounded and the door opened. "I'm sorry to interrupt, Mr. Hoffman."

"It's all right, James," Clay answered. "What do you need?"

"There's trouble at the mine, sir. Word just arrived that you're needed."

Kit's heart landed in her throat as Clay's expression grew hard.

"What's happened?" he asked, heading toward the door.

James, the accountant she'd met at the matinee, stepped aside, allowing Clay to pass through the doorway. "Jester Wilke is downstairs," James said, following close on Clay's heels.

"Hold up, Kit." Mr. Watson grabbed her arm as she started to follow.

"But—"

"I'll go see what's happening. You stay here."

Something snapped inside her. "No," she said, "I won't. I don't mean to sound rude, Mr. Watson, but I'm done having people tell me what to do. I won't wait here, and I'm not returning to Chicago." Head up, she marched out the door and down the steps, and then she had to hitch her skirt ankle high to run toward the stable Clay was entering.

Upon arrival, while still catching her breath, she asked, "What's happened?"

Clay was already cinching the saddle on Andrew's back. "Nothing you need to worry about."

Just like moments before, when Mr. Watson had dictated she stay put, something cracked open inside her. "Yes, it is. It's my mine, too." Stepping forward, she persisted, "Furthermore, I'm not going back to Chicago. Never again will I sit around and have people dictate to me what I can and can't do. I wasn't just lonely the last year, but my whole life, and I won't go back to that. Grandma refused to leave the house empty, and I wasn't allowed to go anywhere by myself. Do you know what that meant?" she asked, while the frustration that had let loose continued to flow. "It meant I never went anywhere. I never had a say in anything. Well, that's over. Right here and now. You want to know what else? That's the real reason I came out here—to get away from it all. And I'm not going back. Ever."

The last bits of air left her chest and she refilled her lungs, drawing a cleansing breath.

"Are you finished?" Clay asked.

"Finished?"

"Yes. Did you get all that off your chest, or is there more?"

She let out a sigh, briefly examining how there was no pressure left inside her. "No, I think I'm done." Stepping forward, she added, "I'm not leaving. My family is here."

The air seemed to take on a sizzle as they stood staring at each other. There was no way to know if he believed her or not, but she felt a connection of sorts that had her insides flipping end over end.

Finally, he let out a long sigh. "I have to go. I'll let you know as soon as I get back, and we can finish talking with Mr. Watson."

It wasn't until he rode off that Kit realized her initial intention had been to go with him to the mine. Rachel stood in the stall, and the notion of saddling her had just occurred to Kit when she heard her name being called. Recognizing Mr. Watson's voice, she sighed as she turned to the doorway.

"Let's go to the hotel, where we can talk," he said. "I've brought something your grandfather wanted you to have."

It was several hours later when Clay returned to the

stable, and though a good portion of his mind was on the mine, Kit was still at the forefront. As he unsaddled and rubbed down the horse, he couldn't help but grin at how adorable she'd looked, standing there with a straw hat covered in flowers sitting cockeyed on her head as she bristled about going back to Chicago.

He took a breath and held it to a count of ten, telling himself he should insist she go back. Even though Theodore said Oscar had claimed Kit would head out here the first chance she got, Clay knew she'd eventually grow tired of it. Had to. She was used to the city. Had lived there her entire life. Her departure would leave an emptiness greater than Miranda's had if he didn't watch out.

"Clay?"

As he spun around, the expression on Kit's face turned his insides into a mush. He already was in deeper than he had been with Miranda. That was a given.

"I saw you ride in," she said.

He crossed the space and took her upper arms. "What's happened?" The little hat was gone and her eyes were dull. Both of which had his nerves on edge.

"Nothing." Holding up a single sheet of paper, she added, "Just this. It's a letter Gramps wrote me. Mr. Watson gave it to me."

Taking the note with one hand, he used the other to guide her out of the stable. "We'll go to my office," he said.

Once there, he took her into the back room and sat her down on the cot. Taking a seat beside her, he asked, "What's this say?" The paper burned his skin like hot metal. Oscar had already left enough stipulations and secrets. What else could there be?

"You can read it," she said. "If you want."

Holding in a sigh, he unfolded the sheet of paper.

My Dearest Kit,

So you've made it to Colorado. Beautiful, isn't it? I always knew you'd like it there. If you're reading this, you also know about your mother. I'm sorry, Kitten. I just couldn't tell you. I suspect now you understand why Grandma could never leave the house empty. She was afraid Amelia would come home and no one would be there.

Please don't be angry about Grandma keeping you caged up like a bird. She was just afraid you'd fly away, too. And, Kitten, if you have to blame someone, blame me, not your momma. Amelia wanted to take you with her, but I couldn't let both of you go, and she loved your father so much she couldn't stay where everything reminded her of him. You'll understand that one day. Might already.

Well, darling, I just had to tell you how sorry I am, and I hope by the time you're reading this, you'll have started a new life in Colorado. Clay was the son I never had, and I know he'll be good to you. Trust him. I do.

You've also met your brother, Sam. My greatest wish is for the two of you to get to know each other. He's a good kid, and I love him. I told him that, but I'd be obliged if you'd say it again for me.

I won't ask you to take care of Grandma because I know you will, and since you're reading this letter, Grandma's either right there beside you or up in heaven next to me and the angels.

Well, Kitten, your old gramps is gonna sign off now. I just had to find a way to let you know how sorry I am, that I love you, and that I know you'll be happy in Colorado.

Love,

Your grandfather, Oscar P. Becker

P.S. I gotta say, writing this here letter lightened my old soul, Kitten, just like your grandma said it would. Don't look back, Kit. Look ahead and soar with the eagles flying over those mountains.

Clay cleared the roughness out of his throat. He'd almost heard Oscar's voice as he'd read the words, and that brought a sting to his eyes. "That's a nice letter," he said, unable to come up with something better.

"Yes, it is." She took the paper and sat staring at it for some time. "I know what it says, but I still don't understand how she could have left me behind."

"Well, Kit," he started, and the smile on her face said she was thinking the same thing he was. Oscar almost always started a sentence with "well." He grinned and gave her a one-arm hug. "Oscar once told me that sometimes we can't understand things because we're thinking about them too hard. If you let it go for a while, then the answer will come to you."

She laid her head on his shoulder. "I remember him saying that, too."

The moment was tender and quiet, yet his insides started stirring like they did every time she was near. He needed to take Oscar's advice and quit thinking about her so much. Maybe then it would stop.

Sitting up as if startled, she said, "The mine. What happened?"

The trepidation in her eyes made him disguise his concerns. "Just some things had been stolen."

"Stolen?"

"Yes. I sent some men out to find who did it, so there's nothing to worry about." He'd do enough of that himself. What One Ear Bob wanted with two cases of dynamite would keep Clay up at night. It was only his suspicion that it was the trapper; there was no proof yet. He'd set up extra guards around the mine and watching out for Sam. Though he'd had to be discreet in that. The kid took his self-reliance seriously and had once again balked at the suggestion he move into town.

Between Sam and Kit, Clay might never sleep again. Especially when she looked at him as she was right now. Those big brown eyes were sparkling like gold nuggets, pulling him in and igniting a fever. Then she smiled. Her petal lips curled up sweetly, reminding him just how delicious they tasted.

"Where's Mr. Watson?" he asked, in an attempt to detour his thoughts. Or maybe he just wanted to make sure no one would walk in on them.

"At the hotel," she said, lifting her chin, bringing her lips closer to his. "I think he was as afraid of the bridges as I was."

Not kissing her was no longer an option, and the way her smile widened as their lips touched sent a flare up inside Clay. Maybe it was fate, or Oscar manipulating things from the other side, but just as Clay's lips were about to brush over hers again, a knock sounded on the door.

Pulling back, he took a moment to catch his breath

before he dropped a kiss on her forehead. "Come on, we had better go find Mr. Watson." The best thing would be for her to return to Chicago.

Hours later, Kit read the letter one more time before she carefully folded it and tucked it in the side pocket inside her trunk. She would give her mind a break from wondering about her mother. It was already easier than she anticipated. Nothing else really compared to thoughts of Clay. Mr. Watson had said he'd be in town for a week, waiting for her to decide if she wanted to stay or not. Of course she was staying. A week wouldn't change her mind.

Kit crawled into bed as a long sigh escaped her lungs. Clay hadn't kissed her like he had last night, and she imagined it was mostly because he thought she'd leave like the other woman had. Convincing him she wouldn't might become as frustrating as the process of discovering Sam's identity had been.

When sleep finally pulled her in, it was filled with wonderful dreams that had her smiling brightly the next morning, and the day after. Actually, every day for the next week. Kit had breakfast with Clay and Mr. Watson, usually lunch as well—after Clay spent a few hours in his office, while she visited with Clarice and helped with the children. Then they'd eat the evening meal together, sometimes at the hotel, other nights at the society house. Every night, after Mr. Watson went up to his room, she and Clay would take a walk. Though he didn't kiss her again, her world had never been so close to perfect, and that Saturday when she fell asleep, she once again dreamed of living in his house, complete with a Christmas tree all lit up with candles.

Sunday morning she was once again dressed in her short-sleeved blue dress and waiting at their usual table when he walked into the hotel. Mr. Watson had left the day before and today, she and Clay were going out to see Sam, which only added to her growing bliss. They'd gone out to see him a few days ago, with Mr. Watson, but this time it would be just the two of them riding side by side.

"Good morning," Clay said in greeting, squeezing her shoulder as he sat down in the chair next to hers.

"Good morning."

"I received a cable from Mr. Watson," Clay said. "He arrived in Denver just fine, and wants you to know the bridges get easier with every trip."

"I'm glad to hear that," she answered, though she had no plans to find out for herself anytime soon. There was still a wariness about Clay, and that had her wondering about the woman who had left. Kit wanted to ask Clarice, or even Mimmie Mae, but it was Clay's private business, and therefore she hoped an opportunity would arise where she could ask him, and convince him she was different.

Mimmie Mae delivered coffee and took their order. As soon as she walked away, Clay asked, "Are you excited to see Sam today?"

"Yes," she answered. "Mimmie Mae is packing a picnic lunch for us to share with him."

"I'm sure he'll like that," Clay said.

Kit hoped so, but even more, she hoped Clay would like it, too. Rarely did a thought cross her mind that didn't include him, and she liked that. Liked him. More and more every day. The silly fluttering inside her body had grown, too, there was now an aching need that lived inside her, and at times, when he looked at her just right, it grew so strong that normal functions, things as simple as walking, became difficult.

Today was no different, and by the time they'd traversed the hill and spent several hours visiting with Sam, an inexplicable energy swirled inside her. Deep down she wondered if it was because she had been let out of her cage, as Gramps's letter had described. She was a different person here from who she had been back in Chicago, and that, too, was exciting.

After they had finished their meal, Clay reached over and covered her hand with his. "I'm going over to the mine, have a look around while you two visit."

"We can come with you," she suggested.

"No," he said, squeezing her hand and offering a gentle smile. "I'm sure there are still a lot of things you two wish to discuss after Mr. Watson's visit. I won't be long."

Kit watched him leave, and though she and Sam talked, mostly about their mother and grandparents, her mind remained centered on Clay. She wondered how long he'd be gone. She knew it wouldn't be long, but a connection had grown between them, and being separated even for a short time had her feeling as if a piece of her was missing.

She and Sam were sitting outside the cave, on chairs they'd carried out, sipping lemonade Mimmie Mae had provided, when a lull in conversation had Kit asking, "Are there miners at the mine today?"

"No," Sam said. "They don't work on Sundays. A few of them live at the shack a short distance away, though. Hoffman has them taking turns, watching the hills."

"Why?"

"'Cause of the dynamite that was stolen. Don't worry,

though. The only person that's been around is old
One Ear."

"Who's that?"

"An old trapper that knew my pa," Sam explained.
"I met up with him in Black Hawk. He stopped by last
night to see how I was faring."

She recalled the animal-skin-covered man she'd met
in Black Hawk, and though his appearance had made
her quiver then, it didn't lessen the thrill of a few minutes alone with Clay. "I think I'll walk down to the
mine, too."

"Want me to come along?"

"No. I remember the way, and I'm sure you'll want
to look at what's in that." She gestured to a set of saddlebags Clay had brought out to Sam.

Her brother hitched the waistband of his britches as
he stood and puffed his chest out, but she saw the shine
on his cheeks and the glimmer in his eyes. He'd been
glancing at the bag for the past hour.

"I'm sure it's books. He knows how much I like
them."

She checked the pins in her hat as she stood, making sure it was secure. "Well, then, you have a look at
them. I won't be gone too long."

"If you don't see him right away, come back and get
me," Sam said, kneeling down next to the bag. "I don't
want you wandering so far you get lost."

She waved in agreement, as her feet were already
skimming across the grass. Eventually she'd have to
curb her appetite for Clay's undivided attention. He was
an extremely busy man with all his mines and businesses, but the infatuation she had for him was so strong
and alive, as if there were a separate being living inside

her that wanted nothing else but to be at his side, and right now it was all that held her attention.

Jittery with excitement, she hurried down the hill, around boulders and scrub, but paused when she heard a gruff and angry-sounding voice. She slowed her pace and then crouched down to ease her way around a large cluster of boulders. Her heart hit the back of her throat painfully, and she covered her mouth, holding in a scream.

Clay stood just inside the large brace beams of the mine entrance, and outside, several feet away, was a burly man with a fur vest and hat. Her lungs locked when she recognized him as the same one she'd seen all those weeks ago in Black Hawk. He was saying something, but the pounding in Kit's ears didn't allow her to hear what. Her eyes were fixed on the barrel of the gun he had pointed at Clay.

With her mind screaming at her to react, Kit spied a pile of boards a short distance away. Crouching, hoping the man wouldn't see movement out of the corner of his eye, she inched her way around the boulders and toward the pile. He shouted at Clay, who responded, but Kit still didn't hear the words, the pounding of her heart being greater than ever. But as she crept toward the planks, she kept one eye on the burly man and his gun.

Slowly, so it wouldn't catch the man's attention, since he was now only a few yards away, she eased a board off the top of the pile. It was heavy and long, and took all the strength she could muster to lift it high and re-adjust her hold.

Once it was balanced in her arms, she swung one end over her shoulder and letting out a wail that pierced her own ears, she ran forward, intending to club the man across the shoulders.

It all happened at once. The board struck, vibrating up her arms so hard she went over backward as a shot sounded, quickly followed by an explosion that shook the ground below her. Debris started hitting her, falling from the sky like huge chunks of hail. She rolled onto her stomach and covered her head, flinching and yelping as objects pelted her, stinging the skin beneath her clothes. The hailstorm seemed to go on forever, and when it finally slowed, she lifted her head.

Burying her mouth and nose in the crook of her elbow, she blinked away the water in her eyes, trying to make out something, anything, through the thick dust cloud.

She crawled onto her hands and knees, gasping for air and searching the area where she'd seen Clay and expected him to still be standing.

"No," she whispered, not completely believing what she saw. As realization hit, she leaped to her feet and a scream tore apart her throat and heart. The entire entrance was nothing but a pile of boulders and rocks and splintered chunks of brace boards.

"Clay! Clay!" She raced forward and began digging at the pile of rubble. "Clay, Clay, Clay." Tears blinded her, making it impossible to see.

Someone gripped her shoulders. The horror surrounding her was so great that she couldn't think, and just started screaming and kicking, fighting with all the rage racing through her veins.

"Kit! Kit!"

The sound of her name, faint as it was due to the ringing in her head, finally penetrated and she slowed.

Sam had her arms pinned to her sides, and his face was an inch from hers. "Kit! What happened?"

It took a moment to decipher the images flashing through her head, playing out like a performance on-stage. "I came around the corner," she murmured, describing the pictures as they swam into her head. "There was a man pointing a gun at Clay. I hit him with a board and then everything exploded." Breaking out of Sam's hold, she plunged back into the rubble. "Help me, Sam!" She started tossing rocks aside. "Clay's in here. I heard him shout my name before the explosion."

For every rock she threw there were a thousand more that needed to be moved. The overwhelming task didn't daunt her. She'd dig to China and back to find Clay. Fear welled in her throat, but she swallowed it, refusing to think she wouldn't find him. She would, and he'd be just fine when she did.

"Kit! Kit!"

She ignored Sam's shouts. Fighting the tears and anguish threatening to collapse her, she kept throwing rocks.

"Kit!"

"What?" Grabbing another rock, she threw it aside. "Don't just stand there. We have to get Clay out."

"We aren't going to get him out that way. You and I will never be able to dig through all that."

All of a sudden the pile of rubble became overwhelming. A sob escaped and a raw and crushing pain hit her chest. "We have to," she whispered. "We have to."

"Come on," Sam said, tugging her backward. "That pile's not safe. Come back here with me and I'll tell you how we'll get Clay out."

She blinked at the tears and couldn't stop the words from coming out. "What if he's hurt, Sam? What if—"

Sam folded an arm around her. "That's Hoffman you're talking about. It'll take more than a few rocks to hurt him. You gotta keep your hopes up, girl."

He sounded so much like Gramps that Kit's heart caught in her chest, and then her gaze went to the pile of rocks now a few feet behind them. Hope didn't seem to be much compared to that mound.

Sam squeezed her shoulder. "Clay could change the direction the world turns if he set his mind to it. He's just fine on the other side of the pile. Not a scratch on that pretty head of his. I ain't got a doubt, not a one. And you shouldn't, either."

She attempted to keep her chin up as she asked, "How are we going to get him out?" As she glanced around, looking for some kind of aid, she frowned. "Wait, where's the other man?"

"I saw him hightailing it down the hill. But don't worry about him right now, we gotta get Hoffman out."

The vision of such an event, rescuing Clay, had her heart scrambling in her chest. "How?"

Sam forced her down onto a large rock. "The miners in the shack up the track will have heard the blast. They'll be arriving any minute. Tell them to get the mules to move the big boulders and timbers out of the way." He started walking up the hill.

"Where are you going?" she asked.

"I gotta get something from my place. You stay here and keep those miners digging."

Sam took off, sprinting, and Kit jumped to her feet, ready to plunge back to the pile of rubble to dig some more, just as three men emerged from the bushes boarding the rail tracks leading up the hill. "Thank goodness you're here," she shouted, feeling hope rise higher inside her.

Chapter Thirteen

So black around him he couldn't see anything, Clay pushed off the hard ground and searched the empty space around him with both hands, groping for anything that might tell him where he was, or how long he'd been out. He kicked his legs, scattering the debris weighing him down as memories made their way through the throbbing pain in his head. One Ear Bob, brandishing a gun, and Kit flying down the hill with an old two-by-four in her hands.

Clay shot to his feet, cracking his head in the process. Slapping a hand against the sting, he felt the warmth of blood ooze between his fingers. After pulling a kerchief out of his back pocket, he tied it around his head to stop the flow, and moved forward, stooping under the low ceiling. The blackness was disorientating even when he found a wall. Using both hands, he followed it, but had no way of telling if it was the right direction or not. A single word, *Kit,* repeating over and over inside his head, was all he had to guide him.

Fury ate at him. In that split second between the bullet leaving the trapper's gun and hitting the box of dynamite by the door, he'd followed the survival instincts inside him and dived. Not toward her, as he should have, but the other direction, back into the mine. Why hadn't he dived forward? Toward her?

He slapped the wall with all the bitterness raging in his soul, but then paused, listened to the words forming in his mind. If he'd dived forward, by now he'd be buried under thousands of pounds of rock. At least this way he was alive. Just had to dig through those thousand pounds to get to her.

And One Ear Bob. Clay slumped against the wall. If the man had turned the gun on her, nothing would matter. Life wouldn't be worth living.

In the silent doom shrouding him, something snagged his attention. Inside his head, Oscar's scratchy old voice was talking.

"You'd like my Kit, Clay," the old man had told him many times. "She's a scrapper. Sometimes I look at her and can just see the energy trapped inside her. Her grandma does, too. That's why she keeps her under lock and key. I tell Katie to ease up, that no man will ever rule Kit, but Katie's afraid. She doesn't want to lose her like we did Amelia." The old man would sigh then, before he'd say, "Nope, no man will tame my Kit, but the right one, well, he'll love her till the end of time."

Clay cracked a smile. "Well, Oscar," he said, as if the old man was right beside him, as he had been so many times. "You were right. I do like your Kit, and she is a scrapper. Riding the hills dressed as a boy, climbing trees, attacking trappers with two-by-fours." Clay paused then, took a moment to press a hand to the pain in his head, but it was his heart he really felt. "Until the end of time," he whispered. A lump caught in his throat and snagged there.

It wasn't loving her until the end of time that got to him, it was these hills. She was city born and bred, and before long, living out here would make her feel as caged up as she claimed to be back in Chicago. Though she said otherwise, she'd want to leave Nevadaville. Someday. And that was something he wouldn't be able to handle.

"Hoffman! Hoffman!"

Clay snapped his head around. The movement renewed the throbbing, and the pain made him unable to decipher where the sound came from.

"Hoffman!"

"Here! I'm over here!" he answered, having no idea where *here* was.

"I'm gonna light a match. Look for the flare."

"Sam? Sam, is that you?"

"Yes, watch for the flare."

The tiniest flash of light, so faint and brief Clay wondered if he imagined it, happened at the corner of his vision. "Sam, you have to go get Kit!"

"Kit's fine!" Sam shouted. "I gotta try another match."

This time he saw it, a ways off, and dying fast. "I see it. Where is she?"

"She's with the miners. Can you move?"

"Yes."

"I'll light another match. Come toward it. I don't dare move from where I'm at. We won't find the right offshoot if I do."

Clay, crouching and waving his hands in front of him to keep from stumbling, moved toward the occasional flares of light. "Keep lighting matches, and talking. You're a ways off."

It took forever, but finally, when a match flared, it was only a few feet away. "Sam." Relief welled inside Clay. "How'd you get in here?" Before the boy answered, he asked, "You're sure Kit's all right? One Ear didn't hurt her?"

"One Ear did this?"

"Yes. He didn't hurt Kit?"

"No. There's a tunnel off the passage behind me that leads to my cave. It's small, and I hope you'll fit, but it's your best way out of here."

Sensing movement, Clay reached out and snagged the kid's arm. "You saw her. She's all right?" Fear burned his throat.

"She's at the mine entrance, digging her way in." Sam started walking, leading him through the darkness.

"She's all right?" Clay repeated, hoping beyond hope. "Not hurt?"

"Nope, she's not hurt. What happened?"

"One Ear Bob is the culprit who stole the dynamite, and he was in the middle of rigging the entrance. He must have heard me coming, because when I arrived I didn't see him, just the box of dynamite sitting beside the brace beams. He already had a dozen sticks poked in around the beams, caps set and fuses linked."

"What did he wanna go do that for?" Sam asked.

Clay didn't believe what the trapper had said—that Sam was in cahoots with him. And fear for Kit was still forefront in his mind. "Where is he now?"

"I don't know. I saw someone run into the woods. I thought maybe he was going for help."

"And Kit was all right?" Clay asked yet again.

"Yeah, the miners were arriving when I left." Sam grunted, as if moving something out of the way, before he continued, "When I saw One Ear in Black Hawk he said he'd seen my pa just afore he died. Said a griz got him."

"I'm sorry, Sam," he said, taking a moment to acknowledge the kid's loss. When Sam didn't respond, Clay felt the boy had a right to know everything. If for no other reason than to stay clear of the old trapper. "One Ear knows you're part owner in the mine, Sam. He said your father wanted him to look out for your share. He told me if I signed it over to him, he wouldn't blow the place up."

"Don't know why folks think I need looking after so much," Sam said gruffly. "Here's the tunnel. It's small. I hope you won't get stuck."

"I won't get stuck," Clay said, dropping to his knees.

"Don't follow too close," Sam warned. "I don't want to kick you in the face."

Clay waited, giving the kid time to crawl in before he examined the area with both hands and then climbed in. He had to roll his shoulders tight to his chest and inch forward with his forearms. The space was too small for him to rise to his knees, leaving his legs trailing along behind him like a heavy, useless tail, and he could feel blood dripping off the back of his kerchief and onto his neck.

"What happened then?" Sam asked, his voice echoing in the tiny space. "How'd the mine blow up?"

Fear renewed itself inside him, yet at the same time, a smile tugged at Clay's lips as the picture formed in his mind. "Kit came barreling down the hill and hit him with a board." He grinned. "His gun went off and the bullet struck the box of dynamite." Needing to hear she was fine once more, he asked, "You're sure she's all right?"

"For Pete's sake, man, she's fine," Sam answered. "I didn't want her following me, so I put her in charge of the miners. I wouldn't put it past her to have the entrance cleared by the time we get there."

Clay not only heard the humor and respect in Sam's voice, he felt it. "That she might, Sam, that she might," he readily agreed. "How much farther is it?"

"It's a ways yet, Hoffman, just hold your horses. You'll see my sister soon enough."

"She's a good person, Sam. She loves you," Clay said, after maneuvering through a very tight spot. He had to empty his lungs completely, otherwise the sentiments swelling in his chest might permanently lodge him in the tiny crawl space.

"Yeah, well, she loves you, too, Hoffman."

Clay bit his lips, half afraid he might respond.

"You hear me, Hoffman?"

"Yeah, I heard you, Sam."

"What you gonna do about it?"

He knew what he wanted to do—marry her today, or tomorrow at the latest. That couldn't happen, though. He couldn't take the chance. If Kit left, he would have to go after her, and leave all he'd worked for his entire life. She wasn't Miranda—he understood that—but she was a woman. Her mother's daughter. Who had left everything as easily as Miranda had.

"What you gonna do about that, Hoffman?" Sam repeated.

"I don't know, Sam," he answered, blowing out a sigh. "I don't know."

"Well, you best figure it out," Sam said. "The opening's right up here."

Clay experienced a bout of anxiousness that had him wanting to shove Sam out of the way. But since he could barely slither forward, he quelled the urge. However, the air that filled his lungs when he finally crawled out of the space and stood on his feet had never felt so rejuvenating, even though he had to lean on the wall as his aching head spun.

"This way." Sam bolted forward.

Clay followed, holding the back of his head with one hand as they hurried toward the cave entrance. Night was falling and the dusky light changed the color of the grass. Clay had to blink several times to make out the difference between rocks and bushes as his dizziness increased.

Lights, lanterns and torches soon flicked in the distance, and he slowed his pace as everything teetered. Leaning against a big boulder, he regained his balance, and his vision cleared enough to see Kit.

She stood by herself a short distance away, as if overseeing the entire operation of mules and men moving rubbish from the mine entrance. Clay's heart, racing at the sight of her, stopped for a moment when she spun around and planted her hands on her hips.

"Kit!" Sam yelled.

Stomping up the hill, she shouted, "Samuel Edwards, where have you been? We need all the help we can get, and what do you do? Take off for your cave." Pointing behind her as she marched, she continued, "Clay is buried in that mine and I expect no man on this mountain to remain idle until he's out."

Clay waited until she was a few feet away before he

pushed off the rock and stepped up beside Sam. "Go tell the men to stop digging, Sam," he said.

"No!" she shouted, holding up one hand. "Clay," she said, in that exasperating tone of hers, "Clay is…" Her voice faded and then her eyes, locked on his, flashed brightly. "Clay!" In a single bound she was in his arms with her legs wrapped around his hips, her lips kissing every spot on his face. "Clay. Clay. Clay."

His mouth caught hers as his arms tightened around her waist, keeping her exactly as she was, clinging to him with all the strength in her wonderful little body. They kissed, and kissed, and kissed, until his body gave out completely. He tried to stop himself from going down, didn't want her hurt, but it was useless. And then he saw only blackness.

"Why don't you go lie down for a while?" Clarice asked. "I'll sit with him."

Kit shook her head and once again smoothed the hair off Clay's forehead with a hand that refused to quit trembling. "No." Tears threatened to spring up again and she held her breath, forcing them to stay put. She'd cried all the way to Nevadaville, riding in the ore box, holding his head in her lap. He'd collapsed beneath her, and the fear that he'd died had almost killed her. They were at his house now, had been for hours, but he hadn't opened his eyes.

"It'll be morning soon," Clarice said.

Nodding, Kit kept her eyes on Clay, but found the ability to speak. "*You* should go lie down. You've been up all night."

"So have you."

Kit didn't respond. There was no need. She would

stay up as long as it took. Would be sitting right here when he opened his eyes.

"The doc says he's going to be fine," Clarice said with encouragement. "Just needs to sleep it off."

Another nod was Kit's only response.

Clarice's arms came around her then, from behind, and the woman gave her a long hug. "I'll be in the room just down the hall," she said.

"All right," Kit whispered. Reaching up, she squeezed one of Clarice's hands as they slipped away. "I just can't leave him," she admitted. "I just can't."

"I know," Clarice whispered back. "You don't need to. Come get me if something happens."

"I will." Kit let out a ragged sigh as the door closed, but her gaze never wandered. She watched the steady rise and fall of Clay's chest. It was comforting to know he was breathing, but until he opened his eyes, she wouldn't close hers.

The men had carried him into his house, and a good portion of them, as worried as she, were still downstairs. Every now and then she heard a thud or thump that signaled was someone coming or going. The doctor had been there when they arrived and had said head wounds often looked worse than they were, because of the amount of blood, but that Clay should be fine.

Everyone else seemed to have confidence in the surgeon, and she used their faith to conjure up some of her own as the hours ticked by. The words *should be fine* darkened her mind as intensely as the blood stained the front of her dress. She'd rinsed her hands before washing the blood from his face and body, but she could still feel the stickiness, and feared he'd lost too much.

The sun was starting to sneak through the window,

aiding the faint light from the lamp beside the bed to brighten the room, when a muffled moan had her hand pausing on Clay's cheek. Holding her breath, she watched. Listened.

Another moan, and then his eyelashes fluttered, as did her insides. She barely got a glimpse of those blue eyes she adored so much before the corners of his lips curved upward slightly.

"Hello," she whispered, leaning closer.

"Hi," he said, eyes closed again.

"How do you feel? The doctor left some medicine," she said, moving to reach over the back of the chair.

He caught her arm and then his hand slid around her back. "No medicine," he said. "Just you."

"Me?"

Tugging slightly, he said, "Lie down."

He still hadn't opened his eyes all the way, and the gruffness of his voice said he was clearly in pain. "You're hurt, Clay. I can't—"

"Please. My head won't hurt so much if you're in my arms."

Considering that was the only place she wanted to be, and he sounded as if he truly believed it would help, she eased onto the mattress and carefully stretched out beside him. His arm looped all the way around her and pulled her closer, until she was on her side, the length of her pressed against him, her head on his shoulder.

The next moan he let out sounded less pained, almost pleasure-filled. "I feel better already," he whispered, reaching over and grasping her waist with his other hand. "Stay right there. Right there."

"I will," she promised, cupping the side of his neck

with her hand while resting her arm across his chest. It was healing, lying beside him like this. "I will."

His hold relaxed and she knew he'd fallen back to sleep, yet she couldn't convince herself to slip off the bed. Furthermore, there was an incredible awareness inside her that said she was where she belonged. Kit closed her eyes, relishing the thought, and made no attempt to fight the grogginess overcoming her.

When awareness brought her out of a wonderful dream, she had to think only for a moment what had wakened her. The hand roaming up and down her side brought a smile to her lips as she tilted her head.

"Hello," Clay said, those blue eyes once again shimmering brightly.

Happiness floated through her bloodstream like sunshine flooding the window. "Hello."

His lips touched hers and she closed her eyes, savoring the feeling before kissing him in return. She wanted to tell him what she'd discovered. That she loved him with her heart and soul, and that she never, ever wanted to be parted from him. But a knock sounded on the door.

The rattle of the doorknob had her scrambling off the bed, and with both legs twisted in her skirts, she fell into the chair beside his bed as the door opened.

"You're awake," Clarice said. "I expected to find you both asleep."

Kit's face was so hot she was sure the skin was blistered. She loved him, but getting caught lying in his bed wouldn't be appropriate, even given the extraordinary circumstances.

Clay's fingers found hers, threaded between them and squeezed. "We both just woke up."

* * *

Three days later, Clay sat with his back against a boulder outside Sam's cave, wishing the kid would walk up the hillside. He'd—no, they'd—been here since midafternoon, and for the life of him, he couldn't get Kit to go home. There was a dull ache in his head, not from his injury—he was healed well enough from that—but from Kit's stubbornness.

His gaze landed on her, sitting on the other side of the cave opening, flowery hat askew, and he pinched his lips together, stopping the smile before it could form. She should be in town, but no matter what he'd said, she'd refused to stay there. It had been a choice between bringing her with him, or waiting to see who ended up following him—Katherine or Henry or another alias she'd create.

Even frustrated to hell and back, he wasn't mad at her. He tried to be, but one glance at those brown eyes and his fury melted. Along with his heart. And he still didn't know what to do about that.

Feeling his stare, she turned. Clay pulled his gaze away, threw the little rock he'd been rolling between his fingers toward the fire pit and then gestured toward the sun dropping behind the mountaintops. "If we head out now we can make it back to town before dark."

"What about Sam?"

"It doesn't look like he's going to make it home tonight. His trapline runs for miles." He stood and brushed the dirt off the seat of his britches, watching her do the same to the back side of her blue dress. His heart once again took to throbbing elsewhere in his body. The past few days had been like some form of medieval torture, seeing her sitting on the side of his bed every time he opened his eyes. And now that he was better, sitting here alone with her, for hours, was becoming more than he could take.

She, however, would probably kick him in the shin if he came within striking distance. He'd seen her mad before, but today, when he'd discovered Sam had gone looking for One Ear, and he'd told her to stay in town while he went to look for her brother, she'd lit into him like a mother badger.

"Clay," she said, with the same tone of intolerance she'd used half the afternoon. "We both know Sam isn't out setting traps."

He shook his head. "No, we don't know that, Kit." There was a one percent chance that's what Sam was doing, and Clay wanted her to believe that—then he could get to tracking the kid's trail. He'd hoped she'd see the empty cave and agree to return to town. But that hadn't happened.

The miner, the same one the trapper had knocked unconscious prior to setting the dynamite at the mine entrance, had discovered Sam gone two days ago, and had sent others after him. But no one had told Clay until this morning. Time was running out and it was hard telling what One Ear might do now. "Come on," Clay said. "I'll take you back to town."

"Take *me* to town?"

"Us. We. We'll go back to town," he corrected, but knew it was too late.

The glare in her eyes didn't lessen. "You're not taking me back to town just so you can go find Sam on your own." She didn't give him enough time to answer.

"I know that's what you plan on doing, but where you go, I go."

Anger raced in his guts, proving he was wrong. He could get mad at her. "No, you're not."

She folded her arms across her chest. "Yes, I am. I've told you before I'm not leaving your side, and I'm not. I mean what I say."

Clay balled his fist at the desire to grab her by the waist and plunk her on Rachel. He chose reasoning instead, and pointed toward the sky. "When that sun goes down it's going to get cold, and you don't even have a coat." To enforce his statement, he added, "You refused to go get one before we left town."

"Because you would have left without me," she spouted back.

He had been leaving town without her; she'd just caught up to him before he'd made it out of the stable. Changing his bargaining tactic, he said, "Then how about you stay here and wait for Sam and I'll go scout the area a bit?" There were still men cleaning up the Wanda Lou, and he could ask them to keep an eye on Kit while he went after Sam.

"We both know he went after One Ear Bob, for what he did to the mine, and we both know you plan on going after him. Even though there are a dozen men out searching, you still plan on going yourself. With a gash in your head, no less. Dr. Jamison said it would be a few days yet before it was completely healed."

How could someone he was mad at, someone so stubborn he wanted to shake her, be so adorable all he really wanted to do was cradle her in his arms? "Kit," he said, blowing the frustration out of his body with a long sigh.

"He's my brother." She stomped a foot on the ground,

but it was the tears glistening in her eyes that snagged him harder than ever. "And you could get hurt again."

He wrapped a hand around her upper arm. The skin beneath his palm was chilling and he led her into the cave. "Come on, let's find you a blanket or something."

Clay didn't let her stop until he'd set her down on the bed in the back of the cave and draped a blanket around her shoulders. Kit was scared. Sam was out there, tracking that awful man, but she was furious that Clay intended to go after him. There were a million other things going on inside her as well. He still wasn't completely healed, yet he wouldn't rest until Sam was found. She knew that, too.

This far back, the cave was dark, but she saw the worry that darkened Clay's eyes as he sat down beside her. They'd barely spoken since leaving town—except to yell at each other a few times—and she couldn't take it any longer. Arguing with him was horrid.

He looped an arm around her and briskly rubbed the blanket covering her arms. "That better?"

She nodded. It was him that made her feel better, not the blanket. Her body still remembered lying beside him, and longed to do it again.

"Sam's fine. We'll find him."

"I know," she answered. "He's lived on his own too long not to be fine."

"You're right," Clay said.

"It's you I'm worried about. The doctor said you could be dizzy for days."

"I'm fine. I've been hit on the head before."

A chill raced up her spine, making her quiver. He pulled her closer and kissed the top of her head. The action loosened a hard knot inside her. "I don't know what I'd do if you died."

"Kit—"

"I know why my mother had to leave Chicago," she whispered. The past few days she'd come to understand many things.

"Why?" he asked.

Desire leaped to life inside her. She'd tell him—that she now understood how a person could love someone so much they feared they couldn't live without them. But first she had to do something. Know something. Letting the blanket fall, she reached over to cup his cheeks, and brought her lips to his in one swift, easy movement.

"Kit," he said against her lips as he tried to move his head.

She kept right on kissing him, knowing full well he was much stronger than her, and if he really, really wanted to stop her from kissing him, he already would have. Catching his bottom lip between both of hers, she lightly nibbled on it before she ran the tip of her tongue along the curvature of his mouth.

"Kit," he said warningly as he grabbed her shoulders.

"Yes?" she whispered into his mouth, while running her fingertips down the front of his chest and around his sides.

He let out a low growl as his lips caught hers and then led them on a marvelous adventure of tasting. She clung to him as the excitement he instilled in her burst into life with renewed urgency.

By the time the kiss ended, she was warm and tingling from head to toe, and her insides had stirred up that unique desire where she craved something she couldn't explain. A jolt of hot and molten excitement flared in her most private spots, and once again her breasts tingled, felt heavy and tight.

He was looking at her and breathing as heavily as she. After a moment he tugged the blanket over her shoulders again. "You—you should crawl under the covers. It's going to get cold when the sun goes down."

He wasn't angry; she could tell that by his eyes. But the way his body tensed and the deep breath he took said he was battling against something. Another spark ignited in her. She leaned forward, but he jumped off the bed, started toward the door.

Disappointment flooded her. "Where are you going?"

"Just stay there, Kit," he said, walking away.

Chapter Fourteen

Even though Kit was in the very back of the cave, Clay heard her pacing, and willed himself to stay right where he was, sitting on a rock, staring at the dying embers of the fire. One more kiss was all it would take, and he couldn't let that happen. The world was full of tempting, alluring women.

But not one like her.

It was as if someone had drilled a hole and planted a stick of dynamite inside him. And then lit the fuse. It was exhausting, frustrating and downright thrilling.

Knowing what he knew should help him control such things. She'd barely been outside of Oscar's house. Didn't understand the complexities of men and women, and what kissing led to. There she was, as innocent as they came, and here he was, as randy as a stallion.

He loved her, had no doubt, and not acting on that love was worse than not loving. Picking up a pebble, he threw it among the coals, watched the sparks fly up and burn out, suspended in the air. The kiss she'd initiated inside the cave had shortened the burning wick inside him to a very dangerous stage.

"Clay?"

He shot to his feet so fast his back cracked.

"I didn't mean to startle you," she said, standing in the entrance.

"Are you hungry?" His voice sounded squeaky even to him.

"No."

Unable to keep his distance, he walked over and leaned against the opposite wall. "What do you need?" That was a damning question if ever he'd asked one. It set all sorts of visions dancing in his head.

She pulled the blanket tighter beneath her chin and sat down against the rock wall. "You know that letter from Gramps?"

Perplexed, Clay moved closer and sat down beside her. "Yes."

She let out a long sigh. "I understand things better now."

His mind darted back to the bed, to before she'd kissed him. "You mean your mother?"

"Yes."

Compassion struck him like a bullet. He laid a hand against the softness of her cheek. "You can't take the blame for something that wasn't your fault, Kit."

She pressed her face into his palm. "I know."

Clay's heart swelled with care for her. His hand slid beneath her hair and caught her opposite shoulder, pulling her against him.

"Gramps said she loved my father so much she couldn't stay in Chicago," she said.

He rested a cheek on top of her head. "Yes, he did."

She let out a long sigh. "I know how she must have felt."

A quiver touched his spine. "You do?"

"Yes, I do." She snuggled closer. "And I'm more like her than I knew."

Clay closed his eyes, bracing himself. After the mine explosion, One Ear and Sam's absence, she was ready to go home. He knew it would happen, and should have been better prepared.

"But I'm not like that other woman."

His guts clenched, but then released just as quickly. "What other woman?"

"The one you built your house for." He would have bounded to his feet, but she wrapped her fingers around his. "Tell me about her, Clay. Please."

He was ready to get rid of that piece of his past, but couldn't deny the trepidation at telling Kit. Yet she did deserve to know. He had to search his mind to remember what had happened. "Her name was Miranda and she was an actress in Denver. The opera house in Nevadaville had burned down, so I had it rebuilt, and then started building the house, but before either were finished she had an invitation to perform with a troupe in Paris."

"Will she be back?"

"No."

"Are you sure?"

He stared at the stars overhead, waiting to make sure his next words were completely true. They were. "If she does return to Colorado, it won't matter to me."

"Did you love her?" Kit asked.

"Miranda?" he asked, mulling over the question. "I thought I did, but now I know I didn't. Not the way love should be."

Kit tilted her head, gazed up at him with those brown

eyes so full of affection he felt it flow through his veins. "How should it be?" she asked. "Love?"

He was lost. Utterly, hopelessly lost, and one hundred percent sure he'd never love another woman the way he loved this one. "Like this," he whispered, leaning down to capture her sweet mouth.

Kit was besieged by the undemanding pressure of his lips. They were warm and moist, and moved against hers with a tender slowness that made her feel cherished and loved. She slipped her arms up and wrapped them around his neck, completely spellbound.

The gentle command of his tongue easing between her lips had her opening her mouth, and even then the kiss remained featherlight and precious. When Clay lifted his face, she had to work hard to make her eyes open. It was as if she were floating on a cloud somewhere.

"We can't do this, Kit," he whispered, kissing the tip of her nose. "I can't do this."

A profound instinct said he wanted her as badly as she wanted him, and she couldn't understand why he fought it so strongly at times. "I won't leave, Clay. I'm not leaving. Not tonight. Not ever."

"You don't know that, Kit. There may come a day when none of this, none of Colorado, is what you want."

His frustration was so real she felt it inside her. In her very heart of hearts. Things she'd read about finding love, and had imagined were just tales, collected in her mind. *Two become one* repeated itself several times. That's what had already happened. He was living in her heart. She reached up and ran a finger along the ridge of his chin. "Did you go after her? Look for her?"

He frowned. "Who?"

"Miranda."

"No."

"Why not?"

"Because acting is what she wanted."

Kit's heart skipped a beat. She let her finger trail down his neck. "Silly woman. Do you want to know what I want, Clay?"

A little smile appeared on his lips. "A family."

Her eyes misted. "Only if that family includes you."

He shook his head slowly, but the shimmer in his eyes had her toes curling.

"You don't know what you're saying, Kit."

She undid the top button on his shirt and kissed the hollow of his neck. "Yes, I do, Clay. I love you." Her lips trailed the underside of his chin, then up and over the edge of his jaw.

"It's not that easy, Kit."

"You're the one who told me not everything in life should be hard. That some things should just fall into place as they were meant to be." Catching his lips with hers, she combed her hands into his hair, sending his hat to the ground, and arched her back, pressing her breasts against the solid span of his chest. For as tender and sweet as his kiss had been, hers was just as soul-shattering. She felt him strain and struggle, and immersed everything she had in deepening the kiss until his lips parted and his arms tightened around her.

He took control then, driving the kiss until her very soul cried out for a release she knew only he could provide.

Gasping, he pulled his lips from hers. "We can't do this."

At some point during the embrace, she'd crawled

onto his lap, now sat straddling his legs, with her skirt twisted around her thighs. She lowered her weight onto him and the feel of him sent the need swirling in her center to new heights. "Yes, Clay, we can. What we can't do is keep fighting it. It's going to happen. We both know that, and we both know it's exactly what we want."

"Kit," he said once more, though it was more of a groan this time.

"Love me, Clay," she whispered. "Love me the way love should be."

He let out a low, electrifying growl, and grasped her hips, forcing the heat of their bodies to unite even through their layers of clothing. His kisses held her attention, until the next thing Kit knew, she was being lowered onto the bed in the back of the cave. She closed her eyes, surrendering completely as Clay slid her stockings down her ankles. Her dress was next and then her undergarments, leaving her with nothing but Clay's glorious hands and mouth to warm her exposed flesh.

Warm her he did, by kissing and caressing her until she grew restless atop the covers. His mouth was on her breasts, licking and suckling, until the glorious sensations had a need inside her throbbing, begging for more. "Clay," she said between gasps. "I feel as if I might explode, like that mine did."

His husky chuckle made her hips pitch upward. One of his hands was between her thighs, teasing her womanhood with slow, delirious strokes. It was beyond imagining, beyond describing.

She buried her hands in the covers, not knowing what else to do with them, and rode wave after wave of new-found pleasures that had her wanting to moan. The ache inside her was undeniably fierce and fiery, yet sweet and promising.

Growing frantic, she locked her hands onto the sides of his face, dug her fingers into his hair and pulled his head up, where her lips could catch his. He kissed her over and over, and while she was fully participating, her tongue swirling with his, her hands moved to his shirt, tugging open the buttons and pushing it from his shoulders.

He eased off her then, and Kit tried to catch her breath, but watching the outline of his figure, the shimmer of his skin as he shed his clothing, only had her yearnings screaming louder.

When he bent over the bed, she raised both arms, welcoming him with her heart, body and soul. "I thought you'd never return," she whispered, as her hands slid across his bare shoulders to latch on to the back of his neck.

"I was wrong, you know," he whispered back, kissing the side of her neck.

"Wrong about what?" she asked, half wondering how she was supposed to carry on a conversation at a time like this.

"You." His husky chuckle tickled the tender skin over her collarbone.

"Me?"

"Yes, when I said you could tempt the devil out of hell."

She sucked in air through her nose as his tongue licked her nipple, leaving her feverish breast desperate for more. "How so?"

"You are worse than that. You could tempt a saint out of heaven."

everything, his hands, his mouth, his whis-
out a tiny giggle. "Oh, and tell me, Mr. Hoff-
you the devil or a saint?"

icked his way to her other breast. "Well, Miss
Becker," he said teasingly. "Which do you prefer?"

Kit couldn't answer. The havoc of his mouth taking
its fill of her breast was too great to speak through, and
she couldn't even comprehend all the things his fingers
were doing between her thighs.

When the commotion ebbed for a moment, as he
shifted his length above her, she glided her fingertips
along the muscles bulging beneath the skin of his upper
arms, and then slid her hands around his back. "Which-
ever one I'm holding in my arms right now."

They became one then. His entrance was slow and
steady, easing into her gently as his eyes held hers with
a loving gaze. It was profound and stunning. She lifted
her hips, wanting all he had to give.

Her breath wedged in her lungs as a sharp sting
caught her unaware.

He paused, looking at her keenly.

She grasped his backside and pressed her hips harder
against his. "Don't stop, please, don't stop," she begged,
somehow knowing he could erase the pain.

His mouth captured hers, made her forget everything
except the tumult leaping back into life between them as
he moved inside her. She gave in to the astounding sensations, riding the steady, gentle pace he set. Every time
the connection deepened, she thrust her hips upward,
made dizzy by the commotion building in her veins.

Clay's kisses continued, and the vibrations his mouth
caused mingled with those swirling in her torso until
the two became one and grew into a passion that con-

sumed her entire being. The chaos swelled, became larger than anything she'd ever known, filling her with a great obsession of love and need that was capable of carrying her away.

Clutching him, praying she wouldn't float off into some unknown world, she rode surge after surge of delight that stole every last sense she had.

Then, with a startling awareness, she cried out, "Clay!" as a shattering rent split the pressure inside her. The resulting pleasure was immense, and intensified by a number of tinier bursts, spewing delight through her body as he stiffened and shuddered against her, while repeating her name over and over.

She welcomed his weight as he relaxed upon her, and tightened her hold as a great wave of bliss washed over her.

He moved, easing his weight from her, and Kit, not ready to release him, followed his roll, snuggling into the heat of his body with complete contentment.

"Clay," she said, moving nothing but her lips.

"Hmm?"

The smile on her face couldn't have grown any larger, but felt as if it did. She was complete and spent, and that had her ready to share the understanding she'd found earlier. "This is why my mother left Chicago." She tilted her head to gaze at him.

A frown formed as he opened his eyes. "What?"

"She left because living without my father was too painful. I know, because that's how I feel about you."

He stiffened, but his hold tightened, crushing her to his side.

"I don't ever want to live without you." She slid on top of him, to look directly into his face. The handsome,

handsome face she wanted to look at every day. All day. Wiggling, positioning her body perfectly atop his, she said, "And I want to do what we just did over and over again. Until the end of time."

The following morning, Clay, sharing a pot of coffee with Kit by the fire, was marveling at how he could feel so rested and refreshed on such little sleep, yet be more confused than a mule with eight legs. He wanted to kick himself in the ass at the same time as he wanted to haul Kit right back into Sam's bed.

That was not going to happen. He was in love with her, and wanted to marry her, but asking her to stay out here…he couldn't do that. She'd never lived anywhere except Chicago. Then there was the will. If she married before she turned twenty-one, she'd lose her inheritance. Furthermore, what they'd done last night had other consequences—pregnancy. He should never have let it happen.

Letting Oscar down—which was ultimately what he'd done—ate at Clay's conscience. The man had trusted him with his most cherished possession.

A thunder of hooves had him looking up to where Jake Hoover, one of the miners, bounced on the back of an ore car mule. "Telegraph arrived. Sam was spotted over by Georgetown."

"Georgetown?"

"Yup. Want to send some more men that way?"

Clay shook his head. "No, I'll—" Kit clearing her throat had him changing it to "We'll go."

Less than half an hour later, with saddlebags packed from Sam's never-ending supply of beans and peaches, he and Kit rode away from the cave, toward Georgetown, following what Clay knew was the shortcut Sam always used.

Clay had completely given up any thoughts of asking Kit to remain behind. For one, she was too stubborn, plus he didn't want her anywhere but at his side. He would just have to learn to control himself. Not have a repeat of last night.

They rode all day, cross-country on the little-worn trail, without finding Sam, as he'd hoped. That night when they laid down their bedrolls, Clay fought the urge to merge his with hers. They'd slept across the fire from one another once before—and parts of him wished she was dressed as Henry, with that bagful of fish guts again.

Long after they'd bedded down for the night, he was staring at the stars above, trying hard not to think of the night before, when a soft whisper hit his ears.

"Clay? Are you sleeping?"

"No," he answered gruffly from his spot several yards on the other side of the small fire.

"Oh," Kit replied, with chagrin in her tone.

Sighing at the frustration eating at him, he asked, "What did you need?"

"Nothing," she whispered. "I was just cold."

Glancing up, seeing her standing next to him, he held the corner of his blanket up for her to slide under. She did, tossing her own blanket over top his as she snuggled up next to him, nuzzling his neck with the tip of her nose.

When her fingers made their way inside his shirt, he whispered, "Don't, Kit. We need to get some sleep. Tomorrow will be another long day."

To his disappointment—though he tried hard not to

admit it—her hand stilled. But soon, as the wind rustled the trees into a soft melody, just holding her was torture. He shifted, but that just had her snuggling closer. She nipped and nibbled on his neck, and then suckled the area, sending a jolt through him. Her hands under his shirt were moving again, driving him wild by playfully dipping into the waistband of his britches. He held his breath for a moment, fighting to find fortitude.

"Kit, stop it," he whispered, but his hand said something completely different as it bunched the layers of her skirt upward. At last, beneath the layers, he found her, warm and moist. While Kit, being as bold as she was beautiful, found him as well, hot and throbbing against the buttons of his pants she unfastened. He held his breath as her fingers wrapped around him, and swallowed the groan rumbling in his throat.

"Still want me to stop?" she asked into the cavern of his mouth.

"No," he growled, capturing her mouth. They kissed and fondled one another until the tumultuous demand pulsating through him had to be released. Just then, Kit pulled away—her lips, her body, her hands. He groped for her, catching nothing but material. Discovering she was stripping off her pantaloons, he wrestled his britches down beneath the blankets still covering them, and then caught her leg, pulling it across his hips.

Her velvet softness accepted him with absolute perfection, and the drawing, the in and out as he lifted and lowered her hips onto his, was flawless—the perfect amount of friction and pressure. Divine satisfaction as well as pure torture. The heavenly kind. The kind he never wanted to live without.

They soared as one, never leaving the ground beneath

the mountain sky overhead, yet with all the magnificence of eagles in flight over the mountains. His release grew imminent, and he grasped her hips tighter, holding them in that exact spot as her body shuddered and her mouth raced over his face. Fulfillment was so vast he trapped her lips between his. Kissing her was the only way to muffle the cry of ecstasy shooting up his throat that would surely echo across the mountain all the way back to Nevadaville.

He continued to kiss her as the aftershocks left them both quaking, and then, while regaining his ability to breathe, he buried his face in the curtain of her hair.

She bit his earlobe. "Now, aren't you glad I didn't stop when you asked?"

One hundred percent in agreement, he admitted, "Yes." Easing her off him, he added, "And now it's time you get some sleep."

"All right," she agreed.

As she righted her clothing, Clay did the same, and then, when she snuggled up against him, he wrapped both arms around her, encouraging her to use his chest as her pillow. The ground was hard and the air brisk, but he wouldn't have traded places with anyone—not for all the gold in Colorado. And that had him declaring, "Kit, we can't keep doing this."

She kissed his cheek before asking, "Why not?" Propping an elbow on his shoulder, she cupped her chin in her palm. "I love you, Clay."

"I love you, too," he said, not the least surprised by how easily it came out. "And I want to marry you."

Her nose nuzzled his. "I want to marry you, too."

"But we can't."

Sitting up, she stared at him, aghast. "Why not?"

He ran a hand into her hair, cupping the side of her face. "Because the will clearly states that if you marry before you're twenty-one, you lose your inheritance."

"No, I won't—"

"Yes, you will," he interrupted. "It'll go to P.J., and right now I don't have enough cash on hand to pay him outright. That could mean—"

"Oh, good heavens," she said, plopping down. Once her head was settled on his shoulder, she pulled the blanket over them. "For a smart man, you're not very bright."

"Kit—"

"I'm going to sleep, Clay. We'll talk about it in the morning. Maybe by then your senses will have returned."

Chapter Fifteen

The sun had barely peeked over the mountain when Sam came rushing into their camp. "Hoffman. Boy, am I glad to see you. You got a rope?"

Clay, thanking his lucky stars that he and Kit had righted their clothes before going to sleep, leaped to his feet. "Yes, I have a rope. Why?"

"Come on. I'll explain on the way. It's not far." As if it was an afterthought, Sam nodded. "Morning, Kit."

"Hi, Sam," she said, already folding blankets. "Why do you need a rope?"

"'Cause I gotta save my dog," he said, grabbing the ropes from both saddle horns before taking off down the trail. "It ain't far."

Half an hour later, Clay would have given all the gold he had to be somewhere else, doing something else.

He shook his head, for the umpteenth time. "No, Kit. You're not going down there."

"I have to," she insisted, pointing to the edge they stood on and the deep ravine below. "I'm the lightest one here, and the weakest."

"She's right, Hoffman," Sam said, peering over the

edge. "It's gonna take all the strength you and I have to lower her over and pull her back up."

Frustration tore at Clay's throat, leaving a burning path and emitting a snarl that could have come from a mountain lion. He stomped back to where Sam had slept the night before, less than half a mile from where he and Kit had made their camp, and kicked at a rock. There had to be another way down there. But his gaze, making a full circle of the ridge and ravine, said there wasn't. The cliff had an angled overhang, leaving nothing for him to climb down or up.

"How'd your dog get down there, anyway?" he growled.

"I done told you, he must have wandered too close to the edge in the middle of the night. He's just a pup." Sam, lying on his belly, shouted over the edge. "Don't worry, Massachusetts, we'll save you."

A single yelp echoed off the mountains.

"You went all the way to Georgetown just to get a dog?" Clay asked, drawing in another deep breath that didn't calm his nerves any more than the last one had.

"No, I was tracking One Ear." Sam sat up. "I caught him, too. I knew some things about him. Things my pa told me that would put him behind bars. Figured he needed that after what he did to you. So I tied him up and escorted him into Georgetown." Sam's gaze went back to the ledge. "That's why I didn't have a rope. A man doesn't travel in the mountains without a rope. Anyhow, the lawman there, he offered me a reward for catching One Ear, but I said no, I wouldn't take no money for it. But they had a batch of pups, right there in the sheriff's office, so I said I'd take one of them. He's got a black mouth and nose. Smart fella. I'm sure he'll never get too close to another edge after this."

"Clay," Kit said, coming up behind him.

Her touch, the way she ran a hand along his back until it hooked on his hip, had the love he held for her increasing his fears.

"We have to get that pup."

He knew it, and that was the problem. Turning, he folded her in his arms. He'd never known such fear. Nor such love. In a way, he'd always loved her, from Oscar's stories, and what he felt toward her now overpowered anything he'd ever imagined knowing about love. "I don't want you lowered over that edge."

She rested her head against his chest and squeezed his waist. "It's the only way."

The emotions racing through him had the ability to cripple him, but didn't. In the way only love can do, it doubled inside him, made him grow in strength and gave him the courage to admit, "I'm scared, Kit. What if something happens to you?"

"Nothing's going to happen to me. You'll be holding the other end of the rope, and I know you won't let me fall."

The poignancy of her words struck him in the core. His arms tightened around her, never wanting to let go.

She lifted her head. "I trust you, Clay. I always will." Her mouth quirked with a smile, and her eyes grew radiant. "And I love you very, very much."

He understood then what she'd said about her mother not wanting to live without her father. "I don't want to live without you."

"And I don't want to live without *you*," she replied.

Framing her face, he kissed her long and sensually, not caring if Sam saw or not.

When the kiss ended, leaving him somewhat unsteady, she—in her unique way that was so adorable—squared her shoulders and stepped out of his hold.

"All right, then," she said with a determined nod. "We'll need both ropes."

Back near the edge of the ridge, she tucked her skirts between her legs and started looping one of the ropes around her thighs and waist.

"What are you doing?" Sam asked with a deep frown of confusion.

"I've climbed a lot of trees in my life," Kit said, now tying slipknots in the rope. "And Gramps made me wear a safety rope on some of the taller ones." Her gaze included Clay. "He showed me how to tie knots so they won't let loosen."

He still wasn't sold on the idea, but understood there were no alternatives. Stepping forward, he inspected every knot on her makeshift harness. Unable to stop himself, he said, "But you're afraid of heights."

"No," she said, "not really. They only get to me when I'm on a train and it travels over bridges. Other than that I'm pretty good."

Even with fear sloshing in his veins she had the ability to make him smile. Seriousness quickly overcame him when he felt her tremble. "If it's too much, just tell us and we'll pull you back up."

"Don't you dare," she said sternly, "pull me up until I have that pup in my arms, no matter what."

Clay secured the other rope to the harness around her waist, and then, knowing the time had come, he kissed her lips swiftly before stepping away to loop the rope around a tree that looked as if it had been planted in that spot for just this purpose.

"Sam," he snapped, his nerves eating at his skin. "Help her over the edge, then grab the rope behind me."

Sam stepped up and took Kit's waist. "Ready?"

Her eyes met Clay's once more, and he tried his damnedest to include encouragement in his gaze.

She nodded and turned to Sam. "Ready."

It was probably only ten minutes from start to finish. But having her suspended over the edge of that ravine was the longest and scariest length of time Clay had ever experienced. He prayed, he pleaded and he concluded he, too, was facing the greatest fear of his life—loving someone more than anything else. Anything. Ever.

When she finally reappeared near the rim, he pulled her over the edge and carried her as far away from the edge as possible before he set her down to unfasten the ropes. She handed him the dog, a yellow ball of fluff that he instantly passed on to Sam, so Clay could get her out of the ropes and into his arms, where she belonged.

As soon as he let go of the final piece of rope, let it coil with the rest near her ankles, he grasped her upper arms. "You are going to marry me as soon as we get to town. I don't give a damn about the will. P.J. and Sam can have it all. And we can live anywhere you want."

Kit, too happy even to remember that moments ago she'd dangled in midair, looped her arms around his neck and kissed him soundly. "I knew you'd come to your senses. And we'll live in Nevadaville."

"Senses?" Sam said. The dog was licking up one side of his face and down the other. "I think I'm the only with any sense. You ain't givin' me all that, Hoffman.

I don't want no part of running a mine. I done told you that a hundred times."

"Don't worry, Sam," Kit said, before kissing Clay briefly. Enough for him to focus his attention on her. "This is what Gramps wanted," she told him. "You and me. The will says so."

Clay was smiling, but also shaking his head. "I've read that will a hundred times over, and every stipulation. It doesn't—"

She stopped his rant with another kiss. "Did you read between the lines?"

He frowned.

Looping her arm through his, she started walking up the trail, to where they'd left the horses. "Well, Clay," she started, knowing she sounded a lot like Gramps. "Sometimes we can't understand things because we're thinking about them too hard. If you let it go for a while, then the answer might come to you."

He stopped her in her tracks. "Between what lines? The will says—"

She sighed and kissed him again. "That you have to approve any man I marry before I'm twenty-five. Well," she said, grinning. "You approve of the man I'm marrying, don't you?"

"Yes, but if you marry before you're twenty-one—"

"The will says to see stipulation two, right there," she said.

His frown grew deeper, but the grin on his face told her he was thinking, rereading the will in his mind as they walked. She grinned, too. Gramps hadn't been a fool. He knew exactly what he'd been doing when he wrote that stipulation.

He was giving her a family.

Epilogue

Kit paused at the top landing, gazing out the window at the snow floating to the ground like dandelion seeds, barely a dusting, but a perfect match for the fluffy flakes that had fallen and piled up yesterday. Ideal for Christmas Eve. Movement, or maybe just instinct, had her turning toward the bottom of the stairs.

Clay, dressed in a black suit, stood there, near the large decorated tree, and as he caught her gaze, he held up one hand. Her heart tumbled sweetly, and she lifted her burgundy skirt high enough to glide down the steps. He took her hand and kissed her knuckles as she arrived at the bottom.

"You look lovely," he said in that husky way that sent her senses askew.

"You have to say that," she teased. "You're my husband."

"Which means I get to appreciate your beauty more than anyone else." His gentle kiss was one of those she cherished the most. The tenderness made her insides hum like a lullaby.

"How long until the children arrive?" she asked, almost breathless when his lips left hers.

"Not long enough for what you have in mind," he said, running his hands down the length of her back.

She giggled. "You've gotten so good at reading between the lines."

He laughed as he drew her farther into the vast parlor of their house. That beautiful, wonderful house on the mountainside, where love percolated in every room.

"Sam sent a message with the miners," Clay said. "He'll be here for supper."

"Wonderful," she said. "I hope he's bringing Massachusetts with him. I had Mr. Wilson save a ham bone just for him."

Clay laughed. "His cabin is done, too. If the weather holds, we can ride out so you can see it."

She nodded, but didn't instantly agree, knowing he might very soon change his mind about allowing her to ride up the mountain. Switching subjects, she pointed to the packages piled beneath the tree. "I hope the children like the gifts we picked out."

"How could they not?" Clay replied. "You bought practically everything they asked for."

Kit placed her hand on her stomach, thinking of the gift she'd wrapped and tucked under his pillow in their bedroom upstairs. She could barely wait for him to open it tonight. Afraid he might be reading her mind at this very moment, as he had the uncanny ability to do, she said, "Well, thanks to Adeline, the meal will be perfect. She left a short time ago, to help Clarice get the children ready." Feeling her cheeks warm, Kit added, "There will be no burned biscuits for our Christmas Eve dinner."

"I don't mind burned biscuits," Clay said, kissing that sensitive spot beneath her ear he knew drove her crazy.

Giving him a gentle, teasing shove, she said, "Only

because you're too kind. You've endured eight months of my terrible cooking without saying a word. You would rather eat burned food than hurt my feelings."

"You're learning," he said. "And it hasn't been that bad. Besides, you make up for it in other ways."

Her mind flashed again to the gift upstairs, and her hand was back on her stomach. The spot where a miniature Clay—or possibly Kit—Hoffman grew. It had been hard to contain, especially once she knew for sure, but she wanted to keep the secret until he opened the package. She'd bought the frame in Denver, on one of their trips there. Inside the private car he'd had refurbished just for their travels, she held no fear of traveling over the bridges. Actually, Clay kept her so occupied while the train rolled along, she never knew when they crossed a bridge.

The hinged frame was for his desk, and had space for two pictures. She'd put a picture of the two of them, taken shortly after their wedding, in one side, and in the other she'd slipped a piece of paper with a penned message. A large question mark, followed by the words *due to arrive summer 1886.*

"What," Clay said, running a finger down the side of her face, "are you thinking about so hard?"

The desire to tell him had her nerves jittering.

"Your cooking is—"

She kissed him, stopping him from praising something that was awful. He was the most wonderful man on earth. Another subject popped into her head. "I received a letter from Mr. Watson today."

He eyed her suspiciously. "You did?"

"Yes. He's sold the house in Chicago."

"He did?" Clay kissed her brow. "You're still sure about that?"

She nodded. "Yes. There's nothing in Chicago I need. Never really was. It was all out here." Kissing his lips, she added, "Just like Gramps always knew it would be."

Clay took her arms, held her gaze with one filled with love and care. "Some days I wonder how I could have missed exactly what that stipulation said."

"Gramps wrote it that way, so neither of us would know what he was doing."

"The old matchmaker," Clay said, kissing her nose. "Though I'm still glad Watson confirmed we were reading 'see stipulation two as it pertains in direct relation with stipulation one concerning specific marriage of said heir' correctly."

The way he quoted the will made her laugh again. "He knew exactly what specific marriage Gramps was referring to."

"I guess I was just being cautious." Clay tugged her hips against his. "I'd already been robbed."

She frowned. "By One Ear? The dynamite?"

"No, by you," he said, kissing the tip of her nose again.

"Me?"

"Yes, you robbed the heart right out of my chest. Lock, stock and barrel. I'm still trying to figure out how that happened so fast. I didn't feel a thing."

Smiling, she looped her arms around his neck, nuzzled his chin with her nose. "Well, you'd best get used to it, because I'm not giving it back. Ever."

"Ever?"

She laid her head against his chest, held him tight.

"Never, ever." Leaning back, she added, "You're all I'll ever need. Ever want."

"We can still do the Oscar Becker Memorial Community Library here," he said, kissing her forehead. "If it's something you still want."

Knowing she'd soon be too busy with their child, and future children, to worry about a library, she shook her head. "No, I like the addition you had built onto the school. The children have full access to the books, and their parents do as well. Besides, our love for each other is the best tribute we could give Gramps. He knew all I ever wanted was a family."

"Somehow he knew that about me, too," Clay whispered.

He kissed her then, until she was practically dizzy and her stomach was fluttering. It couldn't be the baby moving, not yet, but the thought of the new life growing inside her made the urge to tell him peak. She bit her lip, really wanting to wait until they were snuggled in the big bed upstairs.

A suspicious glitter was back in his eyes. "Kit," he said hesitantly, "what aren't you telling me?"

A knock on the door and the giggles of children on the porch kept the words in her mouth. This once, she'd keep her impulses in check. "I'll tell you later," she said, tugging him toward the door. "Tonight, while we're snuggled in our bed." Then, unable to resist giving him something to read between the lines, she added, "When we're talking about our family."

* * * * *

A MAN FOR GLORY
Carolyn Davidson

With her husband hanged for his secret criminal past, bewildered widow Glory Clark is left all alone to run the farm and care for her stepchildren. Then handsome stranger Cade McAllister shows up on her doorstep, bringing hope and tender feelings Glory has never experienced before in her young life.

(Western)

THE DISSOLUTE DUKE
Sophia James

With a name synonymous with sin, and debauchery so shocking it is spoken of only in whispers, Taylen Ellesmere, Duke of Alderworth, is more surprised than anyone when he finds himself forced to marry Lady Lucinda! Before the ink is dry on the register he turns his back on this sham of a marriage and leaves. Three years later, having barely survived the scandal, Lady Lucinda has placed one delicately shod foot back in the hallowed halls of the *ton* when her husband returns...with an offer she can't refuse!

(1830s)

THE RAKE TO REDEEM HER
Ransleigh Rogues
Julia Justiss

Will Ransleigh, illegitimate nephew of the Earl of Swynford, has the tall, aristocratic bearing of nobility—and the resourceful cunning of a streetwise rogue. He is on a mission to clear his cousin's name that will take him across the Continent into a world of international intrigue—and the arms of Elodie Lefevre, the society hostess who brought shame to his family.

(Regency)

AT THE HIGHLANDER'S MERCY
The MacLerie Clan
Terri Brisbin

To regain control of his fractured clan Robert Matheson must take Lilidh MacLerie hostage as a bargaining tool. But Lilidh is no ordinary captive. She's the woman he once loved—and rejected. Looking into the eyes of her captor, Lilidh no longer recognizes this fearsome leader. She should be afraid—there's no telling what he will do. But something about him both excites and unnerves her in equal measure....

(Medieval)

REQUEST YOUR FREE BOOKS!

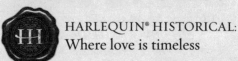

HARLEQUIN® HISTORICAL:
Where love is timeless

2 FREE NOVELS PLUS 2 **FREE GIFTS!**

YES! Please send me 2 FREE Harlequin® Historical novels and my 2 FREE gifts (gifts are worth about $10). After receiving them, if I don't wish to receive any more books, I can return the shipping statement marked "cancel." If I don't cancel, I will receive 6 brand-new novels every month and be billed just $5.19 per book in the U.S. or $5.74 per book in Canada. That's a savings of at least 17% off the cover price! It's quite a bargain! Shipping and handling is just 50¢ per book in the U.S. and 75¢ per book in Canada.* I understand that accepting the 2 free books and gifts places me under no obligation to buy anything. I can always return a shipment and cancel at any time. Even if I never buy another book, the two free books and gifts are mine to keep forever.

246/349 HDN FVQK

Name	(PLEASE PRINT)	
Address		Apt. #
City	State/Prov.	Zip/Postal Code

Signature (if under 18, a parent or guardian must sign)

Mail to the **Harlequin® Reader Service:**
IN U.S.A.: P.O. Box 1867, Buffalo, NY 14240-1867
IN CANADA: P.O. Box 609, Fort Erie, Ontario L2A 5X3

Want to try two free books from another line?
Call 1-800-873-8635 or visit www.ReaderService.com.

* Terms and prices subject to change without notice. Prices do not include applicable taxes. Sales tax applicable in N.Y. Canadian residents will be charged applicable taxes. Offer not valid in Quebec. This offer is limited to one order per household. Not valid for current subscribers to Harlequin Historical books. All orders subject to credit approval. Credit or debit balances in a customer's account(s) may be offset by any other outstanding balance owed by or to the customer. Please allow 4 to 6 weeks for delivery. Offer available while quantities last.

Your Privacy—The Harlequin® Reader Service is committed to protecting your privacy. Our Privacy Policy is available online at www.ReaderService.com or upon request from the Harlequin Reader Service.

We make a portion of our mailing list available to reputable third parties that offer products we believe may interest you. If you prefer that we not exchange your name with third parties, or if you wish to clarify or modify your communication preferences, please visit us at www.ReaderService.com/consumerschoice or write to us at Harlequin Reader Service Preference Service, P.O. Box 9062, Buffalo, NY 14269. Include your complete name and address.

HH13

SPECIAL EXCERPT FROM

HARLEQUIN® HISTORICAL

Read on for an exciting excerpt of
THE DISSOLUTE DUKE
by Sophia James

"I saved the best proposal of all for your ears only."

A streak of cold dread snaked downward. "You want a divorce, no doubt?"

At that he laughed, the sound engulfing her.

"Not a divorce, my lady wife, but an heir, and as you are the only woman who can legitimately give me one, the duty is all yours."

She almost tripped at his words and he held her closer, waiting until balance was regained.

Shock gave her the courage to reply. "Then you have a problem indeed, because I am the last woman in the world who would ever willingly grace your bed again." Disappointment and anger vibrated in her retort as strains of Strauss soared around them, the chandeliers throwing a soft pallor across colorful dresses resplendent in the room. The privilege of the Ton so easily on show.

Scandal had its own face, too!

It came in the way his fingers held her to the dance even as she tried to pull away and in the quiet caress of his skin over hers.

Memory shattered sense and the salon dimmed into nothingness; the feel of his hands upon her nakedness, the smell of brandy and deceit and a wedding quick and harrowing in that small chapel.

Even the minister had not met her eye as he said the

words "To have and to hold from this day forward…"

Taylen Ellesmere had stayed less than a few hours.

Her husband. A different and harder man from the one who had left her and was now back for a legitimate heir.

"If there wasn't a male left in Christendom save for you, I still would not…"

He broke over her anger.

"I will gift you the sole use of the Alderworth London town house on the birth of our first son and pay you a stipend that will keep you independently wealthy in fine style."

Blackmail and bribery now.

"And if the child is a girl?"

"Then I will dissolve all contracts and allow you what I offer regardless. I would not tie you to such a bargain forever should you in good faith produce only a female Ellesmere."

She frowned, barely believing the words she was hearing. "There are other women here who would jump at your offer, Your Grace, if you obtained a divorce and remarried."

"I know."

"Then why?"

"Salvation." He gave no other explanation as he smiled at her, the deep dimple in his right cheek caught in the light. So very beautiful.

Lucinda felt the muscles inside her clench.

Look for
THE DISSOLUTE DUKE
by Sophia James, available next month from
Harlequin® Historical!

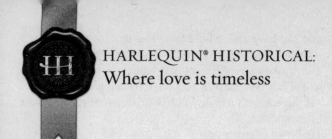

HARLEQUIN® HISTORICAL:
Where love is timeless

CAPTIVE OF THE CLAN

To regain control of his fractured clan Robert Matheson must take Lilidh MacLerie hostage as a bargaining tool. But Lilidh is no ordinary captive. She's the woman he once loved—and rejected!

Rob's touch is etched permanently into her memory and, unaware that he was forced to repudiate their love, Lilidh has never forgotten the man who broke her heart all those years ago. Now, looking into the eyes of her captor, she no longer recognizes this fearsome leader. She should be afraid—there's no telling what he will do. But something about him both excites and unnerves her in equal measure....

Look for

At The Highlander's Mercy

(Book 2 of The MacLerie Clan) by Terri Brisbin in April 2013.

Available wherever books are sold.